NEVER SAY PIE

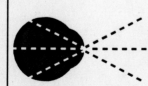

This Large Print Book carries the
Seal of Approval of N.A.V.H.

A PIE SHOP MYSTERY

NEVER SAY PIE

CAROL CULVER

WHEELER PUBLISHING
A part of Gale, Cengage Learning

GALE
CENGAGE Learning·

Detroit • New York • San Francisco • New Haven, Conn • Waterville, Maine • London

GALE
CENGAGE Learning·

Wheeler Publishing Large Print Cozy Mystery.
The text of this Large Print edition is unabridged.
Other aspects of the book may vary from the original edition.
Set in 16 pt. Plantin.

LIBRARY OF CONGRESS CATALOGING-IN-PUBLICATION DATA

Culver, Carol, 1936–
    Never say pie : a pie shop mystery / by Carol Culver. — Large print ed.
        p. cm. — (Wheeler Publishing large print cozy mystery)
    ISBN 978-1-4104-5075-3 (softcover) — ISBN 1-4104-5075-9 (softcover) 1.
Bakeries—Fiction. 2. Pies—Fiction. 3. Murder—Investigation—Fiction. 4.
California—Fiction. I. Title.
PS3603.U628N48 2012b
813'.6—dc23   2012030653

Published in 2012 by arrangement with Midnight Ink, an imprint of
Llewellyn Publications, Woodbury, MN 55125-2989 USA.

For my sister Phyllis,
pie lover, mystery reader,
and proofreader extraodinaire

ONE

"Hanna Denton, pie baker?" The gray-haired woman in the green apron looked up from her list of Food Fair vendors and did a double take. "I didn't think you'd be so . . . so . . . young."

Since I'm not THAT young, I realized she had me confused with someone else.

"Maybe you're thinking of my grandmother Louise who used to own the pie shop in town. She retired and left the business to me."

"Then who's minding the store?" she asked with a puzzled look.

"Nobody, we're closed today." I said "we" because it makes it sound like a substantial enterprise, but my pie shop is a one-woman operation and always has been. Once it was Grannie, now it's me. I hoped to get across how seriously I took my commitment to the fair. I have been known to multitask, but not today. Today I was putting my all into the fair. "I put a sign on the door telling my customers they could find me here at Booth Eleven with all their favorite pies. Lemon Meringue, Blueberry, Double Chocolate Cream, Butterscotch Pecan, and . . ."

"Yes, I see," she said cutting me off a trifle impatiently. "You could have also given us a plug, something like the fair is a happening place for friends to meet and shop, a show-place for fresh fruits and vegetables and hand-made artisan goods." Clearly this woman whose nametag said she was Shirley Nordegard must be in the PR field and more power to her. The new Food Fair was a way for all of us local cooks, gardeners, farmers, bakers, and crafters to expand our market to the world of locals and tourists, if they came. If she had anything to say about it, we'd be mobbed.

"Uh, I didn't quite have room on the sign for all that, but I'm counting on a big crowd after the story about it in the *Gazette* and even a mention in the *LA Times*. Beautiful weather today," I added. No big surprise there. Coastal California between Monterey and San Diego has abundant summer sunshine, except for the occasional fog that drifts in every evening but always disappears the next morning. Just like in Camelot.

I picked up my official folder from Shirley

and drove my vintage station wagon around the Crystal Cove High School parking lot to my assigned spot between nuts and candied fruits. I knew my way around. This was the same high school I'd attended once upon a time. The same parking lot where I'd hung out between classes and after school with my friends smoking a forbidden cigarette or flirting with a certain bad boy, equally forbidden. I was no longer a carefree student, I was a serious businesswoman with a lot to prove: that I was as good a baker as my grandmother, as well as a sales-woman. The Food Fair was a chance to get out of the shop into the fresh air and lure some new customers to a new venue.

The sun was at that moment burning off whatever fog had the nerve to linger and the market was already buzzing with activity. Vendors like me and my neighbors, the nut and fruit people, were unloading their wares from vans and trucks and putting up canopies over their booths hours before the official opening at nine o'clock. It didn't take me long to set up, especially when Manda, the high school girl who works for me part time, came by to help me unpack and my best friend, Kate, showed up to add her decorator's touch to the booth as well as a huge banner she hung with "THE UP-

PER CRUST — Pies made by Hanna Denton from all the best ingredients." I debated about whether to say they were also "the freshest" or "all local," but "the best" covered all the bases and wouldn't leave me open to perjury.

When Kate finished carefully stacking the pies on the table, then cutting up small sample bites of different kinds of pie, she stood in front of the booth to get a customer's perspective.

"Well, how does it look?" I asked, tying an apron around my waist.

"Fantastic," she said. Of course she would say that, she's the one who'd made it look that way. I'd only baked the pies. "Now for your hair and some makeup."

"I thought I was selling pies."

"You're selling yourself too. Don't forget that."

She sat me down on a wooden stool that came with the booth and whisked out a comb and brush, eye shadow and mascara from her shoulder bag. "The eyes. That's what people notice," she explained.

"Funny, I thought they'd notice the pies," I murmured. But if she wanted to give me a quick makeover, who was I to resist?

Then she gave me the same treatment she'd given my booth and same critical look when she'd finished. She stepped back, tilted her head, squinted and finally said I too looked fantastic.

"Just in time," I said. "We open in fifteen minutes."

Finally feeling prepared, I said hello to the guy in the next booth who was selling walnuts, pecans, and several varieties of peanuts seasoned with chili-lime, Cajun spice, or mesquite barbecue. I gave him a sample of Butterscotch Pecan pie thinking of the nut connection and he appeared to be favorably impressed. Then he offered me a small cup of selected nuts and I told him they were spiced just right. Next I introduced myself to the woman on the other side who was selling candied pineapples, cherries, apricots, and even watermelon rind. Who would have thought? She had bins all set up and would mix and match the fruits or just sell small bags already made up.

"I use local honey for sweetener," she explained, offering me a chunk of candied watermelon.

"Then they're really good for you," I said. "And delicious too."

Kate motioned to me and I returned to my booth. "Look who's right across from you," Kate said in a loud whisper.

"Oh, my God, it's Lurline, the cupcake lady," I said. "How did I miss her? I should have known. Everywhere I go, she's there." First she was as cute as a cupcake herself, dressed in pink. And she drove a converted postal truck painted pink, selling cupcakes wherever she stopped. Shirley may have thought I looked young, but next to twenty-something Lurline I was a senior citizen and definitely under-dressed in my jeans and apron. "Just the kind of competition I don't need. Why couldn't I be across from some-one selling broccoli and spinach? Not that they're not nutritious and delicious in their own way, but . . ."

"No, this is better," Kate insisted. "This way people who are interested in dessert will find you here and look who else is around besides the nut guy and the fruit lady. There must be cookies and cakes. It's all good. Go have a look, I'll stay here and mind the booth."

I took her up on the offer and though I didn't find any cookies or cakes, I was impressed by all the vegetables arranged in colorful pyramids. I stopped to look at bunches of baby Swiss chard, potassium-rich red beets, dark green kale, fresh pungent herbs, and English peas in pods. Then I thought about cooking all those vegetables at the end of a long day at the market and I hurried on.

A few booths down the wide aisle I ran into my old high school — I won't say friends, but I did know them from the good old days — Lindsey and Tammy who were selling about a dozen kinds of bread and rolls.

"Wow," I said, impressed by the crowd of customers already lined up for their freshly baked goods. And by the way they'd transformed themselves into bakers. The last time I saw these two girls some months ago they were selling sex toys at home parties. From dildoes to croissants. Talk about versatile. I guess once you've been bitten by the entrepreneur bug you just can't quit.

"You must have been up all night baking," I told them, although they looked just as fresh as their bread. I knew something about the all-night baking thing. It was only thanks to all that eye makeup that I looked as bright as I did. My eyes were riveted on a beautiful flaky brioche that had my name on it. But I cautioned myself to hold back for now. I could easily eat my way through the food stalls, but it was going to be a long day and I had to pace myself.

I swear Lindsey blushed at my comment. Could it be she and Tammy had broken the

13

Food Fair rules and had not baked all that bread themselves? I'd never ask and I wouldn't expect them to tell.

"Hanna," Lindsey said, "this is so much fun. Let's trade. Take a loaf of bread or two in exchange for a pie?"

"Sure," I said. I chose an Asiago Cheese baguette and a crunchy whole grain loaf studded with seeds.

"Oh and try our new Mediterranean Olive Loaf." Tammy pulled out a spatula with a serrated edge and cut me a slice.

"Where'd you get that gizmo?" I asked.

"From the guy who sells them." She waved in the direction of the next aisle. "Ever seen anything like it?"

I shook my head, said I'd see them later when they came by my booth for their pie, and walked away with the two loaves under my arm.

The next booth that caught my eye was called Farmstand Artisan Cheese. A very attractive guy dressed in white chinos and a crisp striped shirt who also caught my eye offered me samples of his best organic cheeses. "All made from raw cow's milk on our farm just out of town," he said in an all-purpose European accent.

"What's that one?" I asked.

"A Triple Cream," he said whipping out

his wide spatula with a serrated edge to cut me a slice which he spread on a cracker. Looked like the same type of knife Lindsey was using. "Smooth, creamy, and elegant," he added.

"Delicious," I said, swishing it around in my mouth like a fine wine.

He nodded his approval of my good taste and gave me a sexy smile that matched his accent. Were either the accent or the smile fake? You never knew. Whatever. He had the perfect personality for a food salesman. What I've found out is that marketing and hustling can be as important as kitchen skills. Something a basically shy person like myself had to keep in mind.

"Firm yet buttery, with an earthy flavor," I added thoughtfully. "Reminiscent of white mushrooms."

"I'm impressed," he said with a grin. "You obviously know your cheese. You'll have to come up to the creamery and let me give you a tour. So tell me, what's a nice girl like you doing up so early on a Saturday morning?"

"Actually I have a booth of my own. I'm Hanna, and I'm a pie baker. Booth Eleven."

"Oh, are you the one with the mini pies filled with organic rhubarb and the warm chocolate chip cookies?"

15

I rocked back on the heels of my clogs. That's all I needed, competition in the form of tiny pies and hot-out-of-the-portable-oven cookies. "No, I'm not. But if you stop by I'll give you a taste of the best pie you've ever eaten. Guaranteed." I know I'm not the best self-promoter in the world, but I've learned I just can't afford to be modest about my pies — no matter what the competition. Granny never was and look where it got her. A long and fruitful career and a nifty annuity package at Heavenly Acres, our local upscale retirement home.

"It's a deal," he said reaching out over his cheese display to hand me his card. "Call me Jacques."

Notice he didn't say his name was Jacques, just to call him that. I could do that.

When I turned around I almost ran into Sam, the chief of police in our little town and the former bad boy I once had a major crush on in high school. He was back, tough and rough around the edges and more dangerous than ever — to me — not to the town, which he promised to protect and serve.

"Sam," I said brightly in my pie sales-woman voice, "what brings you to the Food Fair?" I was glad I'd had the eye and makeup treatment just in time.

16

"Just the usual. Checking for counterfeit goods, drug paraphernalia, and pedestrian safety."

"I know law enforcement is a full-time job including Saturdays, but I hope you drop by the booths and stock up on your fruits and vegetables and maybe a pie or two. You name it, we've got it all in one convenient location. You are a locavore, aren't you?"

"A locavore?" Sam hardly ever smiles, even after turning his life around from one side of the law to the other, but I think I saw one corner of his mouth tilt slightly upward. "Why not? I'm committed to eating locally as much as the next person. I'm here for the food and I'm here because it's part of my job. Mix with the crowd and keep an eye out for any potential criminal activity."

I glanced over my shoulder. Not a pickpocket in sight. But if there were, I'd be protected by the not so long arm of the law. I noticed Sam was wearing street clothes the better to blend in with the local Yuppies. Khaki pants and an Oxford cloth button-down shirt were the uniform du jour for the men in our little corner of paradise. Or shorts, T-shirt, and flip-flops. I'd never seen Sam in a uniform, which I understand police chiefs don't have to wear.

17

He asked where my booth was. I pointed off in the opposite direction, looked at my watch and said I had to get back. He walked with me while he suggested I watch out for anything suspicious.

"Oh, I will. You mean like motorcycle gangs, or cheating at bingo in the church basement?" Either one was so out of the question in Crystal Cove it was laughable.

But Sam didn't laugh. I should have known. He said, "That's right."

I was grateful Sam was there to keep the city safe. So was everyone else. We took our secure little town for granted and we had no reason to think it would ever change. As long as Sam was on duty, it probably never would.

Kate was delighted to see Sam, and me with Sam, since she had this naive romantic idea that we'd be perfect for each other. Even if she was right, she was having a tough time convincing either one of us. I couldn't deny he made my skin tingle and my pulse speed up, both back in high school and now. But I'd be damned if I'd let on I was interested in rekindling a teenage flirtation. I knew enough about Sam to know he had a mind of his own and a will as strong as the Santa Ana winds that blow across the desert and can knock down trees and even power lines.

"You had some customers," Kate said. "Even before we're officially open. I gave them a sample of your lemon meringue pie and they ordered one for next Saturday. Here's their name and address. And look what the cutlery guy brought by for you with his compliments." She held up a six-inch spatula with a serrated edge. "It's some kind of promotion deal. When customers admire the knife you tell them where they can get one like it. Booth Fifty-Six."

"It looks like the same gizmo I've seen two of already today."

"Probably is," Kate said. "He must be handing them out to every vendor, fruits, nuts, everybody. He even gave me a demonstration of how it slices and serves whatever you've got. Not just pies, but meat loaf, lasagna and the edge is sharp enough to cut through steak. Just what you need."

I took it out of her hand and ran my finger gingerly over the sharp blade. Kate said she was going to make the rounds of the fair to see what my competition was and buy some vegetables.

Sam left too. He didn't buy anything from me, but then he had a thing about sugar and butter. He said he never ate it, but most people can't resist a piece of homemade pie if you put it in front of them. But Sam is not most people. There's a good example of his strong convictions. It seemed another one of his convictions was to avoid me whenever possible, even though my pie shop was across the street from the police station. He'd been doing a pretty good job of it since I'd returned to my hometown almost a year ago, except when he wanted to pick my brain or ask me about some resident's background or connections. I told myself I didn't care. I was happy to help if he needed me. But that was not why I'd come back to Crystal Cove. I was here to avoid getting mixed up with men who had an unhappy relationship in their past or a hang-up about commitment. Unfortunately that covered just about all the men in my age group. I was also here to make a living on my own which I was finally doing, thank you very much Grannie for your support.

The Food Fair officially opened and crowds flooded the parking lot. I handed out samples and took orders for pies from some of my regular customers, which I'd deliver later. I sold pies to strangers too and answered questions about our quaint little town. I told how Crystal Cove had been discovered in 1542 by a Portuguese explorer named Cabrillho.

"We're grateful to him for discovering our town, but even better, he also left us his wife's pie recipe for *crosta de torta,* which I still follow faithfully," I told a group of out-of-towners. The part about the discovery was true. As for his wife and the pie recipe I follow, I made that up. Even pie bakers are allowed a little poetic license. I should say *especially* pie bakers are allowed whatever it takes. We wake up with the birds, start yawning during the TV news at night and have no time for a social life. All that, and then we have to compete with cookies, cakes, and muffins.

The good thing was the customers ate up my stories along with my pies. The more customers, the better I got at playing the born-here-in-the-small-town baker role. It was tiring but fun too. By noon I was afraid I'd sell out. Of course that was my goal, but maybe I should have been prepared with more inventory.

Besides tourists, I also saw a few residents I hadn't seen for years, not since I'd returned to town after a stint in the big city. Principal Blandings was one of the people I wasn't all that anxious to run into.

"If it isn't Hanna Denton," said the mustachioed high school principal, looking a little older, a little heavier, and a little less frightening than when I was in high school. "So you're back home in Crystal Cove. How are you adjusting to life in our little burgh?"

"Just fine," I said. "How are you, Principal Blandings? Still terrifying the poor freshmen?"

"Not at all," he said. "I'm the one who put the 'pal' in principal."

I winced. How many times had I heard him say that about being our pal at every single assembly year after year. With a pal like him, who needed enemies?

"And you're the one who put bubble bath in the drinking fountain," he said narrowing his beady eyes.

"I was hoping you'd forgotten that," I said. I hadn't forgotten the remarkable sight of the cascading bubbles or the ten hours of community service I had to do as punishment. "Can I offer you a piece of pie as a peace offering?" I held out a boxed slice of Butterscotch Pecan.

"Thank you. That almost makes up for the time you let the lab rats loose in the halls with your partner in crime, Kate Sullivan."

"What a good memory you have. I can explain about that. We felt sorry for them cooped up in their cages. It was a humanitarian act." I don't think he believed me. Maybe he'd never seen rats imprisoned in a cage. Not from his lofty seat in the principal's office. I wondered what he thought about Sam back in town as the police chief. Some of the things he'd done in high school made me look like Mother Teresa.

"A humanitarian act. That's what your grandmother said in your defense. How is she, by the way?"

"Fine. Here she is now." I waved at Grannie some fifty yards away. I recognized her large straw hat and her posse of bridge buddies from Heavenly Acres.

"Good luck," the principal said. I think he also muttered, "You'll need it," but I'm not sure because he'd quickly moved on to the next booth. Maybe he was afraid Grannie would rag on him about the suspension he'd given me after the lab rat episode. Grannie had a good memory also, and she never forgot or forgave anything negative anyone ever said or did to me.

The only thing she was critical of was my pie baking. Which was good because it kept me on my toes. Kept me inventing new recipes, perfecting the old ones and studying techniques from the masters.

I came out from behind my counter to

hug Grannie and her friends Helen and Grace.

"What a great idea this is," Helen said, beaming at me. "A Food Fair in our own town. No need to drive to Santa Barbara anymore. We've got it all right here. The parking lot is full, the weather is gorgeous as usual, and the food is wonderful." She held out her eco-friendly green shopping bag filled with organic spinach, a long loaf of French bread, and a Mason jar of strawberry jam with a hand-made label. I wasn't sure what she'd do with all that food since the residents at Heavenly Acres had three scrumptious meals provided every day plus tea in the afternoon. But I didn't ask. Especially after she ordered two pies from me for her Saturday night bridge group. I didn't ask if they'd run into the mini-pie baker either. If they did, they were too polite to mention it.

Grannie reached for the sample platter and rearranged the small pieces of pie. Then she tasted my blueberry pie full of plump, sweet farm-fresh berries. She chewed thoughtfully while I tried not to worry about her reaction. She had an exceptional palate as well as a sense of what sold and what didn't. It wasn't an accident that she was such a big success all those years and that I had such big shoes to fill.

"Did you use any lard in your crust?" she asked.

I was sure I told her I chose not to use lard as she'd always done, but she continued to hope I'd follow her recipe with a combination of shortening.

"It's *pâte brisée,*" I said. "All butter crust. More crumbly than flaky, and I like the taste better."

She didn't say anything. If she wasn't going to allow anyone else to criticize my pies, then neither could she, but I could tell she was in the flaky crust camp. While she and her friends were standing there, more customers stopped by and Grannie gave them an earful of praise.

"Hanna has been baking pies since she was old enough to reach the counter," she told a couple trying to decide between Strawberry Rhubarb and Double Chocolate Cream. "You won't find a better pie anywhere in California. She uses the best ingredients, the freshest fruit, and even imported chocolate."

"She ought to know," her friend Grace said with a nod at Grannie. "She's the original pie queen."

"She won the State Fair Bake off two years in a row," Helen added as proud as if she'd done it herself.

Grannie blushed modestly and I'd sold two more pies.

When the crowd thinned and I'd restocked my counter with samples and more pies, I thanked the ladies for their help. "You're the best," I said. "I should hire you to stand out there all day and tout my wares."

"You don't need us, your pies are so good they sell themselves," Helen said.

"It doesn't hurt that she's as cute as a bug either," Grace told Grannie.

"Thanks to Kate who did my makeup and hair this morning," I said. "Otherwise you wouldn't have noticed."

"If you'd like to freshen up," Grannie said. "We'll watch the booth for you."

"That would be great because I'd really like to walk around and see what else is selling. If you don't mind."

They were delighted to play the sales role, which came naturally to Grannie, so I took off my apron, stuffed my wallet in my pocket and first went across the aisle to say hello to Lurline of Lurline's Luscious Cupcakes. Both being competitive, we'd once had a dustup, but had since made up. Kate was right. We both targeted the same customers so her booth across from mine wasn't a bad idea after all. It looked like she was doing as well as I was today. Maybe every day. I didn't know for sure since she usually worked out of her van and went where the customers were like downtown at lunch time to catch the office crowd or out at soccer games at night. At least she didn't have the expenses of overhead like my shop, but then there was the cost of gas to run her van.

I waited while a customer bought a dozen mini-cupcakes. I had to admit they looked adorable and delicious too, my absolute favorite Red Velvet, Coconut Cream, Chocolate Marshmallow, Meyer Lemon, and Strawberry with Buttercream Frosting. "Just wanted to say hello. Looks like you're doing terrific."

"I am," she said. "I've been meaning to come over to see you, but I've been so busy."

"I have too," I said quickly, not to be outdone. "I think we get some of the same customers. The ones with a sweet tooth."

"Definitely. Pie is always good. I mean it's so old-fashioned," she said. I didn't really like the sound of that. I preferred thinking pie was timeless and just as up-to-date as cupcakes. "The one I'm worried about and you should be too is the doughnut booth," she said.

"What?" Why hadn't I seen a doughnut booth?

She nodded. "Haven't you heard? Doughnuts are the new cupcakes."

So she was worried about being passed over by the latest rage in baked goods. Where does that leave pies, I wondered with a little frisson of anxiety.

"They've got a line around the block," she said waving her hand in the direction of the athletic field. "Beignets, churros, crullers, fritters — the whole nine yards."

"Have you tried them?" I asked, feeling woefully out of touch with the latest trend.

"I have." As she talked she sliced up a few cupcakes for her sample tray with a large serrated combination knife and spatula, the same kind I and everyone else had. "The doughnuts are hot from the deep fryer, they're soft on the inside and crisp on the outside. Oh, yes, they're a force to be reckoned with, no question."

"I've got to see this," I said, my mouth watering uncontrollably at the thought of those amazing doughnuts. But truthfully I didn't want to see the line snaking around the athletic field or taste the irresistible beignets, churros, or hot doughnuts. Not now. Even though I longed to sink my teeth into a soft warm doughy doughnut, I needed to be sensible and cleanse my palate with something like an organic carrot and stay positive. Pies are traditional, I told myself. Trends come and go but pies are forever. Pies are the past, present, and future.

More customers came by so I wished her good luck and went to the part of the fair I hadn't seen yet. Something without a bit of sugar or butter. Something that didn't compete with me. These booths were all meat, fish, and chicken. First stop, the sausage stand. I felt obliged to try bites of hot Smoked Pomegranate Sausage, and Chicken Apple with Sherry, as well as Yucatan Cilantro with a South of the Border twist.

I introduced myself to the sellers, Bill, who was as round and robust as their sausage, and Dave, who was so tall and thin I was sure he never ate anything but leafy green vegetables and not many of those. They told me they came up from a ranch down the coast where they raised pigs and they were using guess what to cut the sausage links into bite-sized morsels, the same spatula/knife which they said worked great. I couldn't resist. I bought a package of each of the sausages I'd tasted, and told them to stop by my pie booth.

"Have you seen the reporter from the

newspaper yet?" Dave asked as he wrapped my sausages in a newspaper for me. "He tried everything we've got. Said he's doing a story on the fair."

"Really? You'll get a great review. Your sausage is the best," I told them.

"You like it?" Dave said seeming pleased. "We just started making sausage this year. Everything's changing in the pig business."

"Leaner, more flavorful cuts," his brother added. "We had to learn new ways of feeding and raising pigs. So far we're not sure if it's paying off." He looked anxious as he watched potential customers walk by.

I assured them they were in the right place at the right time.

"The fair has got to be full of concerned culinary adventurers," Dave said. "People who care enough to buy and eat locally. I just hope there are enough of them around."

So far everything at the fair looked and tasted amazing. Who was this reporter and why hadn't I seen him? Whoever he was, he had the world's best job. Walking around tasting things and writing up how fabulous the Crystal Cove Food Fair was. That way for sure more people would come next week and by the end of the summer we'd all be rich and famous.

"What kind of pies are you selling?" Bill asked.

"Today I've got lemon meringue, blueberry, chocolate cream . . ."

"Say no more," he said holding his hand up. "Save me one. Any kind. I'll be by before we close up to pick it up."

We shook hands and I decided that if I ran into Sam again I might casually invite him to a sausage dinner under the guise of helping local merchants by eating their products.

Next my nose led me to a rotisserie chicken truck where the smoke wafted my way and the smell was mouth-watering. There was a line of customers waiting to buy the golden brown birds on the spit. I hoped Grannie and her chums wouldn't mind waiting a little longer while I stood in line. When I got to the counter I asked why their chickens were better than any others. Despite the crowd, the woman whose nametag said Martha took a minute to explain.

"First, they're free-range chickens," she said proudly. "Raised in barns but free to roam in the pastures outside. You won't find any fat, flavorless, industrial-raised poultry on our farm." The way she spat the words out made it clear what she thought of industrial chicken raising. "Sure, they cost you a little more, but they're worth it. We believe you don't just grow a chicken, you grow a relationship."

I stared at the birds rotating on the spit, their juices sizzling on the grill below and I wondered about what kind of relationship they had with the owner.

"Happiest chickens you ever saw," she continued. "That's what I told that reporter."

The reporter again. I ought to get back in case he came to my booth.

"They get all vegetarian diets, without additives," Martha, the chicken lady, said. "They're basted with butter, and seasoned with paprika, salt, and pepper. Try one. You'll never eat another kind of chicken again."

How could I resist. I had to have one. All in the name of research I told myself. I had to find out what sold and what didn't at the market. Now I'd definitely have to invite someone to dinner. This woman's pitch was almost as good as Grannie's. She too was using the new spatula tool to whack the chicken in two for those who only wanted to buy a half. No need to cut one in half for me, I had to have the whole succulent bird.

Next I paused to take a sample of a hand-dipped chocolate caramel studded with sea salt from a woman selling tiny boxes of candy for exorbitant prices. I understood the philosophy. If it cost that much, it must be good.

"These are wonderful," I told the woman.

"Glad you like them. You don't remember me, do you?" she said.

I smiled politely, trying to decide whether to fake it or not. No, I didn't remember her, but she looked about my age and was wearing black tights, ballet shoes, and a black and white tunic. She must have had a friend like Kate because her hair and makeup were perfect.

"Let's see," I said, "class of ninety-four, ninety-five . . . ?"

"I was in your class," she said. "I'm Nina Carswell. Or I was. I married Marty Holloway."

I stared at her in disbelief. Nina Carswell was what we called a dork in those days. Her hair, once lank and stringy was now cut in layers and streaked with blond. Her lips were full, her nose was pert, her thick glasses were gone and her eyebrows were shaped to perfection. How, why, when, and where did this happen?

She nodded as if she knew what I was thinking. I probably wasn't the only one she'd surprised. Marty Holloway. I tried to match a face to the name.

"Marty Holloway, wasn't he . . ."

"He wasn't anything," she said flatly. "Not in high school. But he went to veterinary school and bought old Doc Prentice's practice. He specializes in large animals."

"And you specialize in caramels," I said. "Nice work. I'll be back to buy a whole box."

"Don't wait too long, they're going fast," she warned.

I walked away still dazed to think of how Nina had changed. Obviously I hadn't because she recognized me right away. Even with the makeover Kate had performed that morning I hadn't changed that much. Maybe I ought to work on my looks along with my baking and selling skills. Why hadn't Kate or someone mentioned Nina's transformation so I could be prepared? Not only did she look great, she made amazing candy.

Next I sampled a small piece of wood-fired pizza a few booths away. The seller whose name was Gino did not go to my high school. At least not when I was there. He was at least ten years older than me. He wore a white chef's hat and he offered me a taste of his latest creation topped with sliced figs, onions, tomatoes, and cheese.

"Unusual," I said, trying to decide if I liked it or not.

"Unusually good or bad?" he asked with a pronounced Italian accent. "Maybe I should stick to pepperoni for this area."

I didn't like the implication that Crystal Cove was a backwater where we didn't appreciate gourmet food.

"It's very good," I assured him. "Different."

At this rate I'd have to skip dinner tonight. When I finally staggered back to my booth at least five pounds heavier, Grannie and her friends looked exhausted but triumphant. They'd sold a dozen pies and taken orders for more.

"This was fun," Grannie said rubbing her manicured fingers together. "Wish they'd had a Food Fair when I ran the shop."

"Well, you can come by any Saturday for the rest of the summer and spell me," I said.

"And guess what?" Grannie said. "A reporter from the *Gazette* was here. He tasted everything and he took notes. He's doing another story on the fair."

"So I heard. What did he say? How did he look?"

"Looked darned cute," Helen said. "About your age too. And he wasn't wearing a ring."

I couldn't blame these women. They hated to see someone in my age group like Sam or the reporter unmarried and alone in the world. So they were always on the lookout for Mr. Right for me and for anyone who wasn't attached. I know they meant well. They'd all been happily married and wanted the same for me. They couldn't understand that at the moment I was fine being on my own. I'd been in love only once; it ended badly and I wasn't ready to take the plunge again and risk having my heart broken another time. Not any time soon. Kate warned me about building a wall around my heart, and maybe I had, but flirting was another matter and not off limits. Sam was also definitely another matter. He was definitely worth tearing down a few walls for. If he asked me to, which he hadn't.

"I mean did this guy look like he liked what he tasted?" I said.

"Couldn't tell," Helen said.

Grannie nodded. "He had one of those faces. You don't know what they're thinking."

I guessed we'd all find out what he was thinking when the next issue of the *Gazette* came out. I wasn't that concerned. Why should I be? Everyone loved my pies. Let others make mini-pies, they were only a fad.

I'd stick to the original. If someone didn't like my pies, I was open to suggestions. Pies might be old-fashioned, but as long as they were mouth-wateringly delicious I had nothing to worry about.

Instead of inviting someone to dinner that night, I collapsed in front of the flat-screen TV Grannie bought me and fell asleep watching the Food Channel. Another exciting Saturday night in the life of a small-town pie baker.

Two

Monday morning I was back in my shop, baking and selling pies like one I'd invented in advance for the holidays called Sweet Potato Crunch Pie, made with cream cheese and spices with a walnut topping. I was waiting for the latest issue of the biweekly *Crystal Cove Gazette* to hit the newsstands. It's always a boost to read something nice about yourself. A good review, even from a rinky-dink, small-town newspaper would bring in new customers. I thought I'd probably have it enlarged and post it in the window the way I'd seen in upscale restaurants.

About a half hour later Kate burst into the shop waving the *Gazette* in her hand. She threw it down on one of my small café tables and dropped into the chair like a fifty-pound sack of sugar.

"What's wrong?" I asked. Kate is never not upbeat, so I felt a chill and a premonition of something bad to come.

She held the paper up and stared at me. "Read it," she said. "You'll see what's wrong. The guy is an idiot. They've got to get rid of him."

I snatched the paper out of her hands and sat down across the table. There on the front page was the headline. "Crystal Cove's Food Fair Opens to Huge Crowds and Rave Reviews — With a Few Disappointing Exceptions. By Heath Barr, Food and Life-style Critic."

"Don't tell me, am I one of the exceptions?"

She propped her chin on her palm and nodded sadly.

"He can't be serious," I said, scanning the article as fast as I could, looking for a mention of my pies.

"I'm afraid he is," she said.

"Tell me now, is it really bad?"

"I'm afraid it is," she said.

"Here it is." I stretched the paper out so tightly it ripped in half. "Crust pale and insipid . . . The Chocolate Pie dull and list-less . . . Lemon Meringue too sour, But-terscotch cloying. New owner Hanna Den-ton nowhere to be seen. Afraid to stand behind her pies? I don't blame her." My voice shook, my fingers were numb and stiff.

"Of all the nerve. How could he?" I demanded.

Kate jumped up and folded her arms across her waist. "It's not just you. He trashes other vendors too. He thinks it's his job. He thinks he's the next Ruth Reichl or Anthony Bourdain." She grabbed the paper back. "Look what he says about your sausage man's products — 'Texture too coarse, taste too obvious and ordinary.' And the cheese you liked so much? He says it's overpriced and not as good as Vermont cheese. Why doesn't he go back to Vermont then?" She sat down and pounded my little table with her fist. "You can't let him get away with this."

"What can I do? I won't get asked back to the fair. I'll be blacklisted along with the cheese guy and the sausage men . . ."

"And Lurline and a few others," she added. "Call this critic up and tell him he didn't give you a fair chance. Ask him what his favorite pie is. Invite him here. And if that doesn't work, take out an ad in next week's *Gazette* with testimonials from real people. 'Hanna's pies are the world's best!' Or 'Buttery crusts and tasty fillings. You'll love The Upper Crust.' You'll have no trouble getting endorsements from your fans."

I hardly heard what she said, my mind was spinning with the repercussions of this critical review. I propped my elbows on the table and stared off into space. "This is terrible. Everybody reads the *Gazette.* My career is over."

"Not yet. Not while I'm alive. You're upset. You're overreacting," she said.

"Look what he says about Lindsey and Tammy's bread. 'Dry, tasteless, and stale.' " I jabbed my finger at the paper. "I don't get it, their bread was wonderful and you know I wouldn't say that if it wasn't true. I don't owe them anything."

"Did you read what he said about those rotisserie chickens? 'Overcooked and overpriced'."

"No. That's such a lie. Well, what did he like?"

"The herbs, the honey, the candy. He went ape over the salted caramels Nina Carswell makes. Or whatever her name is now. Listen to what he says, '. . . buttery flavor that lasts a long time on the tongue.' 'A harmonious blend of complex flavors.' Did you like them?"

"I thought they were very good, but overpriced. Maybe I don't realize how much work goes into them and he does. Why didn't you tell me Nina turned into a hottie and married that geek Marty what's his name?"

"I don't know. You didn't ask me, that's why. She never was part of our crowd. The important thing is that you have to meet this guy in person. He'll back down. He'll issue a retraction. He'll admit he was in a bad mood on Saturday."

"A bad mood? He loved those caramels."

"I know. I know. But there was so much he didn't love. I mean if it was just you, but it wasn't. He'll realize he was wrong."

"You think so?"

"I'm positive. Call him now while I'm here. Before you lose your nerve."

She was right. I couldn't sit here whining while my career went into the toilet. Maybe the others weren't worried. Maybe they didn't read the newspapers. As for me, I had to take action.

I pulled my phone from my pocket, pressed the speaker phone option so Kate could listen and called the number of the *Gazette* office located in the middle of the town square. Then I took a deep breath.

I don't know why, but I thought he wouldn't answer his phone. I wouldn't if I'd trashed a bunch of locals like us. I'd be hiding out. But he wasn't. I got connected to a recorded message.

"You have reached the office of Heath Barr, food and lifestyle critic. If I'm not in the office I'm out on assignment. Call me on my cell phone."

"On assignment?" I said with a glance at Kate. "I must have the wrong number. I must have reached the *LA Times* by mistake."

He left his cell phone number so I called it. He answered on the first ring.

"Heath Barr, newspaper pundit," he said.

I almost gagged. Who calls themselves a pundit anyway? "This is Hanna Denton," I said. "The Upper Crust pie baker. I just read your review."

"And what did you think?" he asked. As if he didn't know. As if he expected me to thank him for his frank and unbiased opinions.

"What do you think I thought?" I demanded pacing back and forth across the well-worn hardwood floors that had lasted for the past thirty years. I choked back a retort, bit my lip, and began again. "I'm afraid we got off on the wrong foot. I'm sorry I wasn't in the booth when you stopped by."

"Why is that?"

"I could have told you something about my pies, my background, the history of the shop, and steered you toward one of the pies you might have enjoyed more."

"All that is irrelevant," he said dismissively. "You obviously don't understand how food critics work."

"How do they *work?*" I asked. "And I use the term loosely." I was sincerely curious. I assumed they donned a disguise, went out with an open mind, and tasted food all day. What a job.

He sighed loudly. "I really don't have time right now to explain my job to every disgruntled vendor who calls," he said.

So I wasn't the only one who was disgruntled and who'd let him know. No big surprise there. "I'd like to invite you to come by my shop just off the town square. Taste some of my pies in a different atmosphere. Give me a second chance. When would you have time?"

"I prefer to make a surprise visit. That's what the famous restaurant critics do. Frank Bruni, Ruth Reichl. They even come in disguise. That way you don't have time to chase the rats out of the kitchen or replace the stale cupcakes with fresh ones."

"It's pie. I make pie. And for your information, you are not a famous restaurant critic. You write for a small-town newspaper with a circulation of a few hundred and you are carried away with your own importance."

There was a long hostile silence. I was breathing hard, proud and amazed at myself for standing up to him, instead of toadying to him. I could tell by the way Kate was staring at me she was either shocked or stunned with admiration for my nerve.

"I'm sorry you feel that way," he said stiffly. "I will come to your shop, unannounced as is my custom and in disguise, and you can try to convince me of the quality of your pies. When I have the time. But I warn you, I am very discerning and I am not easily swayed by a lot of hype or sugar and butter just thrown together. My standards are extremely high. Very rare for a small town like this one, I know. I have an idea for you. Yours for the taking. You don't owe me a cent. Here's what I propose. You sponsor a pie contest."

"What?" I staggered backward toward my counter. "Why would I do that?" I prided myself on my self-confidence in the face of competition, but I wasn't ready for a pie contest.

"For one thing, it would prove to the town you are really interested in raising the level of baking quality pies, not just your own, but amateurs as well. Of course it would be an excellent way of promoting your shop at the same time. Free advertising if you will, since the newspaper would cover the event. But of course if you don't have enough confidence . . ."

"Of course I have confidence." But did I really? What if there were dozens of secret pie bakers in town who were better than I was?

"I'll talk to my editor and set things up. I'm sure the newspaper would be glad to host the contest if you don't . . ."

"No, of course I'll do it." No way was I going to let this contest get out of my hands. I had to show that I was open to new recipes and that I wasn't afraid of a little competition from home bakers.

"I'll see that you get the publicity you need. I may not be here, so just drop off the pertinent information at my office. I have a busy schedule."

"I'll do that," I said. What else could I say? He'd trapped me, tricked me into doing something he thought up.

"Busy schedule?" I said to Kate after he'd hung up. "How busy could a small-town so-called pundit be?"

"I heard that part about the disgruntled vendors. How much do you want to bet every one of them has let him have it. Not just you. Before he makes his surprise visit to the shop, you should talk to the others he trashed."

"Good idea," I said. "Who else knows how it feels to be dumped on by a know-nothing. At least we're all in this together. Maybe we can fight back better as a group than one by one. Even though we're competitors we'd never come out against another vendor. Besides I actually liked everybody I met at the fair Saturday. Even Nina. We're not really rivals, unless you count Lurline, but she thinks her rival is the doughnut sellers, not me. I think we could learn something from each other."

"I like your attitude," Kate said. Maybe she thought I'd be falling apart under this barrage of criticism and uninvited suggestions by now. If I was, I knew better than to let it show. "Are you really going to have a pie contest?"

"Do I have a choice?" I asked. "If I don't have a contest, he will, so the answer is yes. I'll pick a date, decide on the prizes, and he'll promote it for me. I can't lose, can I? Unless someone out there is a better pie baker than I am." I looked at Kate, hoping she'd reassure me.

"Even if they are, who would do what you do, get up at five in the morning, make your own crust, get the freshest berries? Live above the store? Work your butt off? No, you've got nothing to worry about. Plus think of all that free publicity you'll get."

I nodded. I hoped she was right about the lack of competition in the hard work department. It sure felt better to take action than to simply sit around and mope. I hated to have to thank Heath Barr for this idea, but maybe I'd have to.

"Call the other vendors," she insisted. "The ones in the same boat as you. Invite them here for a strategy planning meeting. Get rid of that guy. At least make him irrelevant."

"But how?"

That was the question everyone wanted to know the answer to when I called the meeting to order the next Friday night in my shop. How to get rid of the food critic. But no one, even those who'd met him face to face, really knew exactly who he was and how he landed where he was at the *Gazette.*

If Heath had visited my shop during the week his disguise was so good it got past me, and I was on the lookout every day. Was he actually the little old lady who came in for a cup of coffee and bought an apple pie? Or was he the delivery man in coveralls who took home a slice of pecan pie? If he was,

48

I'd been totally punked.

That Friday all the vendors in question were bravely gearing up for another banner sales day at the Food Fair the next day. But they all took time to meet at my shop. We were all worried about attendance the next day. Would customers boycott our booths after reading the damning reviews? Or would they come by because they were curious? Or was our little newspaper so obscure they were totally unaware of what our hyper-critical hometown reporter said about us.

Looking around the crowded shop I was pleased to see they'd all appeared. Everyone I'd contacted, everyone Heath had criticized in his article had all made the effort to drive in from their farms, their stores, their vans, or their kitchens to plot a strategy or just vent their frustration and anger. There was Lurline, the cupcake seller, and Lindsey and Tammy, Jacques the flirtatious cheese maker, and the brothers from the sausage booth as well as Martha the chicken lady. I hadn't contacted anyone who'd gotten a favorable review like Nina or the Italian who made the wood-fired pizza or the beekeeper who made the honey. And definitely not the doughnut people. They certainly didn't need support. They'd be laughing all the way to the bank. Everyone else had escaped the wrath of Mr. Barr and who knows why? Kate had also sampled their goods except for the doughnuts. She said everything was tasty, but no better than ours.

At first there was chaos in my little pie shop. Everyone talking at once. Everyone blowing off steam. Kate had helped me set up enough chairs and tables, then she stayed around to help serve pie, what else? And coffee.

Then I called the meeting to order. I've never been much of a joiner, never wanted to belong to any clubs or organizations with long, boring meetings, but this was different. With an adversary like Heath who had a mouthpiece like the local paper, we needed each other if we wanted to fight back.

"We're here to do just a few things," I said when everyone had been served a piece of seasonal three-berry pie and coffee. "First vent frustration here where we all understand each other's angst. Second, exchange ideas; and finally, plot strategy."

The first part was easy. After a few minutes of angry epithets and name calling, like "know nothing" and "big phony" and "Pathetic excuse for a food critic" the crowd settled down. But moving on to the second and third items was tricky. Some like Tammy wanted to do nothing for fear of alienating our food critic more.

"Nothing? After what he did to us?" said Lurline who was wearing matching hot pink shorts and a hoodie. "I say we boycott the newspaper."

I had to refrain from objecting to any boycott of the newspaper if they were going to promote my pie contest, so I kept my mouth shut.

"That'll show 'em," the long tall sausage brother agreed. "And if that doesn't work, I'll give the guy a tour of our facilities. That goes for everyone in the room by the way. Please come on out to the farm for a tour. We've got nothing to hide. We're proud of our pork products. It's not just sausage. We've got a whole line of meat."

But his brother shook his head. "The guy will never come. He's made up his mind."

"Who is this Barr anyway?" said Jacques. "Where does he get off bad-mouthing the cheese I sell? I don't think he knows what he's talking about. He's a fraud. I say let's expose him."

I smothered a smile. Of all people to call someone a fraud, it had to be Jacques. Away from his cheese booth he sounded completely American. But put him in a sales

51

booth with a decent Camembert in front of him and suddenly he sounded positively Parisian. He even looked the part tonight with his spiky haircut and his slim-cut linen jacket. All he needed was a beret.

"I haven't seen him," I said, "but some of you did. I only talked to him on the phone. I asked him to give me another chance and he said he'd come by the shop. That was Monday and I still haven't seen him. But then he said he'd be in disguise like a real food critic so I couldn't pull the wool over his eyes," I said. "So if he was wearing a mailman uniform or dressed like my dairy supplier maybe I missed him." I didn't mention the pie contest. I hated to give Heath credit for the idea, especially if it worked.

"I don't think so," said Martha, the chicken seller wearing stretch pants and a sweater. It gets cool at night even in the middle of summer along the coast, fog or no fog. We don't have balmy summer evenings like other parts of the country so everyone was dressed warmly. "I think he's a chicken. Which is an insult to my birds. What I mean is that he's afraid of us. He hides behind his byline but he's scared to meet us face to face since he's dumped on us in his article. Otherwise why isn't he here? I challenged him to meet with us tonight, and I invited him to visit my ranch. You all are invited too," she said. "You'll never buy a chicken from anyone else once you see how ours are raised. But where is our critic? Why won't he stand by his words?"

"Right on," Lindsey said. "I told him about this meeting too." She turned to me. "Hope you don't mind, Hanna. I thought it was only fair. So if he had any guts he'd be here."

There was a moment of silence while everyone turned and looked at the door. Nothing. No one. A second later there was a loud knock.

I swallowed over a hard lump in my throat. There was a communal gasp. Had Heath Barr answered the summons? We were all pretty brave without him around, but if he actually walked in now would we really tell him what we thought? That he was all talk, he had no taste, he didn't deserve to be a food critic and so forth and so on. Or would we politely ask him for his credentials, if he didn't mind, and tell him we hoped he'd come back Saturday and give us another chance? Or . . .

The knocking was louder and more insistent. I went to the door. Technically I closed at six, so it couldn't be a customer at this hour. I yanked the door open. Sam was standing there looking grim. As I said, he's not ever Mr. Smiley, but he looked especially stern tonight.

"Oh, hi Sam," I said. "I hope nothing's wrong. Has one of my fellow food vendors violated an ordinance by parking on the wrong side of the street or did someone leave their parking lights on? If there's been an infraction, hand me the ticket, I'll take care of it. Sorry to bother you when you're off duty. We're just having a little business meeting." I didn't like the way he was looking at me, which caused me to run on that way. I hoped it wasn't an official visit.

"Who's we?" he asked.

"We're all food vendors."

He held up a folded newspaper. "Would they be the same vendors that Mr. Barr criticized in his column."

"Some of them are. We're just exercising our right to peacefully assemble under the first amendment. Nothing wrong with that." My nerves were on edge and Sam's long silence didn't help to calm me down. What did he want and if he didn't want anything special why didn't he leave?

I smiled politely and put a hand on the door as if to close it, but he put his foot in the way. "This is serious, Hanna. You can assemble all you want, but I'd like to come in and ask some questions. Like where were you and your friends early this evening when Heath Barr was murdered."

I stepped backward and almost lost my balance. "Murdered?" I felt my knees buckle. "Are you sure? How?"

"With a serrated knife."

I stared at him. The whole room behind me waited in hushed silence. Had they overheard? "Then it was murder," I muttered. No sense hoping he'd committed suicide. I tried to picture the scene, as awful as it was.

"Where?" I managed to say when I found my voice.

"Across the throat."

I gulped. "I mean where did it happen?"

"In his office at the *Gazette*," Sam said. "Before you ask when, why don't I come inside?"

Knowing Sam, I had no choice, so I stepped aside and he walked in. As usual, he wasn't wearing a uniform so I addressed the group. "Everyone," I said loudly so they could hear me over their animated conversations, "this is our police chief, Sam Genovese, with a . . . a . . ." A question? An accusation? An inquiry? I looked at Sam. What was the word I was looking for? "An announcement. Mr. Barr, the local food critic was found dead in his office at the newspaper this evening." I was proud of myself for keeping my voice steady. I purposely didn't say murdered, but murder had to be on all our minds. "No doubt it was while we were all assembled here," I said pointedly. Thus giving us all an alibi.

The room was eerily silent. I hoped Sam noticed that they all looked properly shocked and dismayed. He couldn't possibly think that one of us . . . We were all right here at least for the past hour. And yet who else wanted the guy out of our hair more than we did? Why else would Sam be holding the Monday *Gazette* in his hand? From just a glance, he looked like he'd gone so far as to highlight our names.

As the chairman of this gathering, I thought it best to first introduce the group to Sam. As if we had nothing to conceal. As if we were all eager to help him solve the crime. After all, murder in Crystal Cove could hurt us all where it mattered, in the pocket book. Who wanted to come to a farmer's market if you were afraid you'd be stabbed with a saw-toothed blade for sale in that very market? None of us wanted any damaging publicity concerning our fair. Surely Sam understood that.

I continued to function as best I could in hostess mode. Granny would have been proud of me.

"Officer Genovese, you already know Tammy and Lindsey."

He nodded. We were all in high school together and Sam currently lived in a bungalow next door to Lindsey.

"Jacques is the French cheese vendor from the Artisan Cheese stand." I wasn't sure Jacques was French at all, but he definitely looked European except for his all American Hippie Birkenstocks. He reached out to shake Sam's hand and said something like *"enchanté."*

"You know Lurline, I believe," I said.

She gave him her usual perky smile as if we were just here to have a party. Better than looking guilty, of course, which she probably wasn't. I couldn't picture her slitting the critic's throat on her way to the meeting, but then who could I picture? I looked around the room. And came back to Lurline. Sam being one of the few eligible men in town, Lurline had zeroed in on him some months ago. I'd seen her flirting with him, but then she flirted with everyone, eligible or not.

"Bill and Dave run the Primo Pork and Sausage Stand," I said.

They nodded as Sam checked off something on the paper he held in his hand.

"This is Martha who raises free-range chickens." I gestured in her direction.

She straightened her shoulders, stood, tilted her chin and looked Sam in the eye. "Any questions about Barr you can ask me. I sold that scumbag one of my chickens last Saturday, they're farm raised you know, and he had the nerve to say they were over-cooked and overpriced. Sure they're expensive, but they're cooked perfectly and worth every penny. Come out to the ranch and I'll give you a tour. I have nothing to hide. I didn't kill Barr, but after I read that review I wanted to."

I nodded vigorously. "She's right," I said. "Her chickens are superb. I know because I ate half of mine for dinner that night. And I would have cheerfully stabbed him after reading what he said about my pies. But I didn't," I added quickly.

Sam wrote something on a pad of paper. I wanted badly to look over his shoulder. Was he making a list of suspects? Was I on it?

"You see, Sam, we're all professionals in the food business," I said. "And speaking as an unbiased judge of food I can say that everyone in this room has reason to be proud of his product. I've tasted them all.

Mr. Barr was wrong. He obviously had an ax to grind."

I stopped when I realized that he'd been killed with an ax-like serrated knife. "I mean, he had no business trashing our food at the fair. We didn't deserve it. He was wrong, dead wrong."

I bit my tongue. Dead wrong? What was wrong with me? Blurting the wrong words at the wrong time. Nerves, that's what. I felt a bout of hysteria coming on. The harder I tried to control myself the more likely I'd have an attack of inappropriate laughter. I took a deep breath. I had a horrible irrational feeling that Sam's presence here suggested he already suspected one of us in this room of killing the food critic. Even though I told him we'd been having a meeting and even if we were available, we were not homicidal. But deep down somewhere I too was thinking maybe someone in this room had killed him. I wanted to, they must have too. Sam never said what time he was killed. So could any of us have done it?

"Thanks, Hanna," Sam said in what I thought was a deceptively off-hand way. The others didn't really know his modus operandi, but I wondered if Sam was actually trying to put everyone in the room at ease and off guard and then pounce on them, demanding to know where they were at such and such an hour. Which made me wish he'd tell us what hour did this so-called murder occur and where was I at that time? That's the problem with living and working alone, I might not have an alibi.

"I apologize for interrupting your meeting like this," Sam said. "Sorry it has to be an unfortunate circumstance that brings me here tonight. But my job is to investigate crimes and misdemeanors. As it happens those are few and far between in our little town. Usually what I investigate is a fender bender, a missing pet, or a lost wallet. Yesterday it was a broken clothesline and someone driving on the golf course, which you'll see if you read my weekly column 'The Crime Beat' in the *Gazette*. But today, this time we have a murder on our hands."

He looked around my small shop. Everyone appeared to be suitably horrified. Some were wide eyed with pale faces and nervous fingers tapping on small tables. The tension in the air was so thick you could cut it with one of those serrated knives someone used to slash Heath Barr's neck.

"Are we under suspicion?" Dave, the thin sausage maker, said with a worried frown.

"At this point I plan to talk to everyone who had dealings with Mr. Barr. If you have nothing to hide you have nothing to fear."

"We have nothing to hide," Bill said emphatically. "Say what you want about making sausage, but we only use the best ingredients. Come out and see if you don't believe me." Obviously a super salesman as well as a dedicated artisan, Bill immediately reached into his pocket and handed out business cards to everyone in the room, including Sam.

I wondered if Sam had read that somewhere about nothing to hide and nothing to fear. Nothing to hide? Everyone had something to hide. Especially Sam. He'd spent years in the city before coming back as police chief and had never disclosed much of what happened to him before he became our police chief. Somehow he'd managed to have a career as a big city cop and he'd also made a fair amount of money while he was gone. However he did that, it wasn't by working in law enforcement. That I was sure of.

It turned out Sam asked if they would mind stopping by his office for a very brief interview tonight, since they were here in town anyway. But if it wasn't convenient, he'd be glad to re-schedule.

Everyone agreed to do it then and there. No one wants a visit to the police station hanging over their head. I sure didn't. And so went the evening. The evening we'd planned to get back at the food critic ended in a different way altogether. Somebody got back at the critic all right, but I didn't think it was one of us.

One by one the group filed over to Sam's office at the police station across the street. When they came back they seemed deflated. Not the way you want to start out a weekend of pushing your products. Standing on your feet for eight hours smiling and greeting customers, peddling your pies, your sausages, or whatever takes a lot of energy. And a strong belief in yourself. Selling all day is exhausting, if you're any good at it that is. As Kate said, you're selling yourself as much as your product.

By the time it was my turn to sit in the hot seat across the desk from Sam, I was already feeling drained and on edge at the same time. I wasn't ready for tomorrow's Food Fair yet. I also had a problem keeping my mouth shut when I should, and I knew by now that Sam would take advantage of that. So I waved goodbye to my new friends and told myself to button my lip and only answer his questions with yes or no.

THREE

The police station was empty except for Sam. He had a couple of deputies, but they were only on duty when there was an emergency. I assume a murder qualifies, so maybe they were out interviewing suspects. If there were any besides us. Or was his staff at home with their families? I couldn't picture Sam with a family. If he had one, would he be as good a police chief as he was? The only thing he'd ever told me about the years he'd spent away from Crystal Cove was his tragic story about losing his partner in the line of duty. It was obviously a painful subject so I would never bring it up again and neither would he. Especially if we never got together to talk about anything but a local murder.

Sam's office was small and sparsely furnished, but his desk was large, with stacks of files off to one side. His window was open and the cool air that wafted in smelled as fresh as the ocean. He waved at the chair opposite the desk. I sat, but he didn't.

Instead he leaned against the wall that was painted utility gray and covered with awards and diplomas and pictures of policemen looking proud and serious. He crossed one leg over the other. After a half dozen interviews he looked totally at ease and at home except for telltale worry lines between his eyebrows. He hadn't returned to quiet Crystal Cove to solve murders, but this one had landed square in his lap. Was he worried about his ability to solve it? If so, he never let on. I have to add that Sam, whether worried or not, is more gorgeous than any policeman had a right to be. Since this was his office, I guess his looking at home there shouldn't be surprising. I wondered if he'd learned anything important in the past half hour, like who he suspected of killing the up-tight, supercritical food critic. If he had, I'd be the last to know.

"Go ahead," I said, instantly jettisoning my plan to keep quiet. "I know what comes next. You'll ask me where I was at such and such a time. Whenever Mr. Barr was killed."

"I don't have a time frame, but if you'd like to tell me where you were this afternoon, I'm all ears."

"In my shop baking where I am every

64

afternoon. I have the pies to prove it, some may be still warm from the oven — Dutch Apple, Lattice-topped Strawberry-Rhubarb, Open-face Apricot . . ."

"Okay, okay I got the picture," he said holding his hand out to stop me.

"But I didn't have any customers after two women came in and bought a quiche for lunch."

"That's too bad," he said.

"Too bad that I don't have more customers, or too bad because now I'm a suspect?"

"Both," he said.

"Oh, come on, Sam. You know I'm not a murderer."

"Personal feelings have nothing to do with my job."

"I didn't know you had any."

"That's the way I want it. I deal in facts, not feelings. And if I had any . . ."

"You'd keep them to yourself, I'm sure," I said. Why did I even try to crack this man's façade? It was hopeless. Even when there was no murder in Crystal Cove, he was still all business. He still found material for his "Crime Beat" column in the *Gazette*. But with a real crime on his hands, he was impossible.

I sighed. "What do you want to know?"

"I'd like to see your saw blade."

I reached into a canvas bag I'd slung over my shoulder. I hoped to see some flicker of surprise or admiration for my toting the supposed murder weapon without being asked in advance, but all I saw was a brief raised eyebrow as he donned a glove and reached for the handle of the tool.

"I guess you're surprised," I said. "You thought I'd refuse to surrender my knife or I'd have to dash across the street and retrieve it before I cleaned off all the blood."

"Nothing you do surprises me anymore," he said, exhaling loudly. Then he sniffed the red stain on the sawtooth blade and said, "Obviously you've contaminated your knife."

"If you mean I used it, yes. That's not blood by the way, it's raspberry from the tart I cut up for you. I know you don't eat dessert, but I continue to hope I can change your mind." I reached into my bag again and handed him a generous slice of a ruby-red fresh raspberry tart. "I thought you'd be glad I hadn't cleaned the knife. I guess I was wrong."

He stared at the piece of pie for a long moment. Was he trying to decide whether to use it as evidence of God-knows-what or whether he should eat it?

"The crust is puff pastry," I said, "then a

layer of raspberry jam with fresh raspberries and a glaze on top. It should be served with ice cream or *crème fraiche,* but . . ."

"Thank you," he said brusquely, setting the pie on his desk. "I appreciate the thought and the tart and the tool, but let's get back to your whereabouts this afternoon."

"I didn't have any whereabouts. As I told you I was in my shop. If you'd looked in from the street you would have seen me in the kitchen. What about the others, did they have alibis?"

"I can't answer that," he said with a frown. "That's confidential information."

I leaned forward in my chair. "I know what you're thinking. You're thinking I had a weapon and I had a beef with the victim so that puts me under suspicion. If there's anything I can do to clear my name, I'd be glad to do whatever . . . or . . ."

He shook his head. "Thanks but no thanks, Hanna. All I want you to do is answer my questions. I understand where you're coming from. I know you have a lot of energy and drive. I understand why you're motivated to get to the bottom of this crime. But you have enough on your plate without worrying about my investigation. Your job is to channel your talents into your pie baking and my job is to solve crimes. Just relax, stand back, and let me do what they pay me to do."

I hated hearing that condescending tone he used. If I didn't know him, I'd even call it a holier-than-thou tone. But he really wasn't holier than anyone. Actually he sometimes almost looked a little sheepish when pulling rank. If you'd asked me if Sam resembled an animal, I would have said wolf, but not now.

He'd obviously forgotten that I'd been helpful in solving a murder at Grannie's retirement home only months ago. The only murder anyone could remember in the history of the town. Until now. He could act like I was a simple pie baker with homicidal tendencies, but I don't think he believed it.

"Just for the record," I said, "I wouldn't kill anyone no matter how much they trashed my pies. In fact I've never seen this Barr guy. I don't know what he looks like. I don't suppose you have a photo?"

"You don't need to see what he looks like. I have your statement. I have your cutting tool. Let me know if you come up with an alibi for your afternoon. A customer who came in or a friend who called you. Anyone who can verify your story."

My story? It sounded like he thought I

made it all up. I clamped my mouth shut to keep from saying something I'd regret.

"Until then I know where to find you if I need more information. You're free to go."

"Thank you," I said, choking back a retort. I wasn't ready to go. I refused to be dismissed like a school girl. I had questions for Sam.

"If you won't tell me what the others told you I'll have to ask them myself."

"That's up to you. I can only advise you to keep out of this. My advice to you is . . ."

"I know, stick to baking," I said. If only. "How can you even ask me to do that when you suspect me of murder? Or don't you? And if you don't, I want to know who you do suspect, but I guess you're not going to tell me anything, am I right?"

"Yes," he said loudly as he pounded his fist on his desk. "You are right. I am not going to confide in you in regard to this murder. It's my job, not yours. If I need your help I'll ask you."

In my dreams. He was never going to ask me for help. At least I had the satisfaction of snapping his cool, calm, and collected demeanor. But did that help me accomplish anything I wanted? He still probably suspected me and I had no clue what the others had told him.

So I stood with all the dignity I could muster after being shouted at by the chief of police and told in no uncertain terms not to meddle. I've been through worse than that. I was fired from my job in the city under a cloud of suspicion when I didn't deserve it. I'd fallen hard for someone who didn't deserve me. I came back here when I vowed I never would. When I left at age eighteen, I thought I was too good for this town. Twelve years later when Grannie offered me her pie shop I grabbed onto it like a life saver, which it had been. Maybe Sam was right. I needed to devote myself to my new career and forget about the nasty food critic. And now because Heath was no longer on the scene, I wouldn't have to hold my pie contest. Good thing Sam didn't know anything about that problem or he'd figure I had enough motive to kill the critic.

I walked slowly to the door, chin in the air as if I had a stack of books on my head and was practicing to be a runway model. I turned before I left and looked Sam in the eye. I spoke calmly. For me that is. "Mr. Barr is dead. I'm not guilty and I'm not sorry. You can put that in your police log or in your column."

I didn't slam the door behind me. I closed it firmly before Sam had a chance to respond. Then I stomped back to my shop without a backward glance. Instead of flaking out and turning in early, my adrenaline was pumping and I was much too charged up to do anything but work. As I sometimes did, I used baking as a therapy tool and went out of my way to think up some savory new items for the fair the next day so I wouldn't dwell on the investigation revolving around me.

First I made individual Argentine *empanadas* with ground beef, chopped hard-boiled eggs, onions, green olives and spices, all encased in a flaky puff pastry crust. Next I put together a batch of cheese *bourekas,* those Middle-Eastern cheese-filled pastry pockets. I thought people would want something small and savory to munch on as they strolled the market on a warm sunny Saturday. It's always good to introduce the locals to different tastes as well as the old reliable standards like the pies I'd told Sam about. I'd see how business was tomorrow and then make any adjustments to my menu for next week.

I wondered if anyone but us vendors knew about Heath's demise. Whoever knew, whoever didn't know and didn't care . . . we'd all be back at the fair, one week after we'd been soundly bashed by the critic. The good thing was we had no need to be afraid of being criticized by him ever again. As for myself, I could kiss my pie contest good-bye now that Heath was out of the picture. As far as I knew, the *Gazette* had never had a food critic in the past and maybe would never have one again. I wished I knew who to credit for the loss of his presence. Not that I approve of murder. But I wasn't crying buckets over it either. Maybe if I'd met the man I'd feel sorrier that he was dead.

The next morning I arrived early at the fair after a restless night. I didn't sleep well. Maybe because I was not only worried about a killer on the loose, I was even more worried about being mistaken for that killer. By the chief of police of all people. I dressed in layers, a pair of cut-off denim shorts then some stretch pants, a tank top covered with an oversized sweater which felt good at eight this morning, but by noon would be way too heavy. Then I packed my station wagon to the brim with pies, along with my portable cooler. The awning and the structure of the booth would be set up by the fair work crew. All I had to do was arrange my pies and sell them.

My stalwart student worker Manda arrived at the fair shortly after I did and after we set up and unpacked the pies, I took advantage of her presence to walk around before the opening bell.

I loved that time of day. Sellers were unloading their trucks and vans as the sun was just warming the pavement of the school parking lot. The fresh-picked leafy green vegetables looked crisp and succulent. The corn in green husks was piled high, waiting to be shucked. Strawberries, peaches, and nectarines were at their prime, oozing juice and sweet flavor. Everything was so calm and peaceful it was hard to imagine anything bad happening around here. In fact, I couldn't help thinking positively. Something good was bound to happen. Sam would catch the murderer. It would be a stranger, an outsider. No one we knew. Why would a stranger kill Heath Barr? I had no answer for that. But when we found out we would all be relieved and grateful to our police chief. I would sell all my pies.

I was dying to talk to my fellow vendors to find out what happened when they met with Sam the night before. After their interviews they'd each taken off without saying much and looking shaken. I hoped they too would be feeling more upbeat to-day.

But it didn't look promising. As the sun

73

rose and the booths opened, none of my new friends seemed willing to talk to me. What had Sam done to them? Threatened them with arrest if they got in touch with me or each other? Warned them that I was a problem? Told them I was trouble with a capital T? Or was it just my imagination?

First I dashed across the aisle to approach Lurline, who said she was too busy to talk. She did give me a lemon coconut cupcake though. Maybe that was to divert me, or to buy me off. If I could be bought off, cupcakes were the way to do it. I said I'd see her later and walked back to my pies licking the frosting off my lips. And wondering. Was it just my own anxiety or was Lurline acting strange?

Later when I had a chance for a brief break, I dropped by the sausage booth. Bill said he was short-handed. Dave couldn't make it and he was all by himself. I murmured something sympathetic and he told me again I should come by to see their ranch. "You can't appreciate our pork products until you see how we coddle our pigs. Fresh air, good food and movable pens, and healthy soil. You ever see how pigs live?" he asked.

I had to admit I hadn't. Even more than seeing how the pigs lived in their movable pens, I wanted to hear how his interview with Sam went, but this wasn't the place to ask him about it. There were too many potential customers milling about, all in search of the best buys in home-grown pig products. I also wanted to see how they raised pigs to sell and how they made their sausage. I knew what they said about sausage making. You may love the final product but you don't want to watch them make it. But I did. I really did. Since I couldn't discuss anything about the murder here or what had happened in the police station, I decided then to take Bill up on his offer.

As for Jacques, the European cheese maker, he was not his usual outgoing self. Maybe he was saving himself for the paying customers. Or worried the police were going to corner him and ask more questions. Or just into his performance as a cheese salesman extraordinaire. He was setting up to make sandwiches out of his white cheddar cheese, torpedo onions, escarole, and sourdough bread. "All the ingredients are from our own Food Fair," he announced to the crowd that was starting to gather to watch this French chef with his white chef's hat and large striped apron. No wonder he didn't have time for me. But I made time for him. He was the epitome of what it takes to make it at the market. He looked great. He talked fast with a to-die-for accent. He was enthusiastic. And had some fantastic food to sell. He had a small hot plate where he was grilling the sliced onion with chopped garlic.

"Brush the bread with some of the olive oil in the pan," he said waving his brush in the air with a flourish. No wonder he attracted a crowd and the fair had barely opened. He had a flair for drama. After he assembled the sautéed onions, the cheese, the escarole between two slices of sourdough bread from Lindsey and Tammy's bread booth, he flipped the sandwiches into the pan and cooked them until the cheese was gooey and oozing out onto the crust. It all looked and smelled heavenly. When he cut up the sandwich into little sample bites my mouth watered, but standing at the edge of the crowd I didn't get even one bite.

Frustrated I hadn't had a chance to grill Jacques as he was too busy grilling the sandwiches, I bought a high moisture Jack cheese studded with rosemary from him. He thanked me, then he leaned forward and said, "How are you doing?"

"Okay," I said. "You?"

He nodded, then waited on some other customers. I sensed he was disturbed —

either by Heath's murder or by Sam's questioning him. He certainly wasn't his usual flirtatious self. Or maybe I was the one who wasn't my usual self. I left to go back to my booth so Manda could go to her SAT class at the high school. Who knows what would have happened if I'd done better on my SATs. I might be chief of police now myself. Sometimes I thought my life would have been more exciting if I'd gone into law enforcement — not police chief, but something like bounty hunter or private investigator where intuition would be an asset. Sam was competent and very smart and good at what he did. He was also authoritative, which is important. I told myself making a profit off of pies is challenging enough and the job has been good to me.

I wished Sam would hurry up and solve this mystery. Not just to clear my name and my friends' names and let us get back to normal life, but for his own sake and his reputation in town.

I hated having him tell me to go back to the kitchen. I knew where I belonged. I was kidding myself thinking I could do both — bake pies and help find clues. On the other hand, I was involved in this murder whether Sam liked it or not. I'd had a run-in with

Heath and that put me on the suspect list. How could I not be involved? I sighed.

There was nothing I could do. I didn't have training and even if I did, Sam would never let me get near a suspect. Unless he didn't know about it. All I could do for now was to keep my eyes and ears open and if I heard something, I'd pass it on to the authorities. In the meantime, Sam was right. Baking pies was my job. I was good at it. I needed to concentrate on what I did best.

"I need a gimmick," I said to Grannie and her chums when they stopped by.

"Nonsense," Grannie insisted. "You have quality pies. Why do you need a gimmick?"

"Because everyone else has one," I said, averting my eyes from Lurline's booth where she was icing cupcakes with the initials of the customer while they waited. "Actually someone suggested I hold a pie contest." I waited expecting Grannie and her friends to throw up their hands and say, "A pie contest? What for? That's the most ridiculous idea I ever heard." But they didn't.

"How would that work?" Helen asked.

I shrugged. "I'm not sure. Never mind. The person who suggested it is . . . out of the picture." That was for sure. Heath Barr was as far out of the picture as possible. I could forget about the pie contest.

Helen put her hand on my arm. "I actually like the idea of the contest," she said. "You'll be the judge. People will bring their pies to your shop and you'll have a bake-off. The customers can vote."

"Or your grandmother could be the judge," Grace said with a nod toward Grannie. "You could charge an entry fee and give the money to charity. Or not. All you need is a prize."

Now I was getting worried. They were really into this contest thing. I should have kept my mouth shut.

"I have a silver tea service. I never use it," Helen said. "Not since I moved to Heavenly Acres."

"But Helen," I protested, "you might want to have a tea some afternoon for your friends."

"If I do, I'll invite them up on the hill," she said referring to Heavenly Acres Retirement Home located on a hill above town with an ocean view. "We have tea every afternoon in the dining room or on the terrace. It's a lovely atmosphere and very nicely done with the little cucumber sandwiches and all."

"But what about your heirs? Won't they want to inherit your tea set?"

"I offered it to my daughter, she turned me down. So it's yours for a good cause. Whatever the cause. Whether it's to encourage home baking or promote your pie shop."

"That's very generous of you," I said. The way she said it made the contest sound like a public service. "I'll think about it. Are you sure it's a good idea? What if someone out there is a better baker than I am?"

Grannie shook her head in disbelief. Helen and Grace assured me it wasn't possible. Still I had in no way committed myself yet.

Grannie then sidled up to me and said in a loud whisper. "Is it true about the food critic?"

I nodded. "You mean . . ."

"That he was murdered?"

"That's what they say," I said.

She shook her head. "I should never have retired. This town has gone to rack and ruin since I gave up the shop."

"You're not saying I had anything to do with this homicide or any other unnatural death are you?"

"Of course not, it's not your fault. It's the times we live in. I thought I'd be safe up at Heavenly Acres. But now I'm looking over my shoulder. Until they catch the murderer."

"You are safe. Just don't criticize anyone in the *Gazette* and you'll stay safe."

"Then you think it was someone Mr. Barr dumped on who offed him," Grannie said.

I hid a smile when I heard Grannie talking like a mobster. "That's my theory."

"Then Sam will catch him." Grannie thought Sam rivaled any detective, whether Sam Spade, Columbo, or Sherlock Holmes.

"You think it was a him?"

"No woman could have done such a horrible thing," Grannie said with a frown. "Slit his throat with a cake knife."

"Where'd you hear that?" I asked. As if I didn't know. The retirement home was a hotbed of gossip that spread faster than an outbreak of influenza.

"Oh you know. Here and there," she said vaguely.

"Which reminds me," I said, "I want to check out the knife seller. I've never seen his booth."

"Over there," she said with a nod in the direction of the high school. "I passed by it earlier. His display is quite attractive and he's not bad himself. Go ahead, we'll watch the booth."

After that description I expected a guy who ran a booth called The Perfect Edge with a dazzling selection of knives, cleavers, spatulas, and other kitchen tools to look tough, with bulging muscles and maybe wearing camouflage. But this man looked like the grandfather I never had with a smiley face and a thatch of white hair. I didn't blame Grannie for not providing me with a grandfather. She'd had two husbands, the latest after I'd left the nest. And she'd done a great job being mother, father, grandmother, and grandfather to me, all the while running a pie shop too.

"What can I do for you my dear?" the man said with a smile on his round face.

"I'm Hanna over at The Upper Crust. I've got one of your knives." Or I did have one until Sam took it. *And I've got an unmarried grandmother who needs a man in her life.* "It's perfect for slicing and serving my pies."

"Hello there, Hanna from The Upper Crust. It's nice to hear something good about my kitchen knives. If only everyone was as positive as you are. But unfortunately . . ." He stopped and took a deep breath. When he picked up a long serrated bread knife with a smooth wooden handle I saw his hand shake.

I waited, hoping to hear more. But maybe neither of us wanted to bring up the topic of murder.

"As with all tools," he said. "They can be

used for good or bad. Which is what I told the police chief just a short time ago when he confiscated all my remaining stock of the model you mentioned."

I wanted to say, *He didn't accuse you of murder, did he?* But maybe this kindly grandfather figure wouldn't tell me if he did. Maybe he'd be shocked to hear what his knife-spatula had done yesterday. If Sam hadn't told him.

He reached up on the display board behind him where he had all kinds of knives and spatulas hanging in an artful display. Even Kate couldn't have made a better arrangement. He grabbed a knife set and held it out. "I recommend this one. Made of rosewood," he said, "hand crafted. Has to be rubbed with mineral oil to protect the wood and preserve the grain."

I ran my finger over the blade. This was a lovely knife, but not useful for any kind of tough job like cutting meat. *Or cutting throats.* "It's beautiful," I said. If only I and my colleagues had bought this ornamental wooden set instead of the deadly one, would Heath Barr be alive today? That was presuming one of them committed the murder and I didn't really believe that, did I?

I looked at the knives on his counter and focussed on another combination knife/

spatula that I really liked. Charley, the knife seller followed my gaze.

"That's the Italian artisan knife, made by hand in Piedmont by old-world craftsmen. The rest of my knives are machine-made. They do the job but they're strictly utilitarian. I'm the only one in California who sells this beauty. For those who want the best. That's you, if I'm not mistaken," he said with a twinkle in his eye. Ah yes, this was the grandfather I'd always wanted. The kind who would have taught me to ride a bicycle and carved ABC blocks for me in his garage. He put the hand-made knife into my hand and I felt the smooth wood against my palm and the shape that fit my grasp as if it were made for me.

"You're not mistaken that I lean toward the most expensive whatever it is," I admitted. "This is beautiful." I glanced at a small discrete price sticker and gasped. "Maybe after I make my first million. The one I already have works fine. Not as nice as this one, but it's very sharp. Cuts meat and everything."

"The Model X-40," he said. "That's the one the chief took."

"I'm sorry to hear that. It does such a great job I wanted to order one for everyone I know," I said.

He nodded. "Too great a job. It seems there's been a problem."

"I think I know what problem you're referring to. I had a visit from the chief also. I'm guessing he's looking for everyone who ever bought one of your X-40 serrated spatula-knives."

"Sorry I couldn't help him. I don't keep a list of buyers. I know I should. Other vendors do so they can send flyers to their customers to alert them of special sales and so forth. I'm just not organized enough." He shrugged.

"I understand," I said. "I should be doing that too, but I'm not. It's all I can do to get myself and my pies here once a week and keep up with the customers without worrying about keeping lists or records. But it's true, it would be a good business tactic. If I had a list I could send notices about my holiday pies in advance so I could be prepared."

He agreed that would make good business sense. Then he politely asked me what kind of pies I made and I promised to bring him a sample.

Still thinking of Grannie and her single state, I tried to check out his ring finger to see if he was married, but I couldn't tell so I said, "I imagine your wife is a big help with the paperwork." I know it sounded sexist, but I had to say something.

"She was," he said sadly. "Until she passed on three years ago."

I finally tore myself away, wondering how much Sam had told him about the "problem" with his spatula-knife X-40. I took a moment to congratulate myself for finding out that the charming old fellow wasn't married. Now I was getting as bad as Grannie and her friends with their zeal of matchmaking. But how can anyone blame me for wanting to locate Husband Number Three to fill Grannie's life with love and happiness and a collection of upscale cutlery.

So Sam was one step ahead of me. Today anyway. Tomorrow was another day. I might be wrong, but I hoped and believed that I had a better chance of getting people to talk than Sam did. If I wanted to. Sometimes the police can frighten people. I liked to think I could get information from people by coaxing them. Which would you rather be, frightened or coaxed?

I hurried back to my booth with the news I'd met the man of Grannie's dreams.

"What's Sylvester Stallone doing here at the Food Fair?" she asked.

"Not Sly, but a charming artisan who's

adorable. I'll introduce you."

"Not today." She shook her head. "My hair is a mess and I need a facial."

"Okay, next week then. I have a good feeling about this."

"Your friend Kate was here," Grannie said, changing the subject because she was obviously uncomfortable at my clumsy attempt to set her up with an attractive man. "She bought some meat pies and some other stuff and she said she'd be at the picnic tables having lunch." Grannie pointed toward the far end of the food section where hungry customers could chow down on their farm-fresh goods before leaving the fair. "Why don't you run along and have a coffee or something to eat with her? I'm having fun selling your pies," she said. "I've run into a few friends I hadn't seen in ages. Why didn't I think of this?"

"If you're sure," I said.

She nodded emphatically.

Picnic tables had been set up at the edge of the Food Fair to encourage customers to buy and eat and then go back and buy some more food to take home. It looked like it was working. Kate waved to me from the far end of the area where she was wedged in between other happy fair-goers chowing down goodies like homemade mini-pizzas with brioche crust, fresh fruit drinks, kettle corn, and pâte spread on whole-grain crackers.

I squeezed in between two groups on a bench across from Kate and she opened a plastic container of olives stuffed with blue cheese and offered them to me along with a spicy tofu wrap.

"I didn't know you were into health food," I said eyeing the low-cal flax and whole-wheat wrap suspiciously.

"Let's just say I'm into all kinds of food in a big way, from flax to this gooey cinnamon twist. Take your pick." I chose the twist and washed it down with a paper cup of coffee laced with cream she offered me.

After popping an olive in her mouth, she looked to her right and then to her left. Then she leaned forward. "I heard something disturbing."

I nodded. "I think I know what you mean," I said softly.

"Why didn't you tell me?" she demanded.

"It's not easy to talk about around here, especially with my mouth full of blue cheese."

She tilted her head to one side and looked around at the crowd. Probably wondering how safe it was to say anything confidential.

That's when I overheard a man at the

picnic table behind me say something interesting.

"You say it was murder?" he asked in a low raspy voice.

Oh my God, the "M" word. My ears positively sizzled. That was the word I wasn't supposed to say or hear or investigate. No wonder my whole body went on the alert.

"She said it, not me," another guy answered. "You know how women are. Can't keep their mouths shut."

"Can't live with them, can't live without them," the first one agreed. "You know where she was last night?"

I didn't hear an answer and I didn't want to turn around and stare even though I was dying to know who the guys were. I purposely dropped the plastic fork Kate had given me and leaned down to pick it so I could sneak a look at the speakers from the other table. All I saw was a pair of shoes as one of the guys got up to leave. He was wearing sandals, the kind appropriate for wading in swamps with thick rubber soles and brown leather straps.

"I've got to run," I told Kate, standing up abruptly. "Back to work." But I didn't intend to go back to my booth, I wanted to follow the guy who mentioned "murder" and "last night." It couldn't be an accident. It had to have something to do with the one and only murder in Crystal Cove and I had to follow up on it. And it had landed in my lap so to speak. But by the time I turned to go, intending to follow the guy in the sandals, he was gone.

I felt Kate's curious gaze follow me as I walked away, no doubt wondering why I was acting so strange and muttering "Damn, damn, damn," to myself. I tried to tell myself it was probably nothing. I was over-reacting. Playing detective when I was strictly instructed not to. The men were probably talking about a movie or a TV program. No way did a murderer discuss his or any other crime at a food fair picnic table. The whole idea was laughable, but somehow I didn't feel like laughing.

Four

I not only had to postpone Grannie's intro to Mr. Right Number Three, aka the knife seller, but I also had to take over my pie booth that afternoon and let Grannie get back to Heavenly Acres for her afternoon Bridge game.

I was able to forget anything to do with the "M" word for a few hours because business was brisk. I handed out samples, engaged buyers in conversation about my fresh-baked, luscious pies, my quaint little shop, and my colorful grandmother. You name it, I was Chatty Kathy, as Grannie used to call me, praising our charming small town and, of course, my own pies.

Then Sam came by and it all came back to me. I had walked out of his office last evening with my "I'm not guilty and I'm not sorry" statement. Maybe I shouldn't have been so rash. I could have said "I'm not guilty, but I AM sorry." But I wasn't.

He knew that. So why pretend different?

"Good to see you," I said with a smile, hoping he'd forgotten our last conversation. "Have you had lunch?"

He shook his head. "I'm not here to eat."

I stifled what my response would have been — *Well, what are you here for?* Instead I said, "Well then how about something to take home like a bourek or an empanada?" I wrapped a crisp bourek in a special tissue paper and held it out.

He studied it carefully. Either he'd never seen one before or he was a true aficionado of Middle Eastern cuisine. Then he said "Thanks," and actually ate it while he stood in front of my booth watching me talk a woman into buying the last Strawberry Cream Pie from my portable cooler.

"The strawberries are organic and picked locally," I said. "They're so sweet I hardly had to use any sugar."

"How many will it serve?" she asked.

"That depends," I said. "Six large pieces or twelve slivers suitable for dieters."

"Dieters? I never invite dieters to my house. It looks so good I could eat the whole thing right now." She sighed. "But I won't."

"I admire your restraint," I told her, sliding the pie into a box.

When the woman left, I swallowed my pride and apologized to Sam for being snippy the night before. "I shouldn't have said I wasn't sorry Heath was murdered. It must have sounded heartless." I was hoping he'd say, *Hanna, you're definitely NOT heartless,* but he didn't.

He said, "You're not the only one."

I waited hoping he'd elaborate, tell me who else was glad Heath was gone out of their lives. I could imagine everyone who Heath had criticized was on that list, but who else? He didn't say. What he did say was, "That was an outstanding boureka, best I've had since I left San Francisco."

"Was it at that little place out on Geary Street that made the best Mediterranean food? I loved that shop. I don't know how they did it. But I'm determined to find out. So in between traditional pies I keep trying something new. Grannie thinks I'm crazy for deviating from her old standards, but making the same apple pie every fall gets boring."

"It was a place called Aziza," he said. "With hand-woven carpets on the walls."

"That's the one. I used to go there for the stuffed grape leaves and the dolmah."

"So did I."

I looked at him and I wondered how we'd

missed each other. Was it by minutes? Or was it by years? Maybe it was fate. We were not meant to meet again until now. But why? He propped his arm against the post that held up the sides of my booth as if this was nothing but a casual visit by old friends hanging out together at the Food Fair.

I didn't understand. Was he on duty or not? Was this an official visit or what? Had he caught the murderer and now he was taking a break? Whatever it was, it was a big change from the way he'd acted last night. And a welcome one.

"I'm surprised I never saw you there," he said. "And you're surprised I ever ate anything but donuts."

I shook my head. "If you did, you wouldn't be in such good shape now." Then I bent over to brush a non-existent smudge from the counter so he couldn't catch me staring lustfully at his body. "Were you a cop then?" I asked. I thought I'd slip in a personal question when he wasn't on guard in hopes of uncovering something from the mysterious middle part of Sam's life. I knew about his high-school years and I knew about his small-town police chief career, but not much about what happened in between except for an incident where his partner was killed. Would he ever tell me the whole story?

"No, I wasn't," he said. "What were you doing besides eating boureks?"

"I had a job. I went to work, I came home, and I hung out with friends. That's my story. What's yours?" I asked.

"Same," he said.

Just when I was about to give up on his lack of communication skills, Lindsey and Tammy came by on break from their booth, each clutching loaves of their bread under their arms.

"Sam," Tammy said, batting her eyelashes at him just like she did in high school, "any luck finding the murderer?"

Finally someone asking the question I wanted to ask but didn't have the guts to. I watched to see what Sam's reaction would be. Instead of instructing them to mind their own business, he just shrugged and said, "Not yet."

If I'd asked he probably would have given me the lecture where he glares at me and tells me to stick to baking, but somehow Lindsey escaped that fate. I wished I knew her secret.

"But you must have some idea. Who are the 'persons of interest'?" Tammy asked. "And don't say it's everyone. You don't think any of us girls had anything to do with it, do you? Even though we hated his guts."

"Shhh." Lindsey poked her and motioned for her to tone down her rhetoric.

"It's not a secret," Tammy protested. "Everyone must know by now someone bumped off our food critic and good riddance."

I'd never been a fan of Tammy's, not in high school where she was one of the popular girls and I wasn't and not now either, but at that moment I admired her for having the nerve to speak up. Because I sure didn't.

"The investigation is on-going," Sam said cryptically. Of course he'd say that. He was his usual close-mouthed self.

"I told you he'd said that," Tammy said to Lindsey. Then she turned to me. "Hanna, we came to pick up a couple of pies. What've you got?"

"How about a peach and apricot in a cream cheese crust?" I reached for the pie I'd baked in a deep tart tin with the wavy edge and held it up so they could see the browned top. The juices had bubbled over, leaving a crisp fruity crust.

"Ooooh, it's so beautiful," Lindsey said. "I'll take it."

"Take another. I owe you," I said. I sug-

96

gested a tart All-American Key Lime Pie with a graham cracker crust made with lime juice, evaporated milk, and egg yolks. Lindsey snapped that up too and they toddled off with their treasures. If they were suspects in the Heath Barr murder, they sure didn't seem worried about it. I ought to be more like them. Relax. Stick to business. Ignore the murder. Don't try to help the cops.

"You act like you like your work," Sam said when they'd gone back to their booth. I was surprised he was still there. He could have followed Lindsey and Tammy. They definitely wouldn't have minded at all.

"I do like it. I'm selling something that makes people happy. They don't need it, but they want it. They may not be rich, they may not be driving a Mercedes, but almost anyone can afford a pie. I assume someone like Lurline who makes cupcakes or Nina with her caramels feels the same as I do." I took a breath. Enough about me.

"What about you, Sam, do you enjoy your work? With you, it's hard to tell. Would you rather rescue cats from trees and arrest drunk drivers than be challenged by a devious murderer?"

"What makes you think he's devious?" Sam asked.

"Well, he hasn't been caught," I said. I waited for him to say he was ready to make an arrest, but he didn't. "By the way, what makes you think it's a man?"

"Touché," he said with a nod indicating that I just possibly might be thinking straight. "I'm only going on history, which isn't always reliable. Most violent bloody murders are done by men. Which is not to say a woman couldn't slit a man's throat."

I shuddered trying not to picture the scene. "I'm really glad I never met the man," I said. "Aren't you? I mean aren't you glad you didn't meet him when he was alive? Or did you?"

He shook his head. "I would have preferred that to meeting him when he was dead," he said somberly.

"In his office you mean," I said, then I waited for him to confirm or deny it. I knew I was pushing my luck by trying to find out more, but I could always hope.

He didn't comment so I continued along a different line. "I don't think you ever answered my question. If you don't want to talk about your work, how about the town? Are you glad you came back?"

"Now that I know where to find my favorite ethnic food items, things are looking up," he said with a pointed look at the shelf behind my counter.

What? Sam saying something flattering? "If you've got any special requests, I'm always looking for a culinary challenge." I've never believed that old saw about the way to a man's heart, but maybe, just maybe . . . If I could keep my mouth shut and stick to baking. But could I? And would I want to?

Right now I wanted so badly to tell him what I'd overheard at the picnic tables, but I wasn't going to. Even if I had a written confession or caught the killer in the act, I was not going to say a word. If that's the way Sam wanted it, then that's how it was going to be.

He left after I had a rush of customers and I wondered when I'd see him again. You'd think because it was a small town and his office was across the street from my shop we'd be running into each other five times a day and twice on Sunday, but it didn't happen.

On that Sunday I was restless. I knew I had to wait until Monday to follow up on the Heath Barr problem. If you can call a murder a problem. I'm not good at waiting. I'm impatient and my restless nature has gotten me into trouble more than once. So far I've talked my way out of it, but there's always a first time. I wanted badly to pay a visit to the newspaper offices to make sure Heath hadn't told anyone there about the pie contest idea, but they were closed on the weekend. That didn't stop me from walking over to the town square and knocking on the second floor office of the *Gazette* just to see if anyone was there. What do I know about the news business? Maybe they had odd hours, I thought.

But it was closed. Not only closed, but it had a wide yellow tape across the door that said "Crime Scene." So it was true. So Heath had been murdered right there in his office. I didn't need Sam to confirm it. I felt a chill go up my spine. That should have been enough to scare me away, but I rattled the doorknob anyway. Nothing happened. I left and came back to my shop hoping no one saw me at the crime scene.

I had two reasons to visit the *Gazette* headquarters. Besides making sure Heath hadn't shared his idea of a pie contest with the editor, I planned to place an ad in the paper advertising my pies. I wanted the populace to know they could find me at the Food Fair on Saturdays with the same mouth-watering pies available throughout the week at the shop.

I knew it wasn't my job to solve crimes. Sam had made that perfectly clear. He was right. He had the badge of authority to go where mere citizens feared to go, and I didn't. It was none of my business who killed Heath.

It was crazy of me to ever think Sam would appreciate my meddling in his work. He was a private person. Always had been. His parents weren't around much in his life and when they were they weren't very friendly or lovable. He'd been on his own as long as I'd known him and that was in high school. Of course for all I knew he had an ex-wife and four kids somewhere. He didn't mention them but nothing about him would surprise me. I guess he felt the same about me. Did that mean we were destined for each other? Probably not. But I couldn't deny he figured in more than one of my fuzzy romantic dreams. I have a problem with unattainable men — in that they're more attractive than the attainable ones.

Instead of spending what was left of the weekend rolling out crusts and freezing them to prepare for a busy week ahead, I decided to take advantage of the warm sunny weather and take Grannie on a drive out of town. She was as independent as anybody's grandmother could be, but sometimes she looked a little wistful when she asked me what I was doing on Sunday.

Though maybe that was just my imagination, since the activities list at Heavenly Acres was staggering. And she had more friends there than anyone in town. My usual Sunday involved something to do with baking, so she understood why I couldn't join her for shuffleboard or bingo, but when I called to ask if she wanted to see the countryside that Sunday morning, she sounded pleased.

But where to go? She told me I should choose. Should we visit the ranch owned by Bill and Dave? They'd invited Sam, but no one else, to see how their sausages were made, but wouldn't it be okay for someone on a Sunday drive in the country to drop in uninvited to a ranch where pampered pigs were turned into delicious sausages. Or would I be intruding? Did Bill say Dave was sick or just busy? I could always bring a pie. I'd used that ruse more than once. "I brought you a pie," I'd say, then I'd stay for tea or coffee and ask a few questions, perhaps even make a few connections. The downside was if I said "I brought you a pie" I couldn't pretend I was out for a drive and just happened to be passing their ranch and thought I'd see if they were home . . . And just happened to have a pie in my cooler with their name on it.

I wrapped up a double-crust fresh peach pie and called to see if Grannie was ready. I suggested either heading toward Martha's chicken farm or Bill and Dave's ranch. I'd picked up brochures from both booths. I had reason to visit both. They'd both said they welcomed visitors in a general sense. I took that as an invitation. And an opportunity not to be missed.

Grannie said she'd need to be back in time for the Sunday night barbecue on the terrace of Heavenly Acres followed by a folk music concert. She voted for Martha's chicken farm when she heard how the chickens were treated like royalty. So off we went, heading up the PCH, the famous picturesque Pacific Coast Highway. The sea sparkled on one side, surfers in shiny black wet suits paddled out to sea to catch rides on the long rolling waves and on the other side were fields of wild flowers. Not all of the PCH offers views of the ocean. In southern California parts of the highway are almost five miles inland from the coast. Some of that part of the highway passes vineyards and farms or rolling hills and even some urban landscapes for a change of scene.

Grannie rolled her window down and sighed happily. She had no idea I had any ulterior motives for this trip. She appeared to have forgotten about the murder or more likely she was avoiding the subject just as I was, so we could just enjoy the day and pretend it didn't happen. That was fine for her, and for me too. It would be nice to learn something, using a kind of sneaky or subtle way of extracting information, but that wasn't likely.

"We should do this more often," she said patting the arm-rest of her old car, which still ran like new after I'd had the engine rebuilt and the shocks replaced.

"You're usually busy on Sundays. Bridge, church, brunch . . ." I said.

"It wasn't always like that. When I was a child, my parents would take us out for a Sunday drive along this very coast. My father had some stories to tell. He even knew some of the men who built this highway."

"He didn't know William Randolph Hearst, did he?" I asked.

"I don't think so. But they said his house cost as much as the highway to build."

"You say house, but don't you mean Hearst Castle, the mansion where Hearst entertained movie stars way back in the twenties and thirties?'

Grannie checked her guide book and nodded. "It was designed by the wonderful architect Julia Morgan. It says here she was educated at the Ecole des Beaux Arts in Paris. 'Hearst's mother Phoebe Apperson Hearst introduced her to her son and voila, her career was launched. The Hearst Castle was a lifetime job. Hearst was always changing his mind, upgrading and adding to it'."

"I heard he only wanted a bungalow because he was tired of camping in a tent on his property," I said. "From a tent to a castle. I'm sure he could afford it. Read what your book says about the construction of the Pacific Coast Highway."

She flipped her book open to the chapter on the history of the PCH. "They hired prisoners from San Quentin to work on the road," she read. "The inmates were paid thirty-five cents a day and their prison sentences were reduced in exchange for their work. Locals also got jobs. John Steinbeck was one of them."

"Wonder what his job was. Check the map, will you?" I asked, pointing to the glove compartment. "I googled Martha's Chicken Ranch and I've got the directions here." I handed her my printout.

"If I was still driving I'd get myself one of those GPS things that tell you where to go. They've got a voice inside, even tells you when you make a wrong turn. Helen's son has one."

"Good idea," I said.

"I'll get you one."

"You don't have to do that."

"I want to. I have some extra money put aside."

I shot a sideways glance at her. She had a funny secretive little smile on her face.

"I'm glad to hear it. Did you win at bingo?"

"No, but I have a new job."

"What? I thought you said you never had to work again."

"I don't HAVE to work. That's the nice thing. As long as I live within my means. But this isn't for money."

"Are you going to tell me what it is?" I asked impatiently.

"I'm not supposed to tell anyone," said. "Not at first."

My mind was spinning. What could her job possibly be? "Are you going to be one of those undercover mystery shoppers?"

"In Crystal Cove? Where would I shop?"

"I don't know. I just thought you'd be perfect at it. No one would ever suspect you."

"Thank you for your confidence," she said. "Of course if you promised not to tell anyone . . ."

"Cross my heart."

"I'm the new advice columnist at the *Gazette.*"

I almost drove off the road into a ditch. "What?"

"You're surprised," she said with a little smile. "You shouldn't be. Around Heavenly Acres I'm known as quite a sage, in relationships especially."

"So this is a kind of 'Advice to the Lovelorn' column?"

"Partly. We'll see what kind of advice people want. I see myself as a combination of Miss Manners and Dear Abby."

"That's great. You'll be a fabulous Miss Manners-slash-Abby."

"Thank you. Of course I don't get paid. But I figure it's a stepping stone."

"Absolutely. Today the *Gazette,* tomorrow *The New York Times.* Or do they have an advice columnist?"

She shrugged. "I'm available."

"When do you start?" I asked.

"As soon as I get my act together and buy a new computer, one of those easy kind they make for us seniors. Then I'll need some letters to answer. Oh, and this is strictly hush-hush, so not a word to anyone. I'll be going undercover. I'll be known as 'ask

Maggie'."

"That's a good idea. Too bad Heath wasn't undercover. He might still be alive." I hoped Grannie wasn't taking a dangerous job. All the better if no one knew she was the face behind the column.

"Oh, there it is," she said pointing to a sign that said, One Mile Ahead. MARTHA'S FREE RANGE CHICKEN RANCH: *No antibiotics. No preservatives. All chickens raised without hormones. Family owned and operated since 1935.*

"Sounds good," Grannie said, referring to the chicken.

I was especially grateful we'd taken this field trip together. Otherwise when was she going to tell me about her new career? Now the subject was closed until she brought it up again. I hoped one day she'd be able to take credit for her advice. I was so proud of her I was dying to shout it all over the countryside.

"Is this Martha expecting us?" Grannie asked.

"Not exactly. I mean she said if anyone was interested they should come to her ranch. She's proud of the way she raises her chickens, all organic like that. I could have called her . . . but I wasn't sure where we'd end up today." I also wanted to surprise

Martha. Naturally I didn't suspect her of anything but being an obsessive-compulsive free range chicken booster, but I've been surprised before. Sam told me once in a burst of confidentiality that murderers are often just as likable as the guy next door. I've even heard that many people would commit murder if they thought they could get away with it. It was just that Martha seemed like a tough bird herself, unlike her own birds which weren't tough at all.

"If she's not home we'll just find ourselves a restaurant along the coast. Looking in my other little guide book here, *Exploring California Coastal Eateries* makes me hungry. Aren't you?" Grannie asked.

I nodded. "As usual, you've come prepared. You're a good sport to humor me this way. I just want to pop in, see her facilities and we can go have lunch. I don't picture chicken farmers often taking the day off so I'm thinking she'll be around. I don't know if she has a big staff but she seems like the hands-on type to me."

"I didn't know you pictured chicken farmers at all," she said. "Not a big-city refugee like you."

"I'd never met one until I met Martha. You'll like her. She's outspoken and really into this organic free-range chicken farm

109

stuff. Everyone I know from the Food Fair is passionate about whatever they sell. I feel like I found my group at last."

"That's good, you need a group of young people your own age. Though my friends are always glad to see you. In fact you might like to come up for croquet next weekend. We're having a big game."

"Sounds like fun," I said lightly. Croquet. I was hoping I wouldn't be that desperate for excitement. "But I do have friends, you know. I have Kate, who's just great. The problem is all the other people from my class are in a different class, if you know what I mean. They're married like Lindsey and Tammy, or married to their work like Sam, which leaves me . . ."

"Lonely?" Grannie asked.

"No. Not lonely. Not at all. I'm just happy that I've found a group of Food Fair friends." The last thing I wanted was for Grannie to feel sorry for me and rope me into a croquet game. I pasted a smile on my face and patted her knee reassuringly.

"That's good," she said. "This murder is a mixed blessing. Of course it's too bad for this Heath person, but it has just brought the rest of you together closer and faster than it would have."

"Unless one of us did it," I said staring

into the oncoming traffic, half hypnotized, my mind darting from one vendor to the next.

"Is that why we're here? You think maybe . . ."

"No, not really." I shook my head. "We're here because I want to go behind the scenes and see how other food entrepreneurs manage their business and how they live. That's all." I glanced at her, gave her another smile and said, "Really."

She wasn't completely convinced, I could tell by the look in her eyes.

"Don't worry. I don't plan on mentioning the murder at all," I said.

Grannie nodded understandingly. "Then neither will I," she said. A few minutes later we turned off the highway and after a ride down a one-lane paved road we arrived at a large gate with the name of the farm on a wrought-iron sign above it. The two-story white frame farm house was nestled in a grove of tanbark oak trees surrounded by open fields. As we grew closer, we heard the distinctive sound of free-range chickens clucking happily as they enjoyed the sun and fresh air as much as we did. We parked alongside a truck and a van with MARTHA'S FREE RANGE CHICKEN RANCH painted on the side in green.

I thought the smell of chicken manure would permeate the air, but it didn't. Maybe because the total population of poultry was so small compared to the acreage. Which was the idea after all.

Martha came out of the house wearing baggy blue jeans, a Giants T-shirt, and a surprised expression. "Oh," she said. "I wasn't expecting you."

"Sorry, I should have called, but my grandmother and I were in the neighborhood and we brought you a pie."

"Thanks," she said taking it out of my hand. "I thought if you came you'd bring the cop."

Ah, so Martha wanted me to bring Sam instead of a pie. I understood that. He was tall, good-looking, and an authority figure. What's not to like?

"Hanna has told me so much about your chickens I just had to see them for myself," Grannie said with her inimitable winning way. "She's been raving about your spit-roasted chicken." Trust Grannie to come through with the right thing to say. Martha wouldn't have heard words like that from Sam. You couldn't drag a compliment from him, and he'd never gush over a chicken, no matter how succulent.

No wonder Grannie had sold so many pies

in her time. No wonder she had two husbands who doted on her and left her everything they had. She made friends the way other people make coffee, over and over effortlessly wherever she went. I was more determined than ever to introduce her to the knife artisan. As soon as she had her facial.

I saw Martha thaw before my very eyes. I wasn't sure if at first she was embarrassed to be caught in her dungarees or she just didn't like people popping in on her unless they happened to be an example of Crystal Cove's finest law enforcement. Or maybe she didn't want us to see that most of her chickens were stuffed into hen houses instead of pecking around in the pasture as she advertised. Then why would she invite anyone to visit the place? You couldn't hide chickens for very long.

"The reason our chicken tastes so good," Martha told Grannie, zeroing in on her as if I wasn't there or I was too dim to grasp the concept, "is that they're raised outside where they can scratch the soil, eat green plants and whatever bugs they can find. No crowded poultry house around here. Have a look," she said beckoning us to follow her around the back toward the fields. "You'll see what plenty of space and a natural diet can do. No growth enhancers, no meat or bone meal, and positively no antibiotics."

"I'll never buy an ordinary chicken again," Grannie vowed, and I believed her. Of course there was no need for her to buy any chicken or steak or fish ever again. Not as long as she lived at Heavenly Acres. "How did you get into the chicken business?" she asked Martha.

"My father raised a few chickens when I was growing up. Like his father before him. They sold the eggs to the neighbors." Martha paused to lean against a fence, her face tanned and weathered like the farm woman she was. "Dad taught us kids not to get too attached to them because they weren't pets — they were food on the table. At first we begged him not to kill Henny Penny or Chicken Little, but after awhile we got so we could whack the head off a bird with the best of them."

I saw Grannie flinch. She was not a country girl. She preferred her chicken wrapped in plastic at the grocery store. "Do you still . . ." she asked.

"Kill the birds?" Martha shook her head. "I couldn't do it. Not anymore. The chickens still have names. See that Rhode Island Red over there? She's Harriet and the one next to her is her friend Alice. It would be

114

like killing a friend. Beardsley Packing processes our poultry. They're certified and make sure the birds are humanely slaughtered. But not until the chickens are eight or ten weeks."

"So young?" Grannie said.

"That's older than most," Martha said. "Six weeks is the industry standard. Which is another reason our chickens taste better. More time on the ranch. Try one and you'll see."

"I have and you're right," I said. "Your chicken was fantastic."

Martha nodded as if she'd heard it before. After all, she'd had a line of customers at her booth every time I passed by. Despite what Heath said. "Some people buy our chickens for the flavor and some buy just because they want to support organic farming. They know pasture-raised meat is better for you."

Grannie shook Martha's hand and expressed some words of admiration for her operation and her philosophy. As for me I wondered if Martha would have qualms about whacking the head off an adversary like a food critic who dared criticize her chickens unfairly.

I was getting carried away. Martha couldn't even kill her own chickens anymore. And it was time to go. We'd seen the chickens looking as happy as chickens can look, frolicking in a pasture instead of a crowded poultry house, enjoying nature in all its forms including the occasional bug.

"Thanks so much, Martha," I said. "It's been a treat to see your place. I have a better appreciation for what you do."

Grannie was even more effusive in her thanks, which Martha graciously accepted. Before we got into the car and we pulled out of Martha's drive, she did say, "Next time bring the cop." So she hadn't forgotten or given up. I'd have to tell Sam what an impression he'd made on her.

"Well, did you learn anything?" Grannie asked me as we hit the road again. "I assume you were after something besides a look at those hens."

"I learned she runs a first-class operation," I said. "I'd rather be a chicken on her place than . . . some other things," I finished lamely. "What did you think?"

"I was just glad she didn't invite us to lunch. I couldn't stand to eat one of those two-legged creatures she's given names to. It's enough to make anyone a vegetarian."

"Let's give one of those restaurants in your book a try," I suggested.

We had a wonderful late lunch at a place

called Heathcliff on a cliff above the crashing waves. Grannie picked it out after reading reviews from her guidebook. She ordered a classic shrimp Louis, a mound of huge prawns on a bed of lettuce and avocado covered with creamy house-made Louis dressing. I chose calamari, fried in a delicate batter and served with a spicy marinara sauce. The French fries that came with it were twice fried, the waiter explained after I raved about them.

"First cooked at a lower temperature for the inside," he said, "then a high heat where they're fried to order. A sprinkle of salt, a dip in our chef's special sauce and you're tasting paradise. Am I right?"

I assured him he was completely right. "My compliments to the chef," I said.

As the creator of hand-made food I know how much it means to receive a sincere compliment. And how devastating a negative review can be. Heath's review of my pies still rankled a week later. I knew I should forget the critic's comments, especially considering his recent demise, but I just couldn't. I was guessing my cohorts were in the same boat. Although Lindsey and Tammy seemed more upbeat than ever when I saw them on Saturday. As if the critical comments just rolled off their backs like so much fluff.

We had coffee and Grannie insisted on paying. Then she checked her watch and said, "I'd better get back."

"Too bad. I wanted to take you to a pig farm next."

"A pig farm, how delightful. I'd love to go but not today."

"Pigs are not dirty if that's what you're worried about," I said. "They've been given a bad rap. Besides, they have some interesting heritage breeds at Bill and Dave's Blue Sky Ranch. Where else would you get up close and personal with a rare hog like a Large Black or a Tamworth?" The pictures of the very attractive pigs on Dave and Bill's brochure were enough to tempt me to make a visit, even if I didn't have another motive like a murder investigation on my plate. But not today and not with Grannie. I could go alone but I'd rather find someone else to drive there with me.

"We'll go another day. But I need time to freshen up for bridge. Tell me, are you really interested in the pigs or the farmers or do you think . . ."

"I'm not interested in Bill or Dave in the way you mean. And they don't look like murderers. I just want to get a feel for their operation. And for them. Who does what?

How do they divide up the work? How do they get along? Are they doing well? I'm interested in connecting with everyone Heath dumped on in his review. We have a lot in common."

"You mean you're all possible suspects."

I frowned. Had I told her that or had she figured it out? "Have you been talking to Sam?" I asked as we headed back to town on the PCH.

"No, have you?" she said.

"Yes but I wish I hadn't. He told me to stick to baking pies. He does not want my help solving the murder of the newspaper critic."

"Even after you cracked the last murder case?"

"Especially because I cracked the last one."

"That won't stop you, will it?" she asked.

"Not at all. Especially when I'm involved."

Grannie shook her head and advised me not to get involved. She said that solving the critic's murder was not my job.

"I know that," I said. "I'll only do what I have to."

"Stay home and bake pies," she said.

I couldn't believe she'd mouth the same platitudes that Sam did. She, a former single woman who once ran a business. She, a

119

retired pie baker who'd just taken on a new career. I opened my mouth to remind her, then remembered I was sworn to secrecy and wasn't going to bring it up unless she did first.

She pursed her lips in the disapproving way she had. When I dropped her off at Heavenly Acres she'd recovered. She gave me a cheerful wave as if she'd forgotten all about my disobedient ways. It was just as well. I was going to that pig farm with or without my grandmother's approval.

"By the way, the pie contest is off," I said when she turn to wave to me.

"Too bad," she said. "I was looking forward to it."

"Another time," I said.

She smiled and gave me the OK sign with her hand.

FIVE

I'd no sooner parked Grannie's old station wagon in front of my shop when Sam showed up. I could almost believe he might have been watching and waiting for me. Two days in a row where he was actually seeking me out? What was going on? On the other hand, it could have been a coincidence. He walked out of the police station just as I pulled up across the street, but what were the odds? Had he attached a radio transponder to the underside of my car so he could keep track of me? I only wished he wanted to keep track of me. If he did, it was nothing personal. And if it weren't for this murder, I was convinced I'd probably never see him.

"Enjoying the good weather?" he asked as he ambled up to my car, as if we were just neighbors having a little chit-chat on a Sunday afternoon. It was also as if it was a rare event to see the sunshine in our town in the middle of summer. Neither was true.

"Very much," I said. "Don't tell me you are taking the day off? When there's a murder to be solved?" I knew as soon as the words left my mouth I'd overstepped the boundaries he'd set up.

He gave me his thin-lipped, narrow-eyed look as if to say *How dare you discuss my work with me? If I want to bring up the subject I will. But that's not for you to do.*

"No rest for the weary," he said, and his tone was positively friendly. I must have been wrong about the look he gave me. "I hear you've been out to the chicken farm."

"Why yes," I said. I wondered how the hell he knew where I'd been. At least I knew enough not to show my dislike at being under survey. "That's the joy of small-town living. Everyone knows everything about everyone. How about some iced tea and a piece of Key Lime Pie?" Before he could say no, he didn't eat pie, I rushed on. "It's my latest low-fat, summer-time version. Made with nonfat condensed milk, low-fat yogurt, and instead of a heavy whipped cream topping, I made a lovely golden meringue."

While I was talking, I was unlocking the front door of the shop and opening all the windows. He didn't say no, so I asked him

122

to help me drag a small wrought-iron table and chairs outside. I love the sidewalk café look. There was a breeze off the ocean but the sun was still warm. It wouldn't hurt for the citizens of Crystal Cove to see how it's done. That it's okay to stop and relax and drink tea or coffee with a slice of pie in the afternoon. I hoped someone might see us eating and drinking al fresco in front of the pie shop. They'd think, it's so continental. So civilized. And soon they'd take up the custom. Maybe I'd have to stay open on Sundays when the whole town was out and about. Maybe I'd get the aprés-beach crowd. I set two pieces of pie and two glasses of iced tea on the table.

"How did you like the farm?" he asked after he took a bite.

I frowned, annoyed that he was rubbing it in. Why didn't he come out and say, I not only know where you've been, I know where you're going next. "Very impressive. If I had to be a chicken, I'd live there," I said.

"Until the Beardsley Processing van pulled up," he said.

"So you know about that. Were you out there too?" If he was, why didn't Martha say anything?

"I just got back."

"That explains it then," I said. "We

123

crossed paths. Martha must have been thrilled to see you. You made quite an impression on her. I thought maybe you'd come by to return my knife."

"That's not possible. Until after I finish my investigation."

"I suppose you've got quite a collection of knives by now since the old guy who makes them was handing them out."

"I can't comment on that."

I rolled my eyes. "Oh for heaven's sake. So how's your investigation going?"

"Slowly. This guy Heath was a loner. He came to town a few months ago to work at the *Gazette.* No one seems to know much about him."

I was amazed to have Sam telling me something new. I couldn't help following up with another question. "Doesn't he have a family? Someone who misses him? Someone who hated him? Loved him? Although I don't know about that. I only spoke to him on the phone and he wasn't very nice. It wasn't just me. He gave negative reviews to good products. Have you talked to Bruce, the editor of the *Gazette?* Why did they hire him? Why did they keep him?" I moved to the edge of my chair. I leaned forward. This was just what I wanted. A chance to ask questions, maybe have a real conversation with Sam. A sense that I was useful. That I could contribute. That he valued my input.

"I talked to Bruce," Sam said, "and he says Heath convinced him he needed someone controversial for the paper. Someone to shake things up. Someone who'd increase circulation with his pithy reviews. Who wouldn't just whitewash the vendors. And the price was right. Heath was working for nothing."

"Donating his time?" I said. "Why would he do that?" Sam didn't answer. I didn't expect him to. I just knew I had to see Bruce myself. No need to mention I'd been to the newspaper office and seen the crime scene tape across the door, no matter how innocent my trip was.

"So you've been out for a Sunday drive. What else is on your agenda?" he asked, forking a piece of pie while I watched to see how he liked it.

"In terms of field trips? I don't know. My new friends all want me to come by and see their places. The sausage guys, Jacques the cheese maker . . ."

"I plan on a trip to the pig farm too," he said.

"When? Because I could go next week. We could go together," I suggested. "It would save gas." I held my breath. He'd never

125

agree. He was after something more than a few pork chops, that was sure. "At your convenience," I added.

"Okay," he said.

I tried not to act surprised. But why was he doing this? Would I get to ask the questions I wanted to? Was he using me? Or was there some way I could use him?

"I can go this week. If I can get someone to cover for me here." I watched out of the corner of my eye while he ate his pie. Something was going on. One, Sam eating pie. Two, Sam agreeing to go with me to visit a possible suspect. It wasn't like him.

I was feeling so pumped up I forgot not to mention the "M" word. "I know a murder in a small town or anywhere for that matter is a terrible thing, but doesn't this one coming as it has give you a good reason for hanging on to your job?"

"You're referring to the fact that the city council wants to abolish my position."

I nodded. That's what he'd told me. Many small towns had consolidated or farmed out their law enforcement because of budget shortfall. But if he had to solve a murder every few months, this town needed him.

"If I didn't know better, I'd suspect you of this murder," I said.

"What?" I was afraid he was going to fall

off his chair.

At least I had his attention. "You have the motive, which is that your job depends on having something to do like solving murders, and I'm guessing you don't have an alibi for Friday afternoon. Am I right?"

"As it happens I was in a conversation with one of my deputies in my office. Are you satisfied?" he asked. The look on his face was partly amused, partly amazed at the gall I had to even think such an outrageous thing.

"If you ever need a new deputy, I'm available," I said. "I don't know what it involves exactly, but I like to think I could qualify."

He didn't say anything for a long moment. For the second time today I'd surprised him. If I did nothing else today, I'd consider it a successful twenty-four hours. I decided not to wait for his reaction. "You said you were thinking of running for mayor," I said. "What happened to that idea?"

"I'm still looking into the possibility. The election is in the fall. I have an exploratory committee to check out the situation. I want to know who else is running. The good thing is our current do-nothing mayor is finally retiring. I can't believe I'd have much competition, seeing as the salary is minimal. But I don't want to run if I can't win."

"On the other hand, how do you know if you can win if you don't try?"

"Good point," he said.

Again I had the feeling he was humoring me. It was better than being ignored, so I continued.

"Who's on your exploratory committee?"

"Kate's husband and a few other guys."

"What about a woman? What about me?" I don't know what got into me, but as long as I didn't get totally rejected, I decided to keep trying. What did I have to lose, except my reputation and a few sleepless nights of worrying?

"I know a few people in town," I told him. "People who buy pies. People who sell other stuff like Jacques, Lindsey and Tammy, and Nina who sells caramels. You remember her from high school. She married Marty Holloway. I meet a lot more people now that I'm at the market on Saturdays."

"You don't want to spread yourself too thin," he said as if he was my career counselor. "But I'll check with my committee and let you know." He stood as if he was ready to leave.

"Let me call Kate about filling in for me one day this week so we can go to the pig farm." I took my phone from my pocket afraid if I let him go without a definite commitment I might not see him for weeks. No one could say I wasn't trying to keep in touch.

But his phone rang and he pointed to the police station and walked across the street. Maybe that's one reason Sam isn't married, I thought. He's never not on call. He's always working, even when he's not working. He doesn't have a social life, or if he does no one knows about it.

Like Heath, the food critic. No one seemed to know anything about him. Was he married to his job even though his job was a part-time writer for a small-town newspaper? If he was working for nothing, how did he support himself? Did he take kickbacks? Is that why he gave me and my friends bad reviews, because we didn't offer him anything? Someone must know the answers to these questions. I would find out who that was. Then Sam would be happy to swear me in as his deputy and I'd be in on all the excitement in town and have something useful to do on Saturday nights like breaking up fights over runaway livestock or stolen newspapers.

I called Kate to ask if she had some time to fill in for me. She was playing volleyball in her back yard with her husband and two girls. Being my best friend, she called time out and took my call. She didn't hesitate to ask why I needed her and where I was going.

"Does this have anything to do with that murder?" she asked.

"I don't know. It might. But solving the murder is not my job. It's Sam's. If it was I'd be interested in who else hated the guy besides my friends at the market. Hated him enough to kill him."

"Where are you going?"

"Sam and I are going out to visit the pig farmers, Dave and Bill. I'm going because I'm interested in organic healthful farming. Sam's going because . . . I'm not sure. It must have something to do with the murder but I didn't ask. I hope he doesn't suspect the guys who own the place, they're such nice, gentle people. But who knows? Anyway, I need you to mind the store. If you have time."

"I can't do Monday it's a Minimum Day at the kids' school, but I can come Tuesday."

"Fantastic. I owe you for this."

"I don't have to bake anything, do I?"

"No, I'll be sure I've got a big inventory of fresh and frozen pies. All you have to do is sell. Which you are superb at doing. How can I repay you?"

"Well, if you can baby-sit for me then we

could have a date night without kids," Kate said.

"Of course. You know you can ask me any time. I'm free every night, unfortunately."

"I predict your free nights will be over soon. Once Sam realizes he can't live without you," Kate said.

I didn't want to dash her hopes so I didn't say what I thought, that there was no one Sam couldn't live without. But who knew? He'd surprised me before. Maybe he'd do it again if I stayed out of his way so he could solve this mystery himself. I left a message for him that I was free Tuesday to go to the pig farm.

I solved one mystery all by myself on Monday when I went to the newspaper office again. This time the yellow crime scene tape was gone from the outer office door. Yes, at last! I knocked on the door, a list of questions for the editor in my bag about Heath Barr. But when he opened the door he didn't look glad to see me, in fact I thought he was going to shut it in my face.

"Bruce Scarsdale? I'm Hanna Denton."

"The pie woman, yes I know. This isn't a good time."

"I'm sorry. You must be busy." I tried to look around his big bulky body to see who else was there in the office.

He waved an arm toward an empty desk in the reception area. "We had to let our secretary go and we've had a murder on the premises," he said. It was hard to tell which thing upset him most. Maybe everything. His face was pale, almost ashen under a stubble of beard as if he hadn't been home for a few days. Or maybe that was his normal harried editor look. I'd never met him before. I'd put ads in the paper but never in person.

"I'm sorry for your loss . . . losses," I said.

"If you're here about the article Heath wrote about your pie contest, don't worry, it's already gone to press. It's the last thing he submitted before . . ." He stopped, choked up or just *verklempt.* "Nothing stops the presses," he assured me. "Not time or high tide." As if the citizens were out there waiting for the latest news which only his weekly rag could provide.

"I see." So there I was. Stuck with a pie contest. Grannie would be happy and so would her friends, the potential pie judges.

He pulled a small hand-held computer/reading device from his vest pocket, hit some buttons and read to me in a monotone. "Are you a great pie baker? Do you want to taste some fabulous pies? If so, The Upper Crust Pie Bake-off is for you! Sunday at 11:00 AM is the first annual pie contest at The Upper Crust Pie Shop. Wear your apron for photo opportunities, bring your best pie, sweet or savory, with a home-made crust and at least one local ingredient, and your recipe. Prizes galore. Tastings and good times for all.' "

I stood there open-mouthed. Unable to say a word. Tastings? Home-made crust? What more was there to say? It was a done deal. Heath had sure done a job on MY pie contest. Or was it his?

"Now, if you'll excuse me," Bruce said. "As I mentioned, we're short-handed."

Taking a clue from Sam, I wedged my foot in the door. "I can understand that. So is this where Heath actually worked? Where he wrote that blurb? Or did he just come by and leave off his column?"

"Come by? Hardly. He actually lived in his office." Bruce gestured to a door toward the rear of the entry-way.

"And died there too I heard," I said.

He nodded. "What a shock. If I'd known . . . But he said it was just temporary and since he was donating his time and his columns . . . We don't have money to pay a food and lifestyle critic. But he said he wasn't doing it for the money. He just wanted to get some experience as a journalist. He said staying in his office was just temporary until he found a place to live."

Someone yelled for Bruce from somewhere else. "I really have to go," he said. "It's been crazy here. Heath killed right here, the police . . . And suddenly everybody wants to be a newspaper writer."

"Even if they don't get paid? Even if their life is in danger?"

"Looks that way. They say there's no such thing as bad publicity." He nodded curtly. I was dismissed.

I turned to go. Then I looked over my shoulder. He was still standing in there looking at me. *I thought you had to go,* I wanted to say. *So go.* I smiled and waved and walked out the door. But I didn't want to go until I'd found out something. Something besides the fact that I was hosting a pie contest thanks to Heath. I waited a few minutes and opened the door again. No Bruce. The reception area was empty except for a few empty chairs, a scarred end table, and an empty desk. All a testimony to hard times in the publishing business.

I heard voices coming from another office. I tiptoed to the door that supposedly led to Heath's office and temporary home. No yellow crime scene tapes, but the door was locked. No big surprise there. The police had probably taken everything away including Heath in plastic bags. I pressed my ear against the door. I heard the faint sound of music that sounded like the ring tone from a cell phone. I could almost place the artist, but not quite. Could that be Heath's cell phone left behind and still working? Or someone else's phone like a worker from the coroner's office who dropped it? Didn't he miss it? Where was it? Why hadn't someone taken it before now? What I wouldn't give to get hold of that phone. If it was Heath's, the police would have wanted to take it and any messages for him would be on it. And who knew what else?

I took my cell phone out of my purse and scrolled down until I found the number I'd called Heath on the other day. I pressed send and instantly heard the same song. And quickly ended the call. So it *was* his phone. This time I recognized the popular country song "Everybody Wants to Go to Heaven." How appropriate was that? Did Heath have a death wish?

I was getting close to finding out something. My heart was pounding so loud I was afraid everyone in the building could hear it. If Sam had stripped the office and declared it off limits, why hadn't he taken the cell phone? If Heath actually lived in his office and was killed in his office and his phone was still there, what else was in that office?

It was so frustrating. Why hadn't I studied Beginning Lock Picking instead of taking Algebra Two? Of all the useless high school classes, that was the one I needed least. But Locksmithing 101, now that was something I could really use.

I finally gave up and left the office. I went down the stairs and out onto the street. I said hello to several people I knew on the town square, then I walked around to the back of the two-story brick newspaper building. It was as old as Grannie, maybe older. When I was a kid, the boys in the neighborhood got jobs delivering the *Daily Gazette* on their bicycles. Now it was delivered weekly by a man in a car.

I looked up and wondered if one of the windows on the second floor was Heath's. Next to the rear of the building was a dumpster and a fire escape. I wanted badly to reach that fire escape, but it didn't touch the ground. It was probably weight-operated and likely only descended to the ground when activated by the weight of a person leaving the building in a big hurry while flames licked at his or her boots.

If a person could get on top of the dumpster, and stand on the lid, then that person could reach the bottom rung of the fire escape with her hands and pull herself up. That person was me. No one wanted to get into that office and get that cell phone more than I did, except for Sam of course, but he wasn't there. He didn't know I was here and he'd better not find out. Knowing him and how proprietary he was about evidence and crime solving I could just imagine his reaction. He'd explode with fury just when everything seemed to be going so well between us. Who would have thought he'd suggest we go together on a fun trip to a farm? I didn't want to do anything to upset our new and improved relationship. I didn't want to sit by and let a murder go unsolved or a piece of evidence go missing either.

Just then a delivery truck drove up to the back of the newspaper building. Two guys in overalls jumped out and dumped stacks of boxes labeled Orion Pulp and Paper Products on the ground. I had a moment of grief for the fallen trees it took to make that much newsprint. Some day all newspapers would be electronic. But not yet. The men looked at me like they'd never seen anyone standing in back of a building on a Monday morning looking suspicious. I smiled to assure them I was a harmless nobody and walked back to the street where my car was parked. If I was going to do something like break into an office, I'd better wait until dark. Besides, I'd left Manda minding the shop and she had an appointment with her college counselor that morning.

The day sped by even with that cell phone on my mind. I concentrated on pies. I had to leave Kate with an inventory when I took off with Sam for a day. I made a Chocolate S'Mores Pie with a gooey marshmallow topping and a graham cracker crust of course. I followed that with a couple of banana cream pies. Then I switched gears and made a deep-dish Pizza Pie, Chicago style with sausage and peppers.

I kept thinking of the cell phone. I was terrified someone else would hear the phone ringing and find the phone before I got there. I prayed the battery would run down or if someone did hear the Kenny Chesney song that Heath favored they wouldn't give it a second thought.

During midsummer in central California it doesn't get dark until eight or nine o'clock. By eight I was pacing the floor of the pie shop waiting. I'd dressed in black jeans, a black T-shirt, and non-slip running shoes — the outfit of choice for spies and intelligence gatherers. I couldn't wait another minute. I had to have that phone. I had to find out if it was still there. If it wasn't, I was back to square one, where I did not want to be.

Instead of driving to the town square like some other people in our community I walked the five blocks, hoping no one would see me and ask me what the hell I was doing dressed from head to toe in black like a ninja. I should have waited another hour or worn normal summer clothes. But I wasn't thinking like a spy. I was thinking like a pie baker.

Fortunately I saw no one and hopefully no one saw me. That was the good news. The bad news was that when I turned the corner and the newspaper building came in view, I saw two cars parked in front. My heart sank. I never thought anyone would be there. Why now? Why tonight? It's not like it was *The New York Times* and they had to get the news out as it happened. This was a small-town gazette, for God's sake.

I walked around the deserted town square for a half hour. Every time I passed the newspaper office the damn cars were still there. Finally I couldn't wait any longer. Every minute that passed could be the moment when someone heard that phone ring and called the police or broke in, or worse.

I stood next to the big yellow dumpster wishing I had a way to climb up and onto it. Once on the dumpster I could reach the bottom of the fire escape and climb up to the window, which I hoped was Heath's office and which I also hoped was not locked. I didn't think I'd have the nerve or the strength to break the window. Isn't that what "breaking and entering" actually meant? If I didn't break the window I really wasn't "breaking" was I? I hoped I wouldn't be forced to listen to Sam explain exactly what it meant.

The second or third time I walked around the building I saw the ladder. If I'd brought a flashlight, I might have seen it sooner. But if I'd been shining a flashlight around I might have been seen by someone who'd call the police and I didn't want to think about what would happen then.

The ladder was old and wooden and weighed a ton. Propped up against the brick wall it was hidden behind a tangle of vines that clung to the bricks. I dragged it to the dumpster and nearly tore a ligament propping it up. Hoping the rungs weren't rotten, I climbed up, one foot at a time, and finally stood on the half cover of the dumpster. I stretched and reached for the lowest rung on the fire escape.

The adrenaline was pumping through my veins. I was bursting with pride that I'd come that far. Next time I changed ringtones I'd pick the song about coming a long way, baby as a warning not to get too cocky.

The fire escape was rickety and rusty. It must have been there for decades and never used. But it got me to the window I had my hopes fastened on. I pressed my face against the glass. I couldn't see anything. I tugged on the sash of the window. It didn't move. I squeezed my eyes shut to keep from crying. Maybe I would have to break the glass after all because I sure as hell wasn't going to climb down empty-handed.

With a burst of energy I pulled the window sash once again and it jerked open a few inches. Then with my fingers gripping the frame it moved a little more until I could just squeeze in. Before I did, I glanced down for a moment and felt a wave of vertigo. I've never been good at dealing with heights.

A few minutes later I was standing in Heath's office. The air was warm and stagnant. It smelled like disinfectant and cigarette smoke. Heath smoked? I was surprised — it was so rare of anyone in my age bracket to smoke. But then how did I know how old the guy really was? The disinfectant indicated the blood had been cleaned up. I assumed there was a lot of it considering how he'd been killed. I held my breath and wished I'd brought a flashlight. Never mind. If I had, I might be noticed. So I stumbled around the office my arms outstretched so I didn't bump into anything while listening for sounds coming from the other offices. Someone had to be in there with me or why were those cars out in front?

First things first. Find the damn phone before it rang again and brought someone in to look for it. I crawled on the floor, I explored every inch of the place with my hands and knees. Nothing. My eyes were getting used to the dark and I could clearly see the only items in the room were a desk, a chair, and a couch. Presumably the couch Heath slept on. I went to the adjacent bathroom, which had a small window. Light was coming in from one of the town's only street lights. The room smelled like Clorox. There was a medicine cabinet. It was empty. I was starting to worry. I'd risked life and limb and reputation by breaking into this office and for what?

Then I heard voices. Who was it? The janitor talking to himself? Bruce the editor working late? I went to the door and pressed my ear against it.

"Don't forget the ice," a woman's voice said.

I heard footsteps then a man's voice said, "I got it."

Ice? Drinks? A staff meeting? Then why no lights? An assignation? Then why meet here in this dingy office?

I waited what seemed like a lifetime and didn't hear anything else. Hopefully they'd gone to drink their drinks or suck on their ice somewhere else. Now I had to do what I hoped I wouldn't have to do, call Heath's cell phone. If it was here, it would ring and I'd track it down. Unless the battery was dead.

I found his number and pressed "Send."

It rang. I raced around the office like a mad woman trying to track down the sound. I started to hate that song. I imagined whoever was out there suddenly dumping their icy drinks and running to this office, bursting in and demanding to know what I was doing there. Not only that but taking the phone from me. If I had the phone, which I didn't.

I bumped into the couch. It had to be there. I tore the cushions from the frame and tossed them on the floor. The ringing got louder. So much louder I panicked. They'd hear it. I knew they'd hear it. I ripped the inner fabric lining of the couch and slid my hand then my whole arm down past the springs. My hand bumped into the phone and with fumbling fingers somehow I turned it off.

I gripped the phone so tightly my hand froze. I don't know if I heard footsteps or if I imagined it, but I put the couch cushions back and sprinted for the open window, backed out onto the swaying fire escape, and forced my feet to take one rung at a time as I went down to the waiting dumpster. But instead of landing on the lid, I slipped and fell deep into the dumpster itself. I landed with a thud on top of a plastic trash bag. On the way down I scraped my arm, bumped my knee, and hit my forehead on the metal latch.

I sat on the floor of the dumpster for a long moment, many moments while I caught my breath. I listened carefully in case someone was at the window up there calling me, telling me to give up because the police were on their way. Or maybe there was someone quietly hanging out the window looking down, wondering who the prowler was. Waiting for me to stand up and give up. There wasn't a sound. Hopefully the two late-night workers were busy with whatever it was they were doing, proofreading or making hot love before they went to press.

I sat there rubbing my knee, thinking I was lucky the dumpster wasn't full of smelly garbage. Instead there were plastic trash bags full of paper. That figured. This was an office, not a produce market.

I leaned back against the metal side of the dumpster. My head hurt, my knee ached and I was exhausted. I had the phone. No one caught me. And now I wanted to go home. I stood on shaky legs so I could climb up and out of there. But even though my hands could reach the top, the walls were so smooth I couldn't lift myself out. I had to clamp my hand over my mouth to keep from calling for help. I pictured a shriveled corpse turning up in this dumpster weeks or even years from now. It was MY corpse, with one hand tightly clenched around some newspaper reporter's cell phone and no one knew why.

When I finally pulled myself together, mentally at least, I began piling the trash bags in the corner of the dumpster until the mound was high enough for me to climb up and reach the ladder. I swung one leg over the side, then backed down quickly until my feet hit the ground. I didn't waste a minute before I staggered home through the empty streets. Just before I left I noticed there were no cars in front of the newspaper office. Had the drinkers left? Moved their cars to avoid detection? Or were they never there at all? At this point I didn't care. I just wanted to get out of there.

Six

I wanted desperately to listen to Heath's cell-phone messages, but neither my brain nor my body were working very well. I tottered upstairs, removed my dark camouflage outfit, and fell into bed.

The next thing I knew the sun was streaming in my bedroom window and I heard voices outside on the sidewalk.

"I can't believe she's not here," Kate said.

"Maybe she's sleeping in." That was Sam's voice.

Sleeping in? I was a baker. I got up at five every day, rain or shine. Not today. My brain felt like it was full of cotton. I reached for Heath's precious cell phone under my pillow and hid it under my bed. Then I leaped out of bed and stuck my head out the window.

"I'm here. I'll be right down." But I couldn't go down looking like a zombie, not in front of Sam. I brushed my teeth, combed my hair, and pulled on a pair of white linen shorts and a black tank top. I was horrified to see I had a bruise on my forehead and a gash across my knee. It took a bit of work with my makeup kit to cover the evidence of my late-night escapade.

"Sorry," I said breathlessly when I opened the door to the pie shop. "I'm running a little late. Are we on, Sam?"

He nodded and gave me a long look from my sandals to the top of head. His gaze lingered on my forehead. I wished it was because he found me so stunning he couldn't tear his eyes away, but maybe he was thinking, Why did Hanna plaster makeup on her face when she doesn't need it to look beautiful and furthermore why is she acting so strange today?

I forced a smile. "Don't look at me that way, Sam. So I overslept. It happens. Thanks for coming, Kate."

Sam went outside while Kate and I went into the shop and I showed her the list of orders. I opened the freezer and took out a half dozen pies. Kate helped me fill the shelves in the shop and we labeled everything. She took notes on a small pad of paper, then she paused and looked closely at my face. "What happened to you?" she asked.

"Nothing," I said. This was hardly the time to launch into the story of my expedition last night. "I'm fine. Call me if you have any problems." I grabbed a sweater and my favorite deep-dish apple pie which I thought had a nice balance of tart and sweet thanks to the fresh-squeezed lemon and orange juice mixed with the Granny Smith apples in the filling. I hoped the pie would make up for the fact we hadn't told Dave and Bill we were coming.

Kate stood in the doorway as I got into Sam's sporty convertible. She beamed her approval of my not only taking the day off but spending the day with Sam. As we pulled away, I glanced back. Kate had a funny look on her face as if she'd just remembered something important. But she sounded normal. "Have fun you two," she called.

Sam had directions to the pig farm on his GPS which made it seem like this was HIS trip and HIS idea. All the better that I was just along for the ride. If I stumbled on anything out of the ordinary — and how would I know what was ordinary for a pig farm — then I could file it away in my tired brain for later.

We headed inland on a two-lane road. The sun was warm on my shoulders and the breeze ruffled my hair. I snuck a look at Sam, hoping he was having a good time. At least so far.

"It's a beautiful day," I said tilting my face toward the sun, "and I appreciate your inviting me along." Had he really invited me? I was still groggy from last night and not thinking as clearly as I would have liked. "I hope you're enjoying a day off." Let him tell me this was not a day off. Not for him. Let him bring up the Heath Barr murder case. I didn't want to touch it with a ten-foot pole. I'd already gotten way too involved. I'd volunteered for way too many ways of helping Sam, being his deputy, serving on his election committee. He didn't appreciate it. He didn't want my help, so no more.

I considered turning over the phone I'd found to Sam, but then he'd ask me where and how I'd gotten it and . . . I felt his gaze on me so I turned and looked out the window.

"What happened to you?" he asked.

"Nothing," I said blithely for the second time in the last half hour. "What do you mean?"

"You cut your knee. And did something to your forehead."

"Nothing serious. I just bumped into

something in the kitchen yesterday while whipping up a S'Mores Pie. That's the one with the marshmallow topping."

"I know what S'Mores are," Sam said.

"That's right. We used to make them on the beach."

Did he remember sitting next to me on a blanket watching the sun set while someone built a bonfire and toasted marshmallows? Did he remember how our lips stuck together in a forbidden kiss? I did. But maybe he'd had many sunset kisses since then and mine had faded away like the setting sun.

"In the kitchen," I said hastily returning to the subject at hand. "That's where most accidents happen. Statistically speaking. I'm fine."

"Put some antiseptic on that cut and cold compresses on your head."

"I will, thank you. Just as soon as I have a free moment." I hoped to convey the impression that I was busy as a bee, making and selling pies, with no time for any medical care or extra-curricular activities.

There was a long silence while I tried to think of something non-controversial to say. He beat me to it.

"You don't usually oversleep," he said.

I frowned. "How do you know?"

He slanted a look in my direction and I

turned my head to look out the window. I didn't want him studying my face or my knee.

"I work across the street. I usually see your light go on at five in the morning. But not today."

"You're spying on me," I said only slightly surprised.

"I'm just keeping my eye on you. And everyone else in town. It's my job. Wouldn't want anything to happen to you."

"Thank you very much. You know I've been on my own for twelve years now and pretty good at taking care of myself. Despite a scratch or two. I'm just glad you're not my boss," I said. "I may have to withdraw my application to be your deputy what with all my pie orders piling up. Let's talk about your work for a change and your unusual hours." I knew he didn't want to, but I couldn't help asking, "What were you doing up at five?"

"I have a murder case on my hands. I'm investigating everyone who had contact with Heath Barr."

"Including the men who make the sausage," I noted. "Is that why you're going to see them?"

I should have known. He was taking me with him as a cover for doing his own investigation. I would make it look like an outing in the country instead of an official visit. It had nothing to do with me personally. Only that he was using me to gain entry to Bill and Dave's farm without arousing their suspicion that he suspected them of murder. Or something.

"Do you really think someone would kill a critic for badmouthing their food?" I asked. Which was exactly what I thought.

"Let's not talk about murder today. This is my day off," he said.

I looked at his profile. He was clearly lying but what could I say? I played along.

"Sorry," I said.

"How are things in the pie business?"

"Can't complain," I said. "You saw how brisk business was at the fair. I love getting out and away from the shop. The energy there is contagious. I get to meet new people and reconnect with old friends. Hey, I even met our old 'pal' Principal Blandings. I don't suppose you've run into him?"

"He came to see me. Wants me to give a talk at the high school."

"You? What would you talk about? How to get away with murder? I mean . . ." I wanted to bite my tongue. What possessed me to mention the word murder. Because it was on my mind. Not my fault.

"I know what you mean. I was in plenty of trouble in high school, which is why he wants me to tell the kids how to avoid doing what I did."

"Will it include how you turned your life around? I'd like to hear that."

"Sorry, attendance is restricted to students."

"How about a preview?"

"Not today." He meant not today and not ever. He'd never confide in me. I didn't know why I kept trying to pry information out of him.

What happened in Sam's past that was so secret? I didn't believe for a moment he was going to spill his guts to the high school students and not tell me. Never mind. I'd keep trying to catch him at a weak moment. Maybe after a dose of truth serum which I would hide in his coffee.

"I was saying how I'd met some new people and some old friends like Nina Carswell, well she wasn't exactly a friend, but she's selling salted caramels at the market," I said. "Funny, she didn't look like a traditional candy maker. You know with a white apron, gray hair in a bun and a pair of half glasses."

"I saw her," he said. "No apron. No bun."

"Did you notice she's absolutely gorgeous?"

He shot me an amused glance. "I noticed. Quite a change."

I felt a pang of unreasonable jealousy. I liked to think I'd changed since high school too, and for the better, but he'd never said anything. "Do you remember Marty Holloway?" I asked. "She married him and now he's a veterinarian."

"That's interesting," he said.

"How do you mean?"

"I might get a dog, that's all. I'd need a vet."

"He specializes in large animals," I said. "So you'll have to find someone else."

"Not if I get a large dog."

"If you want a pet, you might think about a pig. From the picture on Bill and Dave's brochure, they look cute and I hear they make good pets. If you bought one you'd save it from the ax."

"I'll think about it," he said. I was sure he was thinking about something else besides making a pet of a pig. But what was it? Even more mysterious than Heath's murder was the enigma of Sam. He smiled then, so unexpectedly that I had a dizzy spell and the lush vineyards on the side of the road seemed to be waving their leaves at me. But maybe that was due to my head injury or oversleeping.

"I'm looking forward to seeing the farm," I said. "You know Dave and Bill invited me too."

"I know," he said. "That's why we're here."

Aha. So that WAS why I was along, to make it seem like a purely social call, when I was sure it wasn't. Not likely Sam was taking a day off for fun.

"Do you ever take a day off for fun?" I asked.

"I am. This is it," he said.

Liar.

He pointed to the sign for Bill and Dave's Blue Sky Ranch, The Primo Pig Farm — "Pasture Perfect" "Heritage Pork from Pigs Who Live Their Lives Outdoors." And "The Proof is in the Pork."

"Did you say they don't know we're coming today?" Sam asked as we approached a long driveway with white picket fencing on both sides of the road.

"I don't think so unless you told them. I wanted to see them at work so I could get an idea of what they do. I hope they're not mad we didn't warn them. Maybe they're too busy to show us around."

"How would you feel if they did the same

156

and dropped in on you when you were at work?" he asked.

"I have nothing to hide and I always welcome customers," I said primly. "Frankly I'd be flattered. My door is always open. But we should buy something. Because I'm afraid they might be hurting for sales. I'll buy whatever they have on hand."

We pulled up in front of a white barn with green trim around the windows. The air was fresh and clean. It didn't smell like a barnyard. The pigs I saw were eating at a trough.

"Hanna," someone called. "Is that you?"

"Probably didn't expect me in a classy convertible," I said to Sam.

I turned and saw Bill, the chubby brother, carrying a bucket and walking toward us.

I reintroduced Bill to Sam and told him I hoped he didn't mind our dropping in like that.

"Glad to see *you*," he said. "Didn't know you'd bring the chief of police along."

Sam thanked him for inviting him and assured Bill the visit was strictly social. I must have looked apprehensive, but Bill patted me on the back and said, "Just kidding," with a smile on his round face. "We have nothing to hide but our secret sausage recipe. Bet you two want to see if our pigs are really as happy as we said they were."

"We'd love to," I enthused. "If you've got time to show us around. I know how busy you farmers are."

"Never too busy to show off the place," he said, leading the way to the pasture. "Don't know if I told you our animals graze on the wild greens. Which is why the meat tastes so good. We raise all their food right here on the farm. Make sure it's as organic as the pigs."

"You can't do all that yourselves, just you and Dave," I said.

"We have help. People who believe in organic farming as much as we do." He stopped at the fence and whistled loudly. Several pigs came loping toward us as if to say, "Who are you and what are you doing here?"

"I brought you a pie," I said. "I remember you said you liked apple."

He took it out of my hands and bent over the crust to inhale the scent of cinnamon and nutmeg. He looked so touched by the gift of a pie, I realized this was my reward for hours in the kitchen. Knowing someone appreciated the work that went into it.

"Thanks," he said. "This looks wonderful." He walked over to a small shed and put the pie inside. "It'll be safe in there," he said. "Safe from Dave." He closed the door behind him then he motioned us out to the pasture. He glanced at my sandals with a frown, then he gave me a hand and I climbed over the fence. Sam followed, seemingly as happy as I was to walk through some mud to get the full organic porcine experience.

"They really do look happy," I said, watching the pigs chase each other around the field.

"Who wouldn't be?" Bill asked. "They're free to roam, play, dig in the ground, and roll in the mud." He took us to the barn where some of his sows had just given birth. He let me hold a squirming, slippery baby pig in my arms.

Sam looked at me with surprise, and maybe even a touch of admiration, as if he didn't think I had the nerve to hold a baby pig. I had the nerve but not the skill, the pig squirmed out of my grip until I had to let him slide out of my arms to join his siblings in the straw.

A couple of large pigs came running up to us. Bill scratched their heads and they made noises that indicated how much they loved being petted, if you can call it that.

"What kind are those?" I asked, pointing to a group of long-legged, ginger-colored pigs grazing off to one side.

"Tamworths," Bill said. "I don't think anyone else around here raises them but us. They make tremendous bacon and wonderful pork. Look at those ears," he said leaning over the fence.

"They look so alert," Sam said, "as if they're listening for something."

"They cost an arm and a leg, but they're worth it. We call them the aristocrats and don't they know it," Bill said with a grin. "See how they're looking at us. Dave was against my buying the Reds, but I don't regret it, even if no one else appreciates them, they're special. I've heard them called gentle giants. You can see why, can't you?" he asked eagerly.

I nodded. What made him think no one else appreciated the Reds? Those were some special pigs all right. "But Bill, how can you stand to uh . . . slaughter them?" I gave a little shiver.

"I confess," he said. "We can't. We send them off to the organic food processor. But when they come back as roasts, steaks, and hams and of course our sausage, we take over. We have a smoke room and a curing room and a walk-in refrigerator. Come and have a look."

I turned reluctantly from watching the aristocratic pigs frolic in the pasture and followed Dave to the out-building. I really didn't want to see what happened to them after being processed. I was in denial about the future of those classy animals and I wanted to stay that way.

Before we got to the building, Bill's tall lanky brother, Dave, waved to us from across the field. "Bill," he shouted, "phone."

Bill frowned. "Guess I'd better take this," he said. Then he hurried off, leaving us standing there in rich, organic bluegrass.

"I don't know what to do. Should we go?" I asked Sam after we'd stood there a few minutes.

"Let's see if he comes back," he said.

"They did invite me and you too as well as the other vendors to see the place so I don't feel like we're intruding. On the other hand —" I turned to see one of the large pigs running on his short legs toward us. No, not toward us, but toward me. Although I thought the pigs were extremely attractive on the whole, I wasn't so sure about this one. I didn't like the way he was closing in on me. I don't know how or why exactly, it was more instinct than anything, but I turned around and started running. I heard Sam yelling at me to stop and come back but I also heard those little pig footsteps behind me, gaining on me and I didn't stop until I got to the fence. I panted, I gasped, and I climbed over just as the pig reached the narrow wooden slats. I tumbled forward and landed on my butt on the other side of the fence. This on top of my adventure last night. Half dazed, I looked at my feet splattered with mud. I had to admit the pig behind the fence with his snout pressed against the wood no longer seemed as dangerous. Maybe he just liked running. I felt a little foolish and was hoping no one but Sam had seen me.

Instead of Bill finding me or Sam catching up to me, Dave walked over, helped me up and said hello as if it was not a bit surprising to find me running across his field and leaping over the fence while being chased by his prize pig. Maybe he wasn't aware he had a demon pig on his hands. He was wearing muddy knee-high boots and he seemed out of breath too.

When Sam joined us I introduced them. "Sorry to interrupt your tour," he said. "But this was an important call. We're hoping to get a loan from the bank because, well, my brother has some expensive tastes." He didn't sound happy about it.

"You mean the Tamworth pigs?" I asked. "They're something special. Even I could tell. They're very fast runners."

"So are you," Sam said under his breath.

"Not just the pigs," Dave said. "Wait till you see the smoke room and the curing room. Everything has to be first class. Things were going okay for us, then that damned food critic with his critical review comes alone and bingo, no bank loan."

"Just because of what he wrote about you?" I asked incredulously.

"That set off a whole chain reaction. We were already in debt to the processor, the distributor, and just about everybody else in and out of town. But George Hamill at the bank was ready to make the loan to keep us afloat until he reads the review, he takes another look at our sales figures, and he turns us down flat. Bill was so mad at that smarmy Heath. If anyone deserved to die it was him. But what could we do? The damage was done. You know Bill, he's not taking no for an answer. He left a call in for George to ask for a second chance. That's what this is about I'm sure. What do you think George is going to say?"

I shook my head. I didn't want to hazard a guess.

Dave's lower lip trembled. I looked away. I was afraid he was going to cry. But he pulled himself together. "Come on, I'll show you around. Who knows how long Bill will be," he said.

The smoke house was a nice-looking little wooden structure with a slanted rooftop. Delicious smoky aromas wafted in the air. Dave opened the door so we could catch a look at ten or more chrome-plated shelves full of sausages and brackets for hanging huge hams and shanks of pork.

"I don't want to keep you any longer," Dave said, "but we'd like to offer you a loin or some chops from the freezer to take home with you. We've got sausage too." Even though I was in no hurry to go, maybe Sam was. Being his inscrutable self, I had no idea if he was bored or having the time of his life. Why was he here, really? I didn't believe for a minute he was taking a day off.

"Go ahead," Sam said to me. I realized he hadn't said much about my hasty race across the field. Maybe he expected me to do something impulsive and wasn't surprised. "I'll be out interacting with the redheads."

I watched him amble out toward the pasture, where the pigs appeared to ignore him. Then I followed Dave behind the barn where a huge shiny white walk-in freezer made of fiberglass stood. He led the way between large pallets stacked next to the freezer waiting to be loaded, or so he said. I could only hope he had enough orders to fill those pallets. He opened the door and invited me to go in and choose whatever I wanted, the cuts were all clearly marked and ready for market.

"Thanks, Dave. I'd love some ribs to barbecue but I insist on paying you for them."

He waved his arm and nodded. "I'm going to check up on Bill. God only knows what's happened now."

He closed the door behind him and I was alone with the meat in the sub-zero room. I buttoned my sweater up to my chin to ward off the chill and made a quick tour of the room. No wonder they were in financial trouble. A freezer like this must cost a bundle. Which was okay if you were selling pork like mad. But maybe they weren't. Every shelf was packed with pork and all labeled: ribs, ham, bacon, blade shoulder, shoulder butt and trays of different kinds of sausage.

I was getting cold so I took a five-pound slab of ribs from a shelf and tucked it under my arm. I could just picture myself first marinating the meat in a vinegar, wine and garlic sauce, then barbecuing it out back behind the pie shop for hours on a low heat. My mouth watered. I was halfway lost in a dreamy sequence of myself surrounded by my new Food Fair friends enjoying a juicy barbecue in my patio when I heard a loud thump. I jumped nervously and went to the door. I pushed the door. Nothing happened. I dropped the pork ribs, turned the door lever and shoved the door with my shoulder. It didn't budge.

"Help," I yelled. "Somebody help me. I'm locked in the freezer." I was shivering. Whether it was because of the sub-zero temperature or my near hysterical fear and claustrophobia, I didn't know. Maybe it was some of each. I told myself to calm down. Dave would come back. Sam would look for me. I wasn't alone out here. And yet I was alone, along with about a thousand pounds of frozen meat.

I looked around. The walls, ceiling and roof were all at least four inches thick. No one would hear me screaming so I might as well save my strength. What did I have to fear? (1) Hypothermia. I was feeling colder by the minute. My teeth were chattering. (2) Suffocation. I tried not to take deep breaths, because I once read you lose heat by breathing. I couldn't help it. (3) Frostbite. I imagined my toes falling off and then the tips of my fingers. I wondered how I'd ever be able to use a rolling pin again. I'd have to buy readymade crusts. There would go my reputation.

I thought I'd read that hypothermia victims got dizzy and confused. Since I wasn't in that great a shape from my escapade the night before, and then my frantic chase today by a maddened pig, I already felt confused and vulnerable. Questions rattled around in my brain. But no answers. What was the thump I heard? I'd gotten myself out of a dumpster, so why couldn't I open the door to a freezer? If I had a choice, I'd pick the smelly dumpster, at least there I could breathe. I was in the middle of a working pig farm, so where was everybody?

I must have been losing my mind because I also asked myself if Dave had locked me in there on purpose and then pushed something against the door which was the thump I heard. Maybe he blamed me for them not getting their loan. Maybe he thought it was my fault they got a bad rap from the food critic. Maybe they invited me out there to kill me. But why? I was just as much a victim of Heath Barr as they were. We were in this together. They were my new friends.

I was irrational. I was alert enough to know that. I just had to hold on until Sam realized I was missing. He'd ask Dave where I was and they'd be here any minute to let

me out. But the minutes dragged by. Had
Sam stumbled on an important clue in the
Heath Barr murder? Was he arresting Dave
and Bill? Maybe they'd killed Heath because
he'd not only given them a bad review, now
they couldn't get the loan they needed and
they blamed him. I could understand that.
It seemed logical, but how would I know
without some evidence. I summoned every
ounce of strength I had and I pounded on
the heavy door. I kicked the door and I
screamed. "Get me out of here." Then I
started to cry.

Seven

I finally stopped crying. I sat down on a small metal stool and buried my head in my hands. A few minutes later I heard voices. Someone was calling my name.

"In here. I'm locked in," I shouted.

"Oh my God, she's still in there. We're coming."

"Don't worry. We just have to move the pallet."

It seemed like hours but it was only minutes later Sam and Bill opened the freezer door and I fell out into Sam's arms. I was shaking violently.

"Good God," Sam said, putting his arms around me. "Are you okay?"

As much as I wanted to reassure him, I needed all the sympathy I could get so I gave in and sobbed quietly for a few minutes. Until I finally took a deep breath and stood back on shaky legs. I took great big gulps of fresh warm air and felt glad to be alive and outside again.

"Sorry about that," Dave said, a little casually I thought. "Things like this happen at piggeries, unpredictable things." It was obvious I was just not tough enough for farm life.

"A pallet fell off the stack and landed against the door," Dave explained. "Which prevented you from opening it. No need to worry. We would have found you sooner or later."

"Worry? I wasn't worried, I was hysterical," I confessed lightly. "I'm just glad it was sooner." I looked at Sam. "I think we'd better go."

"Sure you don't want a cup of coffee or something to warm up?" Bill said as he joined us.

"I'm fine," I said bravely. At least I hoped I came off as brave and not a shivering, panic-stricken coward.

"Don't forget your meat," Dave said holding the door to the freezer open.

I took a deep breath, went back in and grabbed the ribs I'd picked out. I insisted on paying for them, then I thanked both brothers and Sam and I got back into his car.

"Want the top down?" Sam asked as we headed up the driveway. He actually looked concerned about me. I wanted to milk the situation, but I just couldn't. That's the problem when you're just too honest for your own good.

I shook my head. "The fresh air feels good," I said. And it did. But when I shivered, he stopped at the end of the driveway, reached behind his seat for a small plaid blanket and wrapped it around my shoulders. I thought his arm lingered, but that was probably wishful thinking.

Wrapped up tight in his blanket with the sun on my face, I leaned back in my seat and closed my eyes. The few minutes I'd spent screaming and pounding my fist against the freezer door seemed like a dream or a nightmare. "I guess you'll think I'm crazy, but when I was in the freezer I thought maybe Dave had locked me in there."

"Why would he do that?" Sam asked.

"Because he killed Heath and I'd found out?" I laughed nervously. "That's ridiculous. I'm kidding. Why would he kill Heath?"

"Because Heath is responsible for their not getting the loan they wanted?" Sam asked.

"Is that really true?" I asked.

"It's true that they needed a loan and it's

true that they blame Heath."

"But you don't really think either one killed him," I said. "I mean they can't even bear to kill their own pigs."

"A food critic is not the same as a pet pig," Sam observed correctly.

I thought about asserting that the pigs were not pets, but instead I asked, "Are you telling me those guys are on your list of suspects?" I sat up straight, the blanket fell from my shoulders and I stared at Sam.

"I'm not telling you anything. You know that, Hanna."

I did know I was pushing my luck so I didn't ask if he'd ruled me out as a suspect. I had to assume he had.

"Relax," he said. "Let's get you something to eat and drink. You look pale."

I hated looking pale, but if it could get me even a small amount of sympathy from Sam and a stop at a restaurant, I didn't care. And I definitely felt tired, cold, and weak.

"What you need is a bowl of hot soup," he said, "and a cold drink."

"Sounds good," I said. I had no idea where he was taking me and I didn't care. I just wanted someone else to decide.

We went to a small rustic restaurant called Castelli's on the main street of Pescadero, a former Portuguese fishing town, now popular with tourists.

We got a table next to the back window where we could admire the large vegetable garden they used in their famous "home cooking." Sam ordered dark beer for each of us and two bowls of their delicious creamy artichoke soup. He was right. I needed a quick infusion of the rich dark beer and some hot soup to warm and nourish me.

After just a few bites I was feeling much better. My mind was working and my internal temperature was no longer ricocheting between extreme hot and cold. "I don't mind being locked in a freezer, if I get something out of it. But I don't think I did."

"What do you mean? You got a slab of ribs," Sam said, slathering sweet butter on a hunk of sourdough bread.

"That's right," I agreed. Maybe it was the alcohol that loosened my tongue, or the savory hot soup, because I said, "I'm glad you could take time off today, Sam. Does that mean you're not terribly busy?"

How could it mean that when he had a murder to solve?

"Actually I wanted to talk to you about a complaint that came to my attention yesterday," he said after a long drink of draft beer.

"Something besides the murder?" I heaved

a sigh of relief. I was thinking pesky raccoons tipping over garbage cans or intoxicated neighbors or maybe a noisy teen party.

"It may be connected. What do you think of this? There was a break-in at the *Gazette* office last night."

I dropped my spoon and the soup splattered on my sweater. Sam looked at me with a laser-like gaze. He knows, I told myself. He knows it was me. But how could he? Was it the bruise on my forehead or the cut on my knee?

"I assume the body is gone," I said. "So it had nothing to do with the murder."

"That's right. So cross the vampires off the list."

"Why would someone break in? Why not just knock on the door and walk in?" I asked, dabbing the soup off my chest. "Was anything missing? A first edition? The cash box? The awards off the wall?"

He shook his head. "Nothing. I know because I previously stripped the place myself." He paused and then he said, "But I didn't find Heath's cell phone. If he had one."

"Everyone has a phone," I said. I tried not to show I was proud I'd succeeded when he'd failed. "And you needed it because it would lead you to his killer."

"Might help."

"You know if I'd killed him, I'd take the phone with me," I said, even though I knew I was skating on thin ice.

"What if the killer couldn't find it and didn't have time to look?"

"Maybe it's still in the office," I suggested, carefully spooning another mouthful of the savory hot soup into my mouth.

"Maybe it was until last night," he suggested.

"What would you say if I told you I have the phone?" I said. I figured it was better I handed it over rather than being handed a search warrant or even arrested for tampering with evidence.

"I'd say thank you very much," he said, "and I'd drop all charges of breaking and entering provided you handed over said phone. I'd tell you to stay out of trouble and stay home at night."

"I didn't say I had the phone," I said. I knew I was beaten, but I hated to be told what to do. "But if I did, I'd like to hear the messages. I think I'd deserve to know who called him and why. I'd like to know who killed him too."

"I understand," Sam said. "But the DA won't. That phone is evidence. I can only hope it's in a safe place."

"Under my bed."

He closed his eyes and shook his head. Apparently he didn't think under my bed was a secure hiding place.

"Ready?" he said, laying a wad of bills on the table.

I stood. He put his arm around my waist. I wanted to think it was an affectionate gesture, but I realized it was a discrete way of hustling me out of the restaurant and into his car. Sam always drives fast, which makes me wonder how he can arrest speeders, but I guessed he and his fellow city cops had a reciprocal arrangement with the California Highway Patrol. Today he drove really fast down the PCH, passing on the straightaways and hugging the curves in his small Miata.

He didn't say much on the way home.

"I know what you're thinking," I said. "Dumb broad hides prime evidence under her bed. What was she thinking? Why didn't I have this conversation with her sooner?"

He pressed his lips together and nodded. "My fault," he said. "I should have known."

"Known what? That I was the one who broke in?"

"Just a lucky guess," he admitted. "Where was the fucking phone anyway?"

"In the lining of the couch."

"If I had a hat, I'd take it off to you. How'd you find it?"

I felt a sudden warm infusion of heat all over. I might have been mistaken, but I thought I heard grudging admiration underlying his words. Whatever kind of admiration it might be, I'd take it. Sure it was partly the soup and the alcohol that caused the feelings of warm fuzziness, but it was also Sam. If I wasn't mistaken, he actually appreciated my efforts. I was so touched I almost didn't realize he was using me and manipulating me so he could claim the phone I found. Okay, so it was evidence in a murder investigation, but I'd found it. It was mine.

"Grit and determination," I said. "Those are the only tools I have. And as long as I can listen to the phone messages I'll hand it over to you."

"Hah," he said. "You're dreaming. I don't make deals. You know you're lucky I don't arrest you for tampering with evidence."

My lower lip quivered. He wouldn't arrest me I was sure, but I didn't like the way he dismissed me. Even more maddening was knowing I'd given away my bargaining chip. He knew I had the phone. He knew where it was and he was going to take it away from me.

"Isn't it interesting," I said, "there were never any crimes to speak of until you came to Crystal Cove."

"Let's hope no one else comes to that conclusion," he said. "Or I'll be out of a job sooner than I want to be."

Back at the pie shop, I greeted Kate and, followed on my heels by Sam, raced up the back stairs to my small apartment above the shop.

I reached under the bed and found the phone. I would never admit it, but I had been worried. I'd been careless with an important piece of evidence. I held it up and Sam took it out of my hand.

"You give me the phone, I don't charge you, remember?"

I thought about pleading loss of memory because of my recent head injury, but then we'd be back on the subject of how I'd gotten said head injury so I sighed and said, "All right. I just hope you realize that I went to considerable trouble to get that phone for you."

"For me or for you?" he asked.

Just then Kate shouted up the stairs that she needed my help in the shop, so I was spared having to come up with an answer. Not that I was against fibbing to Sam, as long as I wasn't connected to a lie detector in his office. He put the phone in his pocket and there was nothing I could do about it.

I stood there watching Sam cross the street with the phone while Kate gave me a rundown of everything that had happened during the day. I finally turned my head and told myself to pay attention. After all, I had to make some preparations for the bake-off contest. Since this was the first annual event and I wasn't sure how it would work, I had to think fast. Which was difficult since my brain had been half frozen only a few hours ago and my head still throbbed from the accident in the dumpster last night and I desperately needed a long hot bath, or at least a foot massage. Preferably both.

"Are you sure you're up for this contest?" Kate asked.

"Of course. Actually I have no choice. At least it will give me some publicity and it might be fun too. Why wouldn't I be up for it?"

She peered into my face. "I don't know. It almost seemed like you were making up the rules for the contest as you went along."

"So? It's my contest."

"And then you overslept. Not like you. Frankly you looked a little ragged this morning. And now you seem rattled. What happened at the pig ranch?"

"Oh nothing much. Except I was chased across a field by a huge wild boar and locked in a freezer with about a thousand pounds of pork, and well, I've had a big day." I knew the pig wasn't a boar, but it made a better story so I stuck it in.

She looked me over, her gaze lingering on my feet. Then she told me to take a shower while she was on hand to hold down the fort. When I came back down in clean clothes and clean feet she told me I looked better. The truth was I could hardly have looked worse.

Bless her heart, she did not ask for details on my story about the pig and the freezer. She didn't ask if I'd gotten stuck in a dumpster last night either. Instead she asked another all-important question. "You and Sam getting along okay?"

"It's touch and go," I said.

"I hope there's more touch than go," she said with a little smile. "On another matter, any luck finding the food critic's murderer?"

"I don't know. Sam won't tell me anything except to butt out. I suppose he'd love to pin it on one of my vendor friends since they all hated Heath."

"Hey, put me on that list. I hated him too. He didn't know what he was talking about," Kate said untying her apron as she got ready to leave. "I don't understand how he got to be a food critic."

"As I understand from the *Gazette* editor, Heath volunteered to write a column, so how could they turn him down? Like every other newspaper, they've got money problems. So it's a matter of you get what you pay for. They paid nothing, they got nothing. Or worse than nothing, they got flawed reporting. They got food reviews that were slanted and I haven't figured out why. What did he have to gain by trashing some and white-washing others for no good reason? If I knew that I might know what or who killed him."

"Does Sam agree with you?" she asked.

I shrugged. "Sam plays his cards close to the vest. Although I don't think he plays cards or wears a vest, but you get the picture. All he'll say is that he hasn't ruled out anyone and that includes me."

"Typical," she said shaking her head sadly. "I wouldn't blame you if you gave up on him. He's not the only single guy in town and I hope he knows that."

"Are you sure? If there are any more single guys like Heath they ought to watch their backs because they're dropping like flies. On the plus side, you'll be glad to know Sam seemed almost sympathetic when I emerged half frozen from the walk-in freezer and then he bought me lunch."

"The way he sprinted up the stairs to your apartment I thought maybe he wanted something in exchange."

"He did want something all right, but it's not what you think. Anyway, thanks for filling in for me. I'm counting on you to be a judge along with Grannie and her friends in my first annual pie contest. Which we have Heath to thank for."

"As long as I get to taste everything, I'm in."

After she left, I paced back and forth, too full of nervous energy and too apprehensive about Heath's recovered phone to do much baking. I thought about Sam across the street listening to the incriminating messages on Heath's phone, knowing there was no hope of my listening to them.

Since Kate was such a good saleswoman, I had no choice but to start baking to refill the empty shelves and my freezer. I flipped through my files looking for something new. Something challenging.

I eyed a recipe for peach cobbler. Fortunately I had a basket of sweet and juicy yellow peaches from the orchards outside town. It was a crime to do much to them but sweeten them, thicken the juice, and bake them with a crust on top. Which I did. Peach juice bubbled up from under the crust. The smell was tantalizing. It wasn't a fancy pie, but it smelled like summer and I had no doubt I could sell it, if I didn't eat it first.

Next I decided to make a classic Shaker Meyer Lemon Pie. Meyer lemons are not as tart as their everyday cousins. Even the peel is slightly sweet, which makes them the perfect choice for a pie. Not everyone knows that Frank Meyer was once sent to China as a plant hunter and it was there he "discovered" the fabulously sweet lemon which now bears his name. The filling is simple — thinly sliced lemons, eggs, sugar, salt, and vanilla all encased in a double crust. I put it in a hot oven for fifteen minutes, then turned the heat down for thirty minutes and presto — magic. The crust was golden and the inside was luscious.

Since it was midsummer I made two more fruit pies, as much to keep busy as to fill my empty shelves. One was a sour cherry pie with a coconut crumb topping, the other was an open-faced apricot pie with a glaze made of apricot jam. It looked as good as it smelled cooling on a rack in the kitchen and I was proud of myself for not giving in to whining about how unfair life was that Sam got to listen to the phone messages I'd turned over to him.

Tomorrow my fruit supplier was coming to replenish my supply of strawberries, cherries, peaches, and apricots, and I'd be ready to plunge in again. New recipes, new customers, but the same old problems.

After I made a savory tart I thought Sam would like, I took a break and went outside from the steamy kitchen to the cool fresh air. I stood in front of my shop and studied the police station, wondering if Sam was over there at this very moment listening to Heath's phone messages without me. If so, did it occur to him how unfair it was that I was left out?

At five I closed the shop and finally ambled over to the police station with a caramelized onion and Roquefort tart. It was a shameful ploy to worm my way into his office, but how else could I get in? It turned out Sam was swamped with the usual kind of Crystal Cove police department activities. For Crystal Cove it was a minor crime wave. No more murders, thank God, just a raccoon in someone's garbage. And a case of loud shouting outside Bartley's Bar and Grill. And then the gunshots reported by someone on Mulberry Street.

"Gunshots?" I said startled.

"I have to check it out," he said, heading for the door.

"Wait, can't I come with you? Maybe I can help. Interview witnesses or call for reinforcements or something. Mulberry Street is a nice neighborhood. Could be a mistake," I suggested.

"No, you can't. This is police business. You have no idea how dangerous this could be."

I clamped my lips together while he strapped on his gun. I'd never seen Sam wear a gun before, and I knew I couldn't wait here not knowing what was happening on Mulberry Street. But I said nothing. I just watched him go. I gave him five minutes, then I got in my car and followed him.

Mulberry Street is lined with large houses on big lots with tall trees and large lawns. When I got there a man was standing on the curb waving to me.

"What happened?" I asked as I pulled up to the curb.

"It was nothing," he said. "Just a car backfiring."

"I knew it couldn't be gunshots in this neighborhood," I muttered to myself.

I watched Sam out on the street next to his official police car with the flashing lights on the roof. I leaned out of my car window, not knowing if it was okay for me to get out. I was surprised to see Nina Carswell, as I would always refer to her, come running out of the house across the street. It wasn't so surprising that she lived in an upscale neighborhood in a large two-story house with flower boxes and a manicured lawn, while I made do with a tiny apartment — the same tiny apartment I'd grown up in. After all, she was married to Marty Holloway, veterinarian, I reminded myself. There was money to be made from people who owned pets, large or small. The really surprising thing was she was barefoot, dressed in a terry-cloth robe, and her hair was wrapped in a towel like a turban. Of course she wasn't expecting a police car to arrive on her street, and I assumed she must have been curious when the PD arrived. So curious she jumped out of the shower or her spa to see what was happening.

I saw her cross the street and walk up to Sam where they had a brief animated conversation. I didn't know why I had to stay in the car if there was no danger so I got out and after Sam had gone somewhere else I said hello to Nina. I told Nina I happened to be driving by and saw the commotion. By that time I noticed Sam was talking to some other neighbors. I didn't think he saw me.

"Oh, my God, I was so scared," she said. Her eyes looked huge rimmed with eye liner, and her face though carefully made up seemed pale to me. "Did you hear the shots?"

"No, but I heard they weren't shots after all," I said in what I hoped was a soothing voice.

"That's what the chief said. I'd better go home. I was in the spa when I heard the gun shots, I mean the car backfiring." She gave a rueful glance at her robe, bare legs, and feet. "I'm still shaking," Nina said. "I was terrified when I heard the shots. I can't believe they weren't shots after all. This is usually a quiet neighborhood."

"Where's Marty?" I asked looking at their big house.

"Out on a house call," she said.

"Sounds like a good business."

"It is, except being the only vet around, he's always on call."

"Good thing you've got your caramels to keep busy." I had no idea if they had kids or not. Or just her job as a candy maker.

"Sometimes it's not enough," she said quietly. She had a sad look in her eyes. Maybe she wanted kids and couldn't have them, or she wanted a real career but Marty wouldn't let her.

"You have a full-time job," she said. She almost sounded envious. "I've never even made a pie." She knotted her hands together and flexed her fingers as if flexible fingers were a requirement for baking. Actually it wouldn't hurt. I wondered if she was lonely. Why else would she be out on the street in her robe talking to me instead of back soaking in her spa? If I had a spa that's where I'd be soaking my sore shoulder and various muscles.

"There's always a first time," I said. "I'm having a pie contest coming up on Sunday. You could make a caramel pie or caramel cream pie or any kind and enter it. It'll be fun." It occurred to me she might need some friends and she ought to show up for the contest where she could mix and mingle.

"Maybe," she said.

I saw Sam waving at me out of the corner of my eye. "See you later," I said to Nina and went over to say hello to Sam as casually as I could.

"I thought I told you not to come. You're lucky it wasn't a gun fight."

"A gun fight on Mulberry Street?" I asked. I didn't wait for an answer. "It must be hard to follow up on these false alarms."

I stood on the sidewalk as neighbors finally went back to their houses. "On the other hand it's a relief. No gunshots, no problem."

"Better than having a murderer at large," he said grimly. "Yesterday it was a lost dog. And a stolen newspaper from someone's front porch."

"I suppose some murders go unsolved for years." If I was hoping to cheer him up, I'd said the wrong thing.

"I haven't got years," he said.

I realized now how important it was that I'd found Heath's phone. So why didn't Sam act more grateful? Or more willing to let me in on listening to the messages.

"Well, good-bye," I said, hoping he'd say let's get together for something. Anything. But he didn't.

All he said was, "Go home, put a cold pack on your head for ten minutes, then go to bed."

I nodded, then I drove myself back to the shop. Sam's car was already in front of the police station. Inside he was listening to the messages on Heath's phone and I wasn't. I knew perfectly well that he wanted me out of police business. That didn't make it any easier to walk away and forget it. My only hope was that he'd share any information

he picked up off the phone. But it didn't
seem likely.

EIGHT

I was too tired to fill a plastic bag with ice. The last thing I did before I fell into my queen-sized bed with the kind of spa/hotel quality sheets Grannie never had was to look out my window to see if Sam's light was still on at the police station. It was. I ground my back teeth together in frustration. Then I swallowed two aspirin and finally fell asleep.

When I woke up the next morning the *Gazette* was on my doorstep. I was afraid to pick it up and read it. I was sure there'd be a story about Heath, at least an obituary. But would there be a story about the break-in at the newspaper office? Or did no one know about it except for Sam and me, and the editor who wanted to keep it quiet?

I sure would have been happy to keep it quiet.

There it was, Heath's picture on the front page. He looked like a normal thirty-something guy with longish hair and a look on his face as if he'd just tasted something he didn't like or maybe he was trying to impress someone by looking critical. They'd also reprinted his last column on the Food Fair. Fine. All I needed was a repeat of the scathing review of my pies. My fellow vendors wouldn't be happy either. I skimmed down to his obituary.

"Heath Winston Barr, *Gazette* Food and Lifestyle critic, is dead of a fatal homicidal attack while in his office on July 7. The question readers are bound to ask after 'Who Did It?' is 'Can anyone be a food critic?' The answer is yes, with this caveat. Not everyone can get paid for his work. Heath Barr fell into the category of volunteer. Which means he loved his work covering the Crystal Cover Summer Food Fair. His reward was honing his palate and discovering the fine foods grown and produced in Central California. Unfortunately someone disagreed with Heath's opinions or his actions, which led to his untimely death at age thirty-seven. The police are investigating the crime and Chief Genovese requests that anyone with information leading to the arrest of Heath's killer please contact the department at 800-734-5782."

I turned the page of the paper and found

another story in the crimes column. This was about the break-in at the newspaper office. "The *Gazette* editor reports nothing missing, but the search goes on for the intruder because of possible links to the murder of Heath Barr."

I didn't know whether to laugh or cry. While I was trying to decide whether to call Kate or Sam first, the phone rang. It was Jacques, the cheese salesman.

"Bonjour, my belle," he said in that charming but faux accent of his.

"Hello Jacques. *Comment ça va?*"

"I was fine until today. Now I am terrible. That horrible man Heath. I thought he was dead but he lives on."

"You're referring to today's newspaper."

"I certainly am, no joking. But forget that. I'm having a party after the market on Saturday night at my farm. I want you to see it. The goats, the cows, the sheep. See how the cheese is made, take a look at the gift shop, drink some wine, taste some cheese, and forget that bastard Heath Barr, may he rot in hell."

"It sounds like fun. Can I bring a friend?" I didn't know if I'd bring Sam or Kate or Grannie.

"Mais oui, certainment," he said. "Go on the website, Foggy Meadow Farm, for direc-

tions. We're about an hour outside Crystal Cove."

"I'll come as soon as I shut my booth down," I promised.

"Do not be misled. We have no fog in our meadow," Jacques added before he hung up."

Next I called Sam. He answered on the first ring.

"Did you see the paper?" I asked.

"Got it here. I'm hoping it will bring about some new leads. So if you don't have anything new to tell me, I have to hang up."

"I've already told you everything I know. I have a couple of questions. Will there be a funeral? Did he have a next of kin? And of course I want to know who killed him."

He laughed mirthlessly. "The answers are 'I don't know, and I don't know.' What I do know is who broke into the newspaper office the other night. There's a reward for information."

"I thought the newspaper was broke. They couldn't even afford to pay their food and lifestyle critic. And they're offering a reward so they can find out who broke in and took nothing? Are you going to collect it?" I asked.

"Nothing?" he said pointedly.

"Nothing the newspaper was entitled to.

Imagine what would have happened if *they'd* found the phone. You'd still be in the dark. Are you still in the dark?" I didn't expect an answer, but I couldn't resist trying to pry something out of him.

"I'm not sure," he said. "I'm still focusing on the vendors that Heath criticized. Unless you've heard something new."

"Sorry," I said. "I've already checked out Martha and her chickens. You can cross her off your list."

"Not so fast," he said dryly. "She looked like a tough cookie to me. She sure didn't want to hand over her knife. I had to threaten her with legal action."

"Can't blame her for that. Any lab results from those confiscated knives?"

"Hanna . . ."

"All right, all right. Forget I asked. Anyway Martha can't stand to kill her chickens, how could she kill a food critic? Which leaves Lurline, Jacques, Tammy and Lindsey, and Bill and Dave."

I picked up a pen and drew circles around the names of the vendors, but I just couldn't cross anyone's name off the list.

"Maybe you should look into the people Heath gave good reviews to like Gino, the pizza man, or Nina."

There was a long silence. Finally he said,

"And their motives would be?" he asked. I was afraid he was just humoring me, but I couldn't resist explaining.

"Maybe Heath was shaking them down. Giving them good reviews in exchange for money. They got tired of it, went to his office to pay him off but murdered him instead. He deserved it. I mean that's what they might have thought. He wasn't a nice person."

"Gotta go," Sam said. Without even thanking me for my theory. "I've got another call."

I sat down at my kitchen table and asked myself why I bothered to talk to the man. I had bared my soul to him, traipsed all over hell and back to get information and he didn't appreciate it one bit. I was going to tell him about the party at Jacques' and ask if he wanted to go with me, but it was too late. I'd go alone. I threw a discarded apple core from the basket on the floor across the room in the direction of the galvanized trash can in the corner. It landed with a satisfying thunk. "Take that," I muttered.

If Sam was invited to the party I'd ignore him completely. I'd do my sleuthing on my own and refuse to share my information with him. I'd be the life of the party, square dancing in the barn, taking wagon rides around the farm and finally watching the wheels of cheddar cheese age. I didn't need Sam to have a good time, in fact he could be a damper on a good time. Grannie would be more fun. But I didn't think she'd agree to go with me. Never mind, this was a chance to bond with my fellow vendors, and I'd find out if Jacques was all talk or if he was interested in me.

I didn't have any hope that Sam was interested in anything but solving the murder of Heath Barr. How I wished Heath had never come to Crystal Cove. And I wasn't the only one. Heath himself, as he took his last breath before his throat was slashed, must have wished the same.

I needed a challenge in the pie department so I painstakingly pitted the sour cherries the delivery man had dropped off from his farm for a Twice-Baked Sour Cherry Pie. I'd made my usual all-butter crusts earlier, rolled them out into thick disks and refrigerated them. I heated my oven to 425 degrees and rolled one into a twelve-inch circle. I pre-baked the crust for a half hour while I prepared my sour cherry filling, adding sugar and tapioca to the cherries. I took the golden brown crust from the oven and filled it with the cherry mixture. Then I cut my remaining crust into half-inch thick rounds. I laid the rounds of dough on top of the pie, brushed them with cream and baked it again until my crust was dark golden brown and the filling was bubbling and smelling delicious. I was grateful to be able to forget Heath's murder for an hour while I baked.

But with my pie baking in the oven I stood at the huge restaurant sink filled with dirty bowls and spoons thinking, why did Heath come here? Was it a career move? Did he think there was a future for him at the *Gazette* even though they refused to pay him? Was it the food fair that brought him here? Even after he saw the facilities and realized what his unpaid job was? Or did he come to our lovely little town because of some woman. If so, who was she? I needed to find her and ask her. I could start by asking Lindsey, Tammy, and Lurline, who were sure to hear more gossip than I did. I knew that he'd dumped on them, but that just enforced one of my theories.

If Heath was pursuing someone, maybe she was married like Lindsey and Tammy. I let my mind wander and I decided maybe whoever killed Heath couldn't get away from him except by killing him. I couldn't see how anyone would want to be with him. But then I'd only had one conversation with him. That was enough for me.

When the pie was done I was so happy with it I thought I'd make one like it for Jacques' party.

The week dragged by. Or slid by, depending on how you looked at it. Sam left me alone, which made me wonder if he'd solved the murder but just didn't tell me. Maybe he was already working on another case. Or he found me boring company and had discovered someone more interesting than a pie baker — like a cupcake maker. I refrained from calling him or knocking on the door of the police station. Instead I worked hard, baking, selling, schmoozing with customers, encouraging them to sit outside at my sidewalk café. I even ordered two tables with bright umbrellas and had them set up on the sidewalk with the others. And still Sam didn't drop by. Not that I cared. I was just glad to see my business taking off.

Since my pie contest was a done deal I had to make time to promote it with posters around town at the library and in store windows. I had to. Grannie and her friends were judges and I had a call from Nina who asked me if I was sure she should enter.

"Of course you should," I said. "There will be loads of people here and they're all amateurs like you. You have an advantage being in the candy business already. You deal with sugar and butter every day." Then I told her about a web site with lots of pie recipes.

She thanked me and said she'd give it a try.

Fortunately my bruises were gone, my head didn't throb and I was ready for a big weekend, the fair, the party at Jacques' and the contest on Sunday. Who said life in a small town was boring? Not if you make your own excitement.

What happens when life gets a little too exciting, for some people that is? Good question. On Saturday I was at the fair again, happily selling peach pies with lattice crust, strawberry-rhubarb double-crust pies, the local favorite — olallieberry pie, apple fritters, and double chocolate tart in a graham cracker crust. I didn't expect to see Sam, so I didn't worry about making anything savory. I was just handing out samples and answering questions like,

"Do you have a cookbook I can buy?"

Answer: "No, but I recommend *The Pastry Lover's Guide to Perfect Pies.*"

"Do you use all organic ingredients?"

Answer: "Our ingredients are all wholesome and natural."

"What's the most popular pie you sell?"

"Apple is the all-American pie, but my

customers are very adventurous. Today's special is wild Huckleberry with Crème Fraiche." Wild huckleberries were hard to find. I paid some kids top dollar for them when they were in season and put bags of them into my huge stand-alone freezer.

When Grannie came by she volunteered to take over and I accepted immediately. I was glad she wasn't too busy with her advice column yet to help me out. As I left I saw she'd immediately attracted more customers. I probably should have her come more often. I never knew if she was glad to be done with pie sales or if she ever missed the whole scene. She'd rolled up her sleeves and was chatting up a few customers so I took advantage of my freedom and made the rounds. I'd promised to introduce her to the knife man, but did I have time to do it the right way? With a proper buildup and a casual manner?

The first thing I noticed was Nina was not at the caramel booth. Instead a man was standing behind the counter looking bored. No samples. No customers. It had to be her husband, Marty Holloway, though I didn't recognize him. I'd never really known him.

"Hi," I said. "Where's Nina?"

"She's taking a break," he said.

"Oh. Maybe I'll run into her," I said.

"I doubt it," he said. "She's out of town."

Out of town? She'd just officially entered my pie contest. "So you're filling in for her," I said. "You must be Marty. I'm Hanna."

"I heard about you," he said.

The way he said it made me wonder what exactly he'd heard. I looked at the display of caramels. The boxes were stacked on top of each other and looked almost industrial. Not a sample in sight. It wasn't what Nina would have done. "How's business?" I asked.

"So-so," he said. "Waste of time if you ask me."

"It's good of you to fill in for her, you must be busy with the large animals and everything," I said.

"You got that right," he said. "But she paid for the booth rental, and she had the candy, so . . ." He shrugged.

"Right. It's really delicious. She's a great, what do you call it, 'confectioner.' Well, I better get back to my booth. I sell pies."

"I know," he said.

I walked back to my booth. I couldn't help thinking of my theory, the one that Sam pooh-poohed. I proposed looking at the vendors that Heath praised instead of the ones he'd trashed. I had this idea that if he shook down someone like Nina, she could

202

have promised to pay him for a positive review but changed her mind. When he tried to force her, threatened to tell her husband she'd taken the money from their savings, she killed him. I smiled to myself admiring my clever solution even though Sam didn't agree. But she had a serrated knife, which I presumed Sam had confiscated by now. Back to my original question, how could any woman sneak up on a big guy like Heath and slit his throat?

Then I wondered, where was Nina? Had she skipped out of town right before my pie contest because Sam was on to her? If he suspected her, he wouldn't tell me. On a related matter, wouldn't you think a veterinarian would have more social skills than Marty did? Didn't they have to have a bedside manner sort of like a doctor to attract patients? Since I didn't have a pet, maybe I was all wrong. Or maybe I'd caught Marty on a bad day, a day when he would rather not be there. Then why was he? Filling in for the runaway Nina so no one would suspect she was on the lam. He wasn't working the booth just to sell a few caramels, but for appearances. If only I could brainstorm with Sam. Unfortunately I had to brainstorm by myself, with no one to tell me if I was making sense or not.

I went back to my booth to relieve Grannie so she could meet up with her friends. I had just begun explaining how I only used local Meyer lemons from the tree in my back yard for my lemon tarts when a trio of two men in suits and one woman with a briefcase came marching down the aisle and stopped abruptly in front of one of the vegetable stands. I stepped out in front of my booth so I could listen in while the officials, if that's who they were, demanded to inspect the scales the vendor was using.

I stood there frozen with dismay watching as they went through a series of tests. The man who was wearing a blue blazer said the household scales in the booth were faulty and until he could provide commercial scales, the vendor couldn't weigh his stone fruit. After this week he'd have to give it away or sell it by the piece or stop selling it. I could hear the waves of discontent all the way down the aisle. Not just me but everybody. Commercial scales were expensive. No ordinary vegetable and fruit seller wanted to invest in them.

Of course I wasn't in any danger of being shut down since I didn't weigh any of my products, but still, I hated to see the long arm of the law reach into our own folksy, small-town food fair. What would Heath say if he were here, I wondered. And what about Sam? Did he know anything about this crackdown? No, that couldn't be.

I'd just returned to my booth after watching the same scene play out several more times with the scales and the fruit and vegetable vendors. I was feeling lucky that I had nothing to worry about from the bureaucrats when the committee of three descended on my booth.

"Any of your wares made with milk, eggs, cream or other dairy products?" a woman in a skirt, low-heeled shoes, and a green jacket with the county insignia on the front asked.

"Yes, many of them," I admitted.

"Where is your refrigeration unit?"

I showed her the large cooler in the back of my station wagon. She positively sneered as if I'd buried my pies in wet sand to keep them cool.

"I'm afraid you'll have to improve your methods of refrigeration before you can sell these pies."

"All of them?" I asked.

"Just the ones with the ingredients I mentioned."

I was livid. My cream pies were kept frosty cool and safe in my cooler. The others like strawberry-rhubarb and peach didn't need refrigeration.

"This is a small-town food fair," I explained unnecessarily, I thought. "We make food for our friends and customers in our homes and bring it here to sell. We're not a big commercial establishment."

"Obviously," she sniffed. "We are only here because we are following up on a complaint of non-compliance."

"Who complained?" I demanded. Then I had a sinking feeling I might know who did it.

She leafed through a small notebook. "I'm under no obligation to tell you."

"Was it Heath Barr, newspaper reporter?" I asked.

She looked startled, but said nothing. She didn't need to. Her face said it all.

"You might want to put a check by his name. He's no longer alive. You won't be hearing from him again."

"Is he the man who was murdered with the — ?" she asked wide eyed.

I nodded.

She put her notebook in her briefcase and crossed the aisle to talk to one of her colleagues. They both turned to look at me as if they suspected me of the murder.

Welcome to the club, I thought. I just hoped I'd discouraged them. Maybe they'd be afraid to tinker with the Crystal Cove Food Fair and the natives who worked there or they might find their throats slit too. Not that I said that. I just thought it.

I checked with my neighbors who weren't harassed by the inspectors. Apparently candied fruit and spicy nuts were not suspect. Lucky them. I wondered how Lurline fared. After the committee had moved on I went across to her booth.

"They couldn't have found anything wrong with your cupcakes could they?" I asked.

"They wanted to know where I made the cupcakes, if it was a certified commercial kitchen."

"Is it?"

"Of course not. I make them at home."

"Did Heath know that?"

"How could he?"

"I just wondered, because guess who reported us all," I said. "Before he died."

Her lower lip curled. "That slime bag."

"Exactly."

"So it didn't do any good to kill him. He's like a vampire. His legacy lives on."

I gave her a second look. Her baby blue eyes had turned dark with anger. I believed for one brief moment she could have slit Heath's throat. She was small but she was tough. And she wasn't sorry he died. Who was?

I explained to her about my refrigeration problem and how I couldn't possibly afford a portable refrigeration unit. Just as the fruit and vegetable vendors couldn't afford commercial scales.

"We're screwed," I said clenching my hands into fists.

She stood on tiptoe to look for the inspectors. They were now on the far edge of the parking lot.

"I don't care," she said, "I'm going to keep selling. That woman said she was going to inspect my commercial kitchen. Over my dead body. Look, I've still got customers," she said in a loud whisper. She did and so did I. "They don't care where I bake my cupcakes." If Lurline was not cowed by those inspectors, why should I be? I was just as gutsy as Lurline and I vowed also not to give in until I had to. I also hadn't learned enough to cross her off my personal list of suspects. In fact I moved her to the top of the Lindsey, Tammy and Lurline list.

After our unwelcome visitors left behind citations ordering us to comply by next week, the market seemed to rebound. I'd almost sold out by four o'clock, even the refrigerated pies sold well, as if my customers had decided that the county couldn't tell them what they could or could not eat. I felt better about everything, but still the citation weighed heavily on my mind.

I didn't stay around much longer. After I packed up with the help of Mandy, I stopped by Jacques' cheese stand to find him fuming over the committee who he referred to as "Nazis" because they'd asked him for, among other documents, his pasture management plan to make sure the sheep and cows were humanely treated.

"They asked me if my ruminant animals are allowed to fulfill their natural behaviors. Can you believe the hubris of those idiots? As if they know what their natural behaviors are and I don't." He paused to catch his breath and recapture his French accent. "Is it true that SOB Heath pulled the plug on us before he bit the dust?" he asked.

"That's what I heard."

"I'd like to know who killed him," he said. "So I could thank him and ask him why he didn't do it sooner."

"What if it was a she?" I muttered, but he didn't appear to hear me.

When he calmed down, he asked me if I was coming to his party that night. I said I was and I was bringing a pie, and coming alone. He handed me a map and said he was dying to show me around the place.

I didn't see Sam at the market at all. Maybe he had better things to do than watch while some county official handed out citations and warnings. I wanted to ask him how seriously I and all of us should take this woman's appearance. On the other hand, maybe I didn't want to know.

Maybe Sam was busy chasing down Heath's murderer. We could only hope. I'd love to forget my list of suspects. I'd love to think about something besides the hateful food critic and his untimely demise. I was not worried the killer was after me. Heath was hated by so many people. I wasn't. At least as far as I knew.

I refused to worry about the county and the end of the fair as we knew it. Somebody would come up with a solution. We'd agree to change our profligate, unsanitary ways and they'd give us some time to comply. Or something. I had a pie contest to think about.

I put my few un-sold pies away, hung a closed sign on my front door and went upstairs to find something to wear that was different from my usual jeans, T-shirt, and apron. Yes, it was a party on a dairy farm, but I couldn't stand another event wearing skinny jeans or cargo pants, gladiator sandals, and a hoodie. Instead, recalling what Heath had said about Foggy Meadow being a misnomer, I found a beaded halter dress I hadn't worn for months, maybe never in Crystal Cove, and high-heels. On second thought, picturing myself touring the pastures and remembering how it felt to be chased by a determined, surprisingly agile oversized pig, I changed into flat sandals, just in case.

Before I took off, I left phone messages for everyone who'd signed up for the pie contest the next day, including Grannie and her fellow judges. I told them we'd gather at eleven the next morning at the shop. I'd have time to set up tables before that, but tonight I was going to try to forget about pie, murder, free publicity, or anything but having fun.

I had no idea if Sam was going to this party or if he was hiding out in his office huddled over his computer using his secure police search engine. If he came to the party or any party, it would only be to further investigate whatever crime he was investigating. Today it was the murder of the newspaper critic. Tomorrow — who knew? That was the reason why he did anything and the sooner I realized that the sooner I'd quit hoping he was interested in me other than as a suspect, an observer, or a witness. It wasn't going to happen.

What better place to look for a killer than a cheese farm where many of the guests had an ax to grind with the victim. As for me, I no longer cared who killed Heath. I just wanted to have a good time at a party. Was that so wrong?

I got into my car, propped the map to the farm on the dashboard and heard a knocking. It was not from the engine but from the driver's side window.

Startled, I looked out to see a strange man's face looking in at me.

NINE

"You're the pie lady?" the man said.

I cranked the window down, vowing that my next car, if I ever bought one, would have automatic windows. Until then I'd be exercising my biceps every day.

"I'm Hanna Denton, the owner of the shop. What can I do for you?" An enterprising business owner like myself wouldn't mind dashing in to get a pie for a paying customer.

"I'm Heath Barr's brother Barton."

"Barton Barr?" I said blinking rapidly.

"Oh, so you've heard of me?" he asked raising his eyebrows.

"No, absolutely not. I just wanted to be sure . . ." I wanted to be sure someone had actually named his or her child Barton Barr. Heath Barr was bad enough.

He must have misunderstood because he pulled out his wallet and showed me his driver's license. Sure enough it was made out to Barton Barr and the address was in Los Angeles.

"Do you see the resemblance?" he asked, leaning down so his nose was only inches from mine.

"To your brother? I've never met him."

"Really? Then why . . ."

"Why would I kill him? I didn't."

"That's not what I meant. Why did you hate him?"

I sighed. I was all dressed up and on my way to a party on a Saturday night, something rare for me and this nutcase who claimed to be Heath's brother was interrogating me. I wished that Sam would meander out of the police station and cite him for loitering or at least bring him in for questioning.

"I don't know why you think I hated him," I said, my foot resting on the gas pedal so I could make a quick getaway if this guy was as nutty as I thought he was. "But if I did it would be because he wrote a nasty review of my pies for the newspaper."

"He was a critic. That was his job," Barton said.

"I understand what a critic does," I said stiffly. "But his reviews were all completely wrong. Not just mine. I invited him in for another shot at my pies but he never showed

214

up. Now if you'll excuse me. I'm sorry for your loss and everything, but . . ."

"Is that the police station?" he asked pointing to the building across the street with the logo and the huge sign. I wanted to say, "No, it's a pancake house, why don't you stop in for a short stack," but I've never been very good at sarcasm.

"Yes, it is," I said.

"I have a beef with the police chief. It's been days since my brother's murder and I understand there have been no arrests yet. On behalf of the Barr family I demand an answer."

"Did he leave any dependents?" I asked.

"Fortunately no," Barton said. "Unless you mean me. Our uncle preceded Heath in death by only a few months. What a terrible burden. First burying Uncle Otto and now Heath. I'm the only one left."

"But you said on behalf of the Barr family," I reminded him.

"That's essentially me," he admitted.

"How sad," I said. "You're an only child now." Of course I'd been an only child all my life and I'd done all right.

"What's really sad is that I have the feeling no one cares about my brother. What are the police doing?"

"I wouldn't know," I said. "I'm sure the

215

chief is doing his best." I should have just shut up. Sam wouldn't expect me to stand up for him, so why bother? Now if I was his deputy I'd have a different attitude. "This is a small town," I continued. "We're not used to murder. I say that as a concerned citizen and an innocent bystander. I myself have nothing to do with the police. I don't think the station is open on Saturday night." I realized that if I really had nothing to do with the police then I wouldn't know or care if it was open on Saturday night.

"I would think Saturday night is just the time when most crimes are committed," Barton Barr said with a smug I-told-you-so look.

"Not in Crystal Cove, they aren't," I said. How I wished I had left two minutes before this man accosted me. If his brother Heath was half as annoying, I could understand the urge to kill him. I couldn't seem to get away from this Barton's narrow-eyed gaze. His grip on my open window frame unnerved me. I was afraid to leave and afraid to stay.

Barton stood up straight and looked across the street, assessing his chances of finding the chief in, I supposed.

"Why don't you go over and knock on the door?" I suggested. "If you really want to see if the chief's in."

"I'll tell him you sent me," he said.

"You do that." Now was my chance. I turned the key in the ignition and sped down the street as fast as I could. When I looked in my rearview mirror he was gone. I was afraid when Barton found that Sam wasn't there at the station, he'd follow me and ask more questions I had no answers for. But after a few minutes on the open road when he didn't show up, I started to relax.

The trip out of town toward the foothills had a calming effect on me. I needed it. Not that I lived in a big city — Crystal Cove was the epitome of small-town friendly and folksiness. But the wide open countryside was another matter. I tried to put Heath Barr out of my mind but I tried to decide if Heath's brother was devastated about his death or not. Maybe Barton just wanted to find out if his brother had left him anything. I could have told him not to get his hopes up since the guy didn't even have a paying job.

However he felt, Barton's arrival on the scene could mean trouble. Not for me but for Sam. Never mind. Sam was a big boy and could handle a simpleton brother who accused him of dragging his feet in this murder investigation better than I could.

An hour later I saw the sign for "Foggy Meadow Farm the home of Honeybrook Cheese — Hand-made, Hand-crafted, Hand-held." The sun was still fairly high in the sky which made the greenery on the other side of the white fences look all the more lush. We don't have rain in California in the summer, so they must have deep wells or spend a fortune on water so their animals could graze. However they did it, the place looked like a picture postcard. Cows and goats grazed on one side of the road and sheep on the other as I drove slowly toward the white frame farmhouse.

There were signs along the way, welcoming guests with balloons, so I knew I was at the right place. Especially when I saw Jacques waving to me from the front porch of the house.

"You found us," he said with a big Gallic smile on his face. Maybe he was French after all. Who else would kiss his guest on both cheeks as he did after I parked my car. Then he gave me a squeeze that could have been Gallic or just definitely bold and somewhat flattering.

"Hanna," he said with a long look at me and my dress, "you look *absolument ravissante*."

I was glad I'd not only dressed for the occasion, but also that I'd taken French at Crystal Cove High School, and I'd curled my hair and did what I could with my makeup. I'd called Kate before I left just so she'd know I wasn't sitting at home another Saturday night reading cookbooks. She was thrilled to hear about Jacques' party and said if she'd been told in advance she would have come by to do my makeup.

"Come up to the house," Jacques said, taking the pie I'd brought out of my hands. "This looks mahhvelous."

"This is all yours?" I asked, looking around at the house, the outbuildings, the pastures, and the animals.

"Not really. Actually none of it is mine. I'm farm-sitting for the Dolan family," he explained. "So I'm here for the summer taking care of the place."

"What about the cheese making?"

"The cheese was made last year or last season. It's aging now. I told them I don't do cheese except for eating and cooking with it. But all I have to do here is turn the wheels and keep the temperature even. And sell. That's my thing. I love the sales part of it. The market and the people. Most of them."

"I saw your demo of the torpedo sandwiches."

"Pretty good, wasn't it?" he said, his eyes sparkling in what I imagined to be a continental sexy way. "I sold out that day. What can I say? I'm a social person. I know what you're thinking. Why be a farm-sitter and bury myself in the country if I love company? Well, it beats working in a factory. Especially when I score a nice place like this one. Otherwise farming is a big fat bore. And lonely. Not that I'm always alone out here, they've got sheep shearers and veterinarians coming and going. What I do is oversee the place. I'm good at that. Giving orders and seeing the big picture."

He wasn't modest, that was for sure, but that's not how he'd gotten this farm-sitting job or any others. He'd had to sell himself. What was so surprising was how involved he was in our local politics and crime scene, considering. "The Dolans will have to give you a bonus," I suggested. "The way you're looking after their interests. A lot of other farm-sitters would have just ignored that know-it-all and his food review and simply brushed it off. But you were right in there fighting for them. I hope they realize what a prize they've got."

"Now you're making me blush," Jacques said. Actually his face did look a little red.

"You're right. I take a personal interest in the farm. I may not have a farm of my own, but one day I hope I will. I may not make cheese either, but I understand the mind of a farmer wherever and whoever he is, especially an artisan who makes blue-ribbon cheeses. I take pride in my work. Like you do."

I could only nod in agreement. He'd obviously thought it all out. Then it was time to change the subject before we both got emotional.

"You don't use a vet named Marty Holloway, do you? I think he only deals with pets."

"I think his name is on my list of emergency numbers. So far there hasn't been an emergency with the dog or the cats. Why? Do you have a sick pet?"

"No, but his wife sells caramels at the Food Fair. Maybe you've seen her. The thing is she wasn't at the booth today. He was and he's a terrible salesman." And a rather unpleasant guy to boot. How did Nina put up with him?

"Some people have it and some don't," he said. "You do."

"Wait, you haven't even been to my booth."

"I came by, but you were so busy you didn't see me."

I was pleased to hear what he said. I always felt I wasn't as good as Grannie, but then I'm still a novice.

"Enough talk of work. You're here to have a good time and forget about those morons who bothered us today. I guarantee they won't be back next Saturday," Jacques said.

"How do you know?"

"I took care of it."

"But how?"

"I called and left an anonymous message at the county board of health about rats spotted at the supermarket in San Pedro," Jacques said, referring to the nearby town where some of our residents shopped. "Now the suits should have something big to worry about besides the Food Fair's scales and our food sample contamination. Yes, that's what they nailed me for. Not any more. Everyone's afraid of bubonic plague, or they should be. With rats in the county who gives a rat's ass about a few minor violations at the Food Fair?"

San Pedro had a new shopping center thirty miles north of us. We locals had all been afraid of their taking business away from us when they opened last fall, but none of us had resorted to out and out lies.

"But, is that fair?"

"Fair? Is it fair to pick on poor farmers

and artisans trying to serve the public with the fruits and vegetables they've raised?"

"No, but I hope they didn't recognize your French accent on the phone," I said.

"I didn't have one," he said with a cockney twang.

I gasped and he laughed.

"No worries, I can be discreet. I'm a man of a thousand voices and almost that many careers. I didn't leave a trail behind me," he said. "Keep moving, that's my motto. One of the benefits of being temporary. I'll be gone before they're on to me. And I won't leave a forwarding address. You know our home-town cop wouldn't allow any vendor to cheat. Even when there's a murderer on the loose. He's there to protect us and our customers. Or he was until the asshole got murdered. Now he's got bigger fish to fry. I hope he gets what he's after."

"Who, the police chief or Heath, the food critic?"

"The cop. Heath deserved what he got, if you ask me. That's what I told the police chief. I felt sorry for him with so much on his plate and the whole town looking over his shoulder, so I invited him to the party."

"Who, the police chief or Heath?" I asked.

Jacques laughed. "Come around back of

the house. We're having drinks around the pool."

"Pool on a dairy farm?"

"Oh, sweetheart, I only work at the best places. What's California in the summer without a pool? My job is to check the pH in the morning and the pool boy comes once a week. I know the drill. You should have seen my place in the Outback. Of course sometimes I hit a rough patch like when I got stuck one summer in Ireland. The ad for the farm sitter said beaches and a river for fishing. Sounded good, right? But the beaches were miles away, cold and frigid, the river'd been fished out by the locals who didn't appreciate my horning in. They weren't fond of the folks I was sitting for either."

"How did you get out of it?" I asked.

"No way out. Had to put in my time. I had my reputation to think of. Once a farm-sitter gets a bad rep nobody wants him on their place."

"Is that where you're from, Ireland? I thought you were French, Jacques," I said.

"I'm from nowhere and everywhere," he said, tilting his cowboy hat back to reveal his tanned features and a shock of streaked, bleached hair across his forehead.

He took my arm and led me up the rise

toward the house. "Did you bring your suit?" he asked when a large pool came into view surrounded by women in dresses and men in casual shirts and jeans. It was all so beautiful, so well-cared for, so rich and lush. I hadn't expected to find this scene way out here.

I shook my head. Who would bring a swimsuit to a dairy farm? "I didn't know you had a pool. You are living the California dream."

"That's the idea," he said. "Never mind the suit. In a few hours we'll all be, how do you say . . . skinny dipping."

I smiled nervously. I'm no prude, but skinny dipping with a bunch of strangers?

"It's not like we're strangers," Jacques said, as if he'd read my mind. "I mean we're all in the same boat, don't you agree?"

"Some might say we're up the creek with no canoe. It means . . ." I didn't get a chance to explain how the saying applied to a situation where a group of former strangers were now bound together as murder suspects. Maybe it was just as well. Jacques was waving to a guy who'd just gotten out of a shiny new black BMW and was walking toward us.

"And who is this lovely creature?" the guy asked Jacques with a nod in my direction.

"She's a cut above your usual breezy."

I didn't know whether to be flattered or insulted. I'd never been referred to as a breezy before. I must have looked puzzled, because Jacques put his arm around my shoulder and explained. "Breezy is a cross between a broad and easy."

"I'm neither," I said. Better to set the record straight right now.

"Hanna, meet my mate Geoffrey."

Again I was confused. Was Geoffrey actually Jacques' partner? Or was it "mate" as in friend in Australia? This time no one explained.

"Hanna works the farm market with me," Jacques said. "She sells pies. Like the one in this box here she brought."

"You made it yourself?" Jacques' tall, attractive friend, Geoffrey, asked. In his ripped jeans, famous name T-shirt, and leather sandals, he looked like an interesting guy, around my age, but how did I know for sure? When there's a murderer on the loose in your town, it's not a bad idea to suspend judgment, of strangers or even your friends.

I nodded and took the pie box out of Jacques' hands. I tipped the cover so they could see the brown flaky crust with the red sour cherry juice oozing from it.

"Whoa," Geoffrey said, his eyes alight.

"Why didn't you tell me you invited a babe who could bake? Is she the one who . . ."

"No," Jacques said curtly. "Bring your suit, Geoff?"

"Do I need one?"

Jacques assured him he didn't and the water was fine.

I listened to the two of them banter for a few minutes as we made our way to the party scene around the pool. Jacques had his arm around my shoulders. I couldn't help being flattered. Especially when the first person I saw was Lurline. Not surprisingly she was dressed to kill in low-rise skintight white jeans. Her midriff was bare and she wore an electric blue stretch tank top and high heels. To top it off I saw a huge tray of little cupcakes on a table on the patio. Who do you think brought those?

Not surprisingly Lurline was surrounded by a group of men. If I hadn't made my entrance in my best dress with Jacques I would have felt old and dumpy next to her. But he had a way of making me and probably every other woman he knew feel young, sexy, and desirable.

It was best that I ignore Lurline for the moment. Fortunately Jacques introduced me to various people, then when some of the other vendors arrived I seized the chance to talk to Tammy and Lindsey, who'd brought their husbands. They'd also brought a couple of baguettes from their bread booth, which went really well with some of the exotic cheeses on the buffet table by the pool. Which all went extremely well with some wine that a good-looking young guy behind a portable bar was pouring. A couple of inflatable rafts floated in the pool. Some cool jazz music floated out from the house on large speakers. I hadn't been to a party like this for years, maybe never, that combined a working country farm atmosphere with sophisticated music, food, and drinks. That Jacques really knew how to throw a party.

"What a life Jacques has," Lindsey said to me as Tammy went off with her husband to see the milking machines. I watched her go, remembering she was still on my long list of suspects. Maybe I'd talk to her later, though what would I say? I knew perfectly well how she felt about Heath's demise.

I admired Lindsey's Palazzo pants and a gauzy see-through shirt. Holding a glass of local dark red Pinot Noir, she looked like an ad for California wine in a slick magazine.

"Makes you want to be a farm-sitter too, doesn't it?" I asked.

"You didn't fall for that line, did you?" Lindsey said. "He's more than that, Hanna."

"Yes, he's a great salesman and a cook as well."

"That's not what I meant." She lowered her voice. "Haven't you heard? He's in the Witness Protection Program of course."

I've never thought Lindsey was the brightest crayon in the box, but being raised by Grannie to be polite, I didn't gasp and tell her she was obviously crazy. I just nodded as if I agreed. On the other hand, was Lindsey capable of making up a story like that? Of course it was possible the story was true, which would explain Jacques' peripatetic lifestyle, hopping from farm to farm. But instead of working for the farm-sitting placement agency, he was placed by the FBI. Just in case it was true I decided to follow through and see if she could back up her story.

"So what's his background? How did he get to be in the program? He must have done something. Was he in a gang or did he work for the mob? Does he know something that puts him in danger?" I asked.

Lindsey's mouth was full of a wedge of the prize-winning triple cream cheese I'd seen on the buffet table so she couldn't answer right away.

What I really wanted to know was how she knew this. If she was out blabbing to me about his identity, didn't that mean his cover was blown and he'd have to move on?

Just as I'd considered the possibility, Lindsey put her finger to her lips. "Don't tell anyone I told you," she said.

"I won't," I promised. "But how did you find out?"

"He told me," she said.

Okay, now I was sure she was wrong. Anyone who said he was in the Witness Protection Program wasn't. He must have been lying because the whole premise was to protect the witness and as soon as someone found out, they were doomed. Whoever was looking for them would track them down and kill them. Jacques was obviously pulling her leg.

"But he didn't tell me who he really is," she said. "Jacques isn't his real name."

"No kidding," I said. My one-track mind went back to the mystery du jour, the murder of our food critic. I still couldn't believe what Lindsey told me about Jacques, but what if she was right? I couldn't afford to ignore it. "What about Heath? Maybe he was in the same program. Maybe they knew each other in federal prison. Which would explain the fact that they both ended up in

Crystal Cove. One was a lousy food critic and the other is an excellent cheese salesman. So now we're left with a clue as to who murdered Heath. It was the mob." I felt flushed with my own brilliant conclusion.

"You could be right, Hanna," Lindsey said cautiously. That should have been a hint that Lindsey was simply making up this story so I wouldn't suspect her.

She stepped closer to me and said in a hushed voice. "Look around. See the guys serving drinks? They're probably Jacques' personal guards or something, don't you think? How could a dairy farmer afford a staff like this?"

If anyone had told me in high school or even yesterday I'd be trading secrets and theories with Lindsey, I'd have said they were nuts. I was about to move away from the cheese table and away from Lindsey before I lost all sense of reality, when she reached for another glass of wine from a passing waiter who she claimed was really a former mob hit man, looked over my shoulder and waved enthusiastically. "There's Sam," she said. "We'll ask him."

"I thought you weren't supposed to tell anyone," I murmured. Wait until Sam heard our theories — he'd run for the hills.

"I'm not, but he's a cop."

Knowing Sam, I was pretty sure he didn't come to the party for purely social reasons. So maybe Lindsey was on to something. Forget the witness protection program, it could have been some other kind of cover-up. Some other tie to the murder of Heath. Just when Lindsey was about to ask Sam what he thought, her husband came up and said they were going for a hay ride. I breathed a sigh of relief as they rode off in a large flat-bed truck covered with straw. So much for the sophisticated atmosphere. No way was I getting into a hay wagon in my good dress. I stayed right there at the buffet table, which looked like the cheese counter at Whole Foods.

"If I'd known you were coming I'd have given you a ride," I said to Sam.

"Thanks, but I may have to leave early," he explained as the wine server returned and Sam snagged a glass of sparkling California white wine. "I'm on call and I didn't want to cut short your evening."

"Very considerate of you. Lots of new crimes to solve, I suppose," I said brightly. "As if you'd tell me."

"I do have something to share with you that may interest you. In fact it's right up your alley. Heard about it from the San Pedro police before I came here tonight."

I tried not to flinch, wince, or exhibit an ounce of more than ordinary interest, but somehow I knew what was coming next. "I suppose they want your help solving some horrendous crime like an unauthorized bonfire on the beach or something."

"Not this time. This was a prank. Someone let a bunch of lab rats loose in the supermarket."

"No," I said, with disbelief.

"Yes," he said. "What does that remind you of?"

"Oh, come on Sam, you don't think I'm still a crazy teenager, do you? I've outgrown silly tricks like that. Not that I approve of keeping lab rats in small cages. I still think it's cruel and inhuman. Just as I did when I was in high school. But I'm too busy . . ."

"I don't think the perpetrator was an animal rights advocate," he said. "I think it was a ploy to divert the county's attention away from the rule-breakers at the Food Fair by steering them to a rat-infested grocery store."

"Good for him or her whoever thought up the ploy. I mean I'm sorry for the poor store owner, but he's a big boy and I'm sure he'll figure it out."

"Is that all you've got to say?" he asked.

"I have a question for you. Are cops allowed to drink while on duty?" I glanced at the glass in his hand.

"I'm not on duty. I'm on call. In addition, I'm undercover."

"Speaking of which, Lindsey thinks Jacques is in the Witness Protection Program."

"Why?"

"You mean you don't know?"

"I can't say."

"Then I assume he is or you would say. You would say 'no, he's not in the Witness Protection Program'."

He shook his head. "I knew I couldn't fool you."

I swear Sam was hiding a smile behind his champagne glass. He'd do anything to point me in the wrong direction. At least he'd dropped the subject of the rats. I thought I'd dodged that rather well.

When Jacques came up, he slapped Sam on the back and said he was glad to see him. "Solve any crimes today?" Jacques asked.

Instead of clamming up the way he would have with me, Sam was totally genial. "Found a lost dog and caught someone trying to steal the 'curve ahead' sign from the highway."

"Any suspects in the murder case?"

Jacques asked.

"Just the usual," Sam said briefly. He looked around at the acres of green grass, the picture-book animals contentedly grazing in the field, the sparkling pool and the well-dressed guests standing around sipping wine. "Nice place you've got here."

"It's not mine," Jacques said. "Wish it was. You've got a great little town here, Chief, with some nice people, especially our Hanna here. Can't believe she's still single. She's not only beautiful but she bakes the world's best pies. Trust me, I know. I've been around the block a few times. Hell, I've even been around the world. If I was going to be around here a little longer . . ." He sighed. "But that's the nature of my job. Here today, gone tomorrow. Something I have in common with our gnarly food critic. Did you say there was a breakthrough in the case?" he asked, taking his hat off and tossing it onto a wooden bench behind the table.

Sam shook his head. Then he looked at Jacques as if he was trying to decide, does this phony Frenchman really think Hanna is beautiful? Or is he permanently full of it? Or was he thinking about Heath and wondering if Jacques killed him. That would explain why Jacques had to be "gone tomorrow." I noticed Sam said not a word to

Jacques about the rat infestation at the grocery store. Maybe it was beyond believable that a Frenchman would be capable of obtaining rats and dumping them at a grocery store and then host a big party. Before Jacques ambled off to greet some new arrivals, he said, "Look around. Don't miss the barn and the gift shop."

I nodded, and Sam said he wouldn't miss it. When Jacques was gone I said, "Well, that lets Jacques off the hook. If this dairy farm isn't his and he's just a farm-sitter as he claims, then why would he care enough to murder Heath for bad-mouthing the cheese that isn't his?"

"Nobody likes to be bad-mouthed," Sam remarked.

"I understand that, but if it's not your cheese, you don't have enough motive to kill the messenger."

He shrugged. I didn't know what that meant. That he agreed or disagreed with me. I sensed this conversation could go on forever. Me floating theories, Sam neither agreeing nor disagreeing with me, just letting me blather on. I was just grateful he'd dropped the subject of the rats. But I was flattered he'd remembered what I'd done in high school.

"Can I ask why you're here?" I said. "Or

is that classified and none of my business."

"I was invited," he said.

"I know. But you must get invited a lot, and yet you're often described as a workaholic."

"Not by you, I hope."

"I try not to describe you at all to anyone. They can draw their own conclusions. Although I sent someone to see you this evening."

"Barton Barr. He came to my office. It was not a productive meeting."

"Did he accuse you of negligence?"

"Nothing I haven't heard before. He wanted to share his thoughts with me as to who killed his brother."

I held my breath. "I hope he didn't say it was me because I think it could very well be him."

"Why would you think that, since he's on a crusade to find the murderer with or without my help? If he did it, why didn't he stay in Los Angeles and out of sight?"

"Because it's a scam and a cover-up. He doesn't really want your help. He just wants to annoy you."

"He did that all right. But why come and knock on my door on a Saturday night?"

"To throw you off. So you'll think just what you're thinking. That it couldn't be him. Did he tell you he's the last member of his family still alive? Doesn't that mean he'll stand to inherit whatever there is now that Heath's dead?"

"I suppose so, but how do we know that there is anything to inherit?" he asked.

"We can find out. I'll do some checking if you like," I said eagerly. I was more than willing to help Sam, and I was eager for this investigation to be over so we could all get back to our normal lives without the shadow of Heath Barr hanging over us.

"I'd prefer you didn't do any checking or anything to do with Heath Barr without my express permission," he said.

"But you're busy. I think you need a deputy. Someone who has a job but could spare some time when you were over-whelmed."

"I'll take that under advisement. You know I'm busy because you see me working at all hours across the street, is that it?"

"I hadn't noticed," I said coolly. But of course I had and he knew it. Good thing I wasn't attached to the lie detector in his office. I could imagine the bells and whistles going off. I was seriously miffed. I'd just shared my best thoughts with Sam and what did I get in return? A cool no, thank you. "I assume you're here at the party because

238

several if not all your suspects might be here too, am I right? Never mind, don't answer that. Don't let me keep you from your investigating. I'm going to look around," I said. "I can't believe this place. Did he say there was a gift shop?"

Instead of going off as I suggested, Sam went with me to a small outbuilding painted white with forest green trim which was actually the gift shop. A woman in a giant apron stood behind a counter filled with the famous Honeybrook cheeses. She was offering samples of a robust blue cheese and a seasonal creamy cheese made with rich Jersey cow milk lightly dusted in toasted red pepper flakes.

"Delicious," I said.

"Glad you like it," she said.

I especially liked the way she didn't push me to buy anything. Was that Jacques' idea or did she come with the farm? "Are you just here for the afternoon?" I asked.

"I work the Food Fair or here on the farm, wherever the family needs me."

"Looks like a great job," I said. I glanced down at the glass display case and saw a selection of cheese knives including the same knife we'd all used at the Fair with the serrated edge.

Sam saw it at the same time. "How much

is the knife?" he asked, pulling his wallet from his pocket.

She consulted her price list and told him it was sixty-five dollars.

"How many do you have on hand?" he asked.

"Just this one."

"I'll take it," Sam said.

I frowned. It looked shiny and new. Obviously never used. So why did Sam want it? To prevent anyone else from using it for illegal purposes? Or to run it by the lab for fingerprints? I didn't ask and he didn't say. Which was typical of our interaction these days. We walked toward the parking lot where he handed me the knife. "That's a replacement for the knife I took from you."

I held out my hand and took it but I was almost too stunned to say thank you. "That means I'm not getting mine back."

He nodded. "That means the subject is closed."

He'd bought me off. For the price of a fancy serrated knife he expected me to buzz off.

TEN

"Now what?" I asked after I put the knife in my car. There were even more people on the terrace now. Dusk was falling, the lights around the pool had been turned on and a chef was cooking something on an outdoor barbecue. What a life. I knew it wasn't Jacques' house or his land, but he got to live there, enjoy the benefits with none of the problems of ownership and act like a landowner and gracious host. Besides that, he'd done all us vendors a favor by getting the county off our backs. I wondered if he'd tell everyone or anyone else that we had him to thank for this huge favor.

"Let's join the others," Sam said. Sam, turning into a social being? Was it possible? Maybe he was being sociable to divert my attention from his squashing my recent theory so brutally. He was after something or someone. And it wasn't Barton Barr. It wasn't Jacques either or he would have acted by now.

On the terrace Sam was greeted warmly by Lurline, who linked her arm in his and ignored me. So who cared? I joined a small crowd that included our host. There were plenty of men at the party who were friendly and seemed impressed when Jacques told them I was the owner of the pie shop in town.

"So you're the woman who got trashed along with Jacques by the so-called food critic?" Jacques' friend, Geoffrey, said.

"That's me," I said. "Along with some others. I don't mean to brag about my pies, but I really didn't deserve to get panned, any more than Jacques or Bill and Dave, the sausage makers, or Martha, the rotis- serie woman. But I didn't kill Heath."

"I know you didn't," Geoffrey said. He said it so emphatically I gave him a second look. If he knew I didn't do it, then . . .

"Any idea who did?" I asked casually.

He laughed. "I'm new in town. I don't know anything about anything except what Jacques tells me. He and I go way back. Why don't you tell me who you think did it?"

"If I knew I'd tell the police. Actually I did tell the police that I thought it was the victim's brother. But my theory was not what you'd call welcomed with open arms.

242

Just a wild guess. But it seems I'm way off base. He has one brother, that's it. And I think this brother's got a financial motive, which is now he gets to inherit the family money. But no one knows if there was any money. So if it wasn't him, I give up and I'm keeping my mouth shut from now on. All I can say is that so many people wanted to kill this guy I'd have to stand in line."

"That guy over there in the civvies, is he the cop?"

"Right. He's the chief of police so he doesn't wear a uniform," I explained.

"So is he on duty tonight?"

It was not an easy question. Sam was talking to Lindsey and Tammy now along with their husbands. Did he suspect them as much or as little as I did of killing Heath, or was he just being friendly? Lurline was still hanging onto his arm. I wanted to think the reason he was looking at her so attentively was because she was also on his list. But maybe not.

"He's always on duty," I said at last. But it looked like he was having too good a time. Instead of frowning or glaring, he was smiling affably and talking to the group. He hadn't talked affably to me. But he hadn't bought them knives either, that I knew of.

I left Geoffrey and made the rounds of

the terrace, talking mostly to town people I knew slightly. We all paused when Jacques announced a square dance in the big barn. Some people groaned, some laughed, and some clapped. Sure enough, when we all obediently filed over there and went in to the huge, high-ceilinged barn I could see there was a huge cleared space on the floor. A guy wearing fancy jeans, a white shirt, and vest, and of course a big cowboy hat, was set up with a console and was already playing music.

Jacques took a small microphone and announced he was pleased to introduce the caller, Texas Jack. He said he hadn't known if the guy was available until he showed up. His excitement was contagious. He seemed so delighted I was even more sure he must be foreign and that's why he was into this authentic American folk activity. I looked around the barn. I thought that women who square-danced usually wore hokey dresses with mountains of petticoats and clunky shoes. And men wore cowboy hats and string ties and cowboy boots. Not tonight. Tonight everyone I saw was wearing California Casual. Oh well. I might have been the only one who not only wasn't dressed for it, I wasn't emotionally or physically ready for square dancing, either.

While the other guests good-naturedly lined up and dosey-doed their partners I quietly headed for the door. It was warm in the barn and promised to get even warmer with all those people dancing up a storm.

I didn't see Sam inside the barn. It would have been quite a sight to see him skipping up and down the floor and bowing to his partner, but I felt claustrophobic even in that lofty barn so I stepped outside, hoping no one like Jacques would see me and insist I stay for the fun. Instead I headed back to the terrace next to the pool. I'd had enough and was ready to go home.

Before I left I stopped for a look at the pool house. Like the rest of the farm, it was first class. Could the Dolans make enough cheese to support this lifestyle? Could anyone? Maybe they were gentlemen dairy farmers. However they did it, I had to admire their taste. The pool house was long and sleek and seemed built to hover over the water. I peeked in, seeing one end was a spa and a Jacuzzi, and in the other end were changing rooms, a sauna, and bathrooms. Under the overhanging roof were spotlights focused on the water.

The evening air was refreshingly cool. Not cool enough for a sauna, but I wanted to see it anyway. I took off my shoes and stepped inside. The small room smelled of cedar. There were fluffy terrycloth robes hanging on hooks. The heat hadn't been turned on so I sat down on a bench and enjoyed a moment of solitude before I went home. Maybe I was more like Jacques than I'd thought. Maybe I too could fit easily into this lifestyle. Maybe his life was the perfect one. It was more than one life, he lived many lives as he farm-sat. Even if his experience in Ireland had been less than ideal, it was different. I knew how fortunate I was to live the life of a pie baker. I had my own home and shop, but no boss. Unlike most working people I controlled my own destiny. I decided what kind of pies to make. I decided when to open and close my shop. I decided whether to hold a pie contest or have a booth at the Fair. But I didn't have a pool or a sauna.

Then I heard voices. Someone else was in the pool house. I reached for the door of the sauna, but then sat back and eaves-dropped shamelessly. How else does a person find out anything anyway? I heard Jacques' name mentioned and I leaned forward. It was dark. I couldn't see anything or anybody.

"I don't know why he invited me."

"He cares about you."

"I don't want to be cared about. I want more than that. Did you see him when that woman arrived? Went running off to meet her right in the middle . . ." Her voice faded away.

Who were they talking about? Me? Was she jealous of my relationship with Jacques, which was pretty sad since we didn't even have a relationship.

"I told Jacques this is his last chance. I'm not following him any more."

"Don't do anything stupid," the other woman said.

"Like tell someone who he is? Don't worry, I can control myself. It's Jacques who can't."

The woman laughed. "You got that right. How many times has he done this?"

"Ask him," her friend said.

"I can't. You know how he is," said the woman.

"Gotta love him. He invites the cop to the party. That takes nerve."

"Which one is the cop?" the woman asked.

"The good-looking dude with the cupcake," she said. "I'd like to kill her."

"You can't kill everyone he flirts with. Like the pie woman. Have a talk with her," the woman said. "Get it over with. Do it tonight."

Have a talk with me? What about? Go ahead. I would be all ears. But they'd better do it soon because I was outta there in a few minutes. But was "have a talk" code for "get rid of"? That wouldn't be easy. I was here to stay. And why bother? I didn't know anything about anything. Instead of being scared, I was mad.

"What's her deal?" the woman asked.

My deal? My deal was to mind my own business, which was making pies. Only stuff happened. Stuff that required me to step in and do something, like locate the missing cell phone or steer Heath's brother to the police.

On a related matter, why did everyone think Sam was with Lurline? Because she was hanging on his arm, looking up into his face with unconcealed admiration. She was probably dancing with him right now. I felt like bursting out of the sauna and asking those two what in God's name they were talking about. They'd be so stunned seeing me pop up they'd tell me everything. Who murdered Heath. What Jacques was really doing here. Who ratted on the food vendors. Then I'd go get Sam and tell him. He'd be so grateful he'd appoint me his deputy. Finally vindicated for interfering in police business, I'd get into my car and race home as fast as I could. And tomorrow I'd run a successful pie bake-off using my new knife to cut slices for everyone.

I'd finally have the answers to these questions too. Who's the best amateur pie baker in town? (Which did not include yours truly of course.) What was Jacques getting away with? Was it murder? Or just on the run from the law for some white collar crime like computer hacking into someone's bank account? Was he really farm-sitting at all? Maybe he'd done away with the Dolans and was robbing them blind, while enjoying the life of an artisan cheese baron. Maybe he thought he deserved it after that disaster in Ireland. Or none of the above. Jacques was simply a colorful and entertaining host who took advantage of his job as farm-sitter.

But if there was foul play, I'd uncover it. Then I'd impress Sam with my fearless determination and unsung detective work. While he was dancing the night away I would be putting the pieces of the puzzles together. All of them.

Of course I didn't burst out of the sauna. Coward that I was, I stayed in there until I was sure the women had left, then I tiptoed out of the pool house looking right and left. Nobody. There was music in the distance.

The square dancing continued and I'd escaped.

I stood by the edge of the pool and dipped one toe into the water. It felt refreshingly cool. If I'd brought my suit . . .

The next thing I knew, someone pushed me from behind. I stumbled, and tumbled head-first into the water. I was so shocked I inhaled a bucket of water. The water rushed into my ears, my nose, and my mouth. Coughing and choking and gagging I felt the chlorine burn the inside of my nose. I tried to swim to the surface but I couldn't figure out which way was up and I panicked. I kicked, I flailed my arms around, but I was still underwater. What a stupid way to die, I thought. I thought I heard someone calling me. Was it Saint Peter or my long-ago deceased Uncle George? Finally I broke the surface. I gasped and blinked at the male form standing at the edge of the pool. It was Sam.

"Thanks for rescuing me," I sputtered angrily.

"I was just coming in to save you but you're a better swimmer than I am. Weren't you on the swim team in high school?" He knelt on the tiles at the edge of the pool and held his arm out. I grabbed his hand.

"I can't believe we're having this conversation. I could have a relapse any minute."

Sam then took both my hands and pulled me effortlessly out of the water. I crashed into him and he put his arms around me, which was comforting seeing as whoever pushed me in could still be nearby.

"I'm afraid I'm getting your clothes wet," I mumbled, my mouth pressed against his shirt.

"Should have thought of that before you jumped in," he said.

"I did not jump in, I was pushed."

Sam looked around. There was no one.

"You don't believe me?" I asked incredulously, stepping back to glare at him.

"You've been drinking," he said. "I saw you with a glass in your hand. It was empty. You fell, that's all. It's nothing to be ashamed of as long as you survived."

"I had one drink. I was not drunk. And I didn't fall. I was —"

"Pushed, I know," he said. But he didn't believe me or maybe he didn't want me to believe I'd been a victim of foul play. He had enough on his plate without worrying about a prankster hanging around the pool who was probably just another guest who'd imbibed too much. Or was it? I gave a nervous shiver.

"Go take your wet clothes off," he instructed, pointing to the changing rooms. Obviously he was tired of this conversation and wanted to get back to the party.

I went inside, took off my designer dress and underwear and wrapped myself in the luxurious robe from the sauna. I wrung my dress out and went back outside. Sam was standing at the edge of the pool staring into the depths as if there might be a man-eating shark waiting at the bottom.

"There were two other women here," I said. "I wasn't alone. I'm not saying they pushed me in, but I overheard an interesting conversation."

"Which you would like to share with me," he said. He sounded resigned to hearing me out.

I felt so warm and safe, thanks to the robe and the presence of the chief of police that I sat in one of the deck chairs and stretched my legs out. Sam pulled over a chair and sat next to me. He turned to face me. He was waiting as patiently as he could for me to unload what I wanted to tell him.

"It was two women," I said. "They were talking about Jacques and they even mentioned me. In fact they said they were going to have a talk with me. Now I realize that was code for drowning me."

"Why? Why would anyone want to drown

you? What do you know that they want kept quiet?"

"Nothing. Nothing that you don't know too. Everything I know I've shared with you. Why don't they pick on you for a change?"

"Who's they?" he asked.

I shook my head. "No idea. My only enemies are Heath and his brother. Heath's dead and I don't think his brother was invited to the party. These two were in the pool house and I was in the sauna. If they'd known I was in there —" I shuddered at the thought. "They could have turned on the heat and locked me in. And I'd be steamed by the time someone found me."

"Are you sure you don't have a persecution complex? Accidents happen."

"Especially to me," I said.

"First it was the walk-in freezer. Then the pig chasing you across the field. Am I missing something?"

"I suppose you think I brought those things on myself because of my inquisitive nature."

"It has occurred to me."

I stood up. There was no convincing Sam and with him here the someone or someones who'd shoved me in the pool weren't going to try again. "I'm going *home.*"

"I'll drive you."

"I can manage. Thanks anyway."

"I'll follow you just in case. Keep your cell phone on. Or did it get soaked?"

"My purse and phone were in the sauna, safe and sound."

It's against the law in California to use a hand-held wireless cell phone while driving and I didn't have a head set. But Sam conveniently overlooked the law, or maybe he didn't notice I was holding the phone to my ear when he called me to make sure I was okay, although he was close enough since he was tailgating me all the way back to town. I took his actions as a compliment. Despite his casual attitude to my "falling" into the pool in a drunken stupor I could hope he might be having second thoughts and believed my story. Whatever the reason, he seemed more concerned than he had at the pool and kept up a steady stream of conversation as we drove in tandem back to town. Which was not like him under any circumstances as far as I knew. I was sure grateful for the bathrobe and I'd have to return it to the sauna, preferably when no one was at home to ask any embarrassing questions.

We both pulled up in front of my shop at the same time and Sam opened the car door for me. My legs were not working very well so I tumbled out and he caught me for the second time that night.

After a few minutes he took my keys, unlocked the front door, and carried me up the narrow stairs to my apartment. No easy job. I am not exactly tiny and the staircase is narrow, but somehow he got me upstairs. I was asleep before he even left, dreaming disturbing dreams of being locked into a sauna by Heath's brother.

The next morning I had a headache that I could not blame on excessive alcohol despite what Sam said, but being the consummate professional I am, I started setting up for the bake-off, hauling chairs and tables into the shop from the storage area in the garage and covering them with Grannie's colorful tablecloths.

Fortunately Grannie and her friends Helen and Grace showed up early. They were dressed for success in casual but elegant pants outfits, matching flat shoes and enough jewelry to start a pawn shop. They all three looked much more alert than I did, but none of them had been pushed into a pool last night as far as I knew. Instead they'd had the time of their lives.

"We had the best time last night," Grannie said hanging a colorful pink begonia in the store window.

"What was it, a bridge game?"

"No, it was karaoke night," Grannie said. "They played all the oldies. You should have heard me."

"I have heard you sing in the shower. I always said you should have a bigger audience," I said.

"What about you? Didn't you go to a party?" Grace asked me, putting knives and spatulas on the serving tables.

"Yes, at the Foggy Meadow Dairy Farm where a guy from the Food Fair works. It's out on Route 92. Have any of you ever seen it? It's a beautiful place. Very upscale. Like the cheese they make."

"That's the kind of man you should cultivate, someone with property." Grannie said, and the others nodded in agreement. Grannie had waited to get married until she found a man with money and property. The others had done well too. Otherwise they wouldn't be at Heavenly Acres, which cost an arm and a leg.

"Unfortunately it isn't his farm," I explained. "It's the Dolans'. Jacques is what's known as a farm-sitter. He takes care of people's farms when they're on vacation. For all I know he doesn't have a cent of his own, but he sure knows his cheese and how to throw a good party."

"Jacques," said Helen thoughtfully. "He sounds French and you know how they can be very sexy. Does he look like Yves Montand?"

I had to admit I didn't know who she was talking about.

"Good looks are not enough," Grannie said, coming into the kitchen with her hands on her hips. "Sexy and romantic are all well and good, but you want someone who's around for the long term. This Jacques may return to France and then where will you be?"

"I'll be right here with you," I said. "Jacques is really cute, he's got a to-die-for accent, and he's a lot of fun. You'll have to meet him," I said so the whole gang could hear me. As usual, they quickly responded and they didn't disappoint.

"Cute and fun? Is that what you're looking for? You're not seventeen anymore," Grannie said with a disapproving look.

"Take your time to look around and find someone to take care of you," Helen advised.

"I think I can take care of myself," I said. "I want a partner, not a caretaker."

"I know how you feel," Grace said soothingly. "I was young once. There's no rush. You deserve someone special. So hold out for what you want. Someone with a solid career, money AND good looks and someone who treats you like a queen."

I knew Grace was referring to her late great husband who'd left her plenty of money. I had no idea if he was good-looking. I'd have to take her word for it.

"I don't think they make them like that anymore unfortunately," I said as I filled the coffee maker with the finest Arabica beans. I'd never met a guy with money and looks who'd treat me like a queen and I wasn't expecting one. If I followed these instructions and adopted Grace's standards I'd never get married. Of course I wasn't doing so well with my own lax standards so what was the difference?

"As for looking around, there aren't many men in town in my age bracket. And the ones that are, are dropping like flies," I said.

"You're referring to that critic, I suppose," Grannie said. "I'm glad you didn't fall for him."

"Not likely. How could I fall for anyone who didn't like my pies?" I thought of Sam, who fell into that category. Wasn't that a sign to back off and quit hoping he'd come around? The pies, it was all about the pies. Pies were a symbol of all that was good in the world. They were sweet or savory, crisp on the outside and soft on the inside. They underwent a transformation in the oven from a soggy mixture to a crisp juicy product when baked. Every society in the world had their version of pie. The English had the popular steak and kidney pie at every corner pub. The Spanish had their empanadas, the Greeks their spanakotyropita, the Aussies their meat pies and so on.

"Sometimes it's necessary to make compromises," Helen said. Maybe she realized as I did, that no mortal man living within driving distance of Crystal Cove could meet all their qualifications.

The bell over the front door of the shop rang and the first of the pie bake-off contestants arrived with a Boston Cream Pie in hand. She was followed by Nina with a pecan caramel pie. It was so beautiful I wondered if she'd really made it. Never mind. I was not cut out to be the pie police. A deputy maybe, but I could never arrest a friend. I was glad to see her after meeting her not-so-wonderful husband and I welcomed her warmly, praised her pie, introduced her to Grannie and her chums, and offered everyone a cup of coffee. Nina looked like she needed it even more than I did. Her makeup was as perfect as her pie, but her eyes were red-rimmed. Lack of sleep? Or crying over something. I hoped it wasn't her pie. I've been known to do that myself and it's not worth it.

A few minutes later the shop was full of contestants. Some I knew, like Tammy and Lindsey, and Martha and her sister. But others were new to me and would hopefully turn into fans unless they were such great pie bakers they didn't need The Upper Crust. I should have nixed the pie contest idea when I could. Damn that Heath for forcing the issue. I started to worry. There were some dynamite-looking pies on the table. What if one or several of the bakers started their own home pie-baking service and gave me a run for my money?

Of course Lurline came with a giant cupcake in a pie shell. I smiled and told her it was brilliant. But what was it? A giant cupcake or a pie shaped like a cupcake? Whatever it was it was meant to be a public relations promotion for Lurline's you know what. In fact her pink van was parked at the curb outside my shop so that no one could miss it.

Grannie, who was standing at the door beaming and ooohing and ahhhing over each and every pie, was handing off pies to her two friends. If this was such a good idea, why hadn't she thought of it? Soon the long extended table in the middle of the room was covered with pies of every shape and form. Actually most of them were pie-shaped.

"What a job you've given us," Grannie whispered to me when she finally closed the door. "How do we taste all these pies? You know with wine tasting they spit out the wine after they taste it."

"Don't you dare," I cautioned her.

"Just kidding," she assured me. "We'll manage."

I was just about to rap on a champagne glass to get everyone's attention. It was an impressive sight I can tell you — about twenty or twenty-five women, each standing behind their pies, which were displayed on the long table. Then the door opened and a woman I'd never seen before walked in. She was about fifty, but as everyone knows, fifty is the new forty, and she looked it. She also looked like she'd heard "When in doubt it's better to be overdressed than under-dressed." She wore a form-fitting jump suit which I guessed was the latest in the fashion world. Along with high-heeled gladiator sandals. Up until that moment I hadn't seen anyone in Crystal Cove who looked like they'd stepped out of a fashion magazine.

But the most surprising thing was that she

spoke in such a deep voice I was instantly caught off guard. For a moment I remembered reading about a woman who'd appeared in an article on transgender relationships.

"Hello everyone," she said in a booming voice. "I'm Gay Grimshaw, the new food and lifestyle critic for the *Gazette.* Here to do a story on the pie bake-off for the newspaper. Which one of you is Hanna Denton?"

ELEVEN

Grannie caught my eye with such a shocked look on her face I was momentarily stunned into silence. Was it someone she knew? Or was it just the voice combined with her looks that surprised my grandmother? When I recovered, I said, "I am," and I went to the door. The new food critic shook my hand so firmly I thought she'd crushed my fingers. She looked so professional with a camera hanging around her neck and a briefcase under her arm that I didn't think to ask for her credentials.

"You're taking Heath Barr's place I suppose," I said.

"That's right," she said. "You knew Heath?"

"Not really. He wasn't very popular around here," I said, careful not to speak too ill of the dead. I hoped she wasn't a friend of his.

"I can see why after reading his column.

He sure did a hatchet job on you." She looked me up and down as if she wondered if I was the one who'd done a hatchet job on him.

I smiled weakly, glad that the contestants were all chatting and the noise level in the shop rose to a crescendo so no one was paying attention to our conversation. "How did you get the job so . . . so soon after . . . ?"

"After he bit the dust? Just blind luck. I needed a job, they needed a food and lifestyle critic and I couldn't be happier. Great job. Great town. But no one knows about it. I'm going to put this place on the map."

I wasn't sure what "this place" meant. She saw my confusion. "I mean the town and your shop." She looked around at the walls, the glassed-in cases, and the tables laden with the contestants' pies. "Nice place you've got here."

"Thank you. I don't mean to criticize Heath, considering what happened to him, but you're a welcome change from your predecessor."

"That Heath." She shook her head. "Hiring him was a mistake and a half. Makes me look good anyway. That's what I told Bruce."

What about killing him? Was that a mistake

too? I knew a lot of people who didn't think so.

"I can't believe they've filled the position so fast." I also couldn't believe anyone would want this volunteer job. Or was it? Especially someone with the equipment she had and the ambition to put me and the town on the map. Where had she come from and what was her goal really?

"Sometimes you're in the right place at the right time," she said brushing her hands together as if she'd just disposed of something undesirable. Like Heath Barr. Was a part-time job for a smalltown, once-a-week newspaper worth committing murder for?

"How true," I murmured. "Actually that's how I got the pie shop here. My grandmother over there retired just as I needed a job and a home."

"That's the kind of human interest story I'm looking for," Gay said her eyes sparkling brightly. "As a companion piece to the pie contest." She lifted her camera and snapped a picture of me before I could protest I wasn't looking my best.

I couldn't help but think — if Heath's job had been as a correspondent for the *Los Angeles Times* instead of the *Gazette* I might have wondered if Gay had had anything to do with his demise, but I brushed the thought aside. She was so much more likable than Heath, we should throw a welcome party for her. If she'd killed Heath in order to fill his shoes, I wasn't going to complain. "I hope you'll stay awhile and taste some of the pies."

"I plan to taste all of them. In the interest of scientific objectivity, of course," she said with a wink.

Now this was a woman after my own heart. But if she was a woman after anyone's heart there was something different about her. Her voice, her handshake, and her manner were hearty in the extreme. I wished I could ask someone like Kate what she thought, but she'd just come in the back door and was tying on her apron to begin her judging duties.

I picked up the glass again, got everyone's attention, and welcomed them to The Upper Crust's First Annual Pie Bake-Off. "My grandmother Louise Denton and her friends from Heavenly Acres as well as my assistant Kate will stop by each pie for a taste and then after a brief consultation, we'll announce two winners, one in the savory category, the other sweet, based on overall appearance, crust, taste, and use of local ingredients. I hope everyone will stay around afterward for pie and coffee."

I made the rounds just looking, leaving the tasting to Grannie, Helen, Grace, and Kate. The pies all looked fabulous. I had overcome any jealousy I'd had and instead congratulated myself on throwing a newsworthy contest. I hoped it made me look confident and self-assured. It reminded me how much I loved the friendly small-town atmosphere contained in my little shop today and I thought I might even do it every year, maybe twice, once in the winter and once in the summer. As I wandered the room I didn't sense any friction in the air. It was billed as a competition, but I hoped no one would mind losing. Martha, my poultry farm colleague, told me she was having so much fun she didn't care about who won.

"Your Snicker's Bar Pie looks scrumptious," I told her. "I didn't know you baked."

"I don't," she said. "I made the crust from chocolate cookie crumbs, then layered whipped cream and chopped Snicker's bars. You can't go wrong with candy bars. They're my secret vice. I had an excuse to buy a whole box to make the pie."

When I stopped to look at Nina's Pecan Caramel Pie she said, "You didn't tell me there was going to be a photographer here. I hate having my picture taken."

"Why? You're obviously photogenic and you look great," I said. "I didn't know the photographer was coming. I'm surprised they'd replaced Heath already. Can you believe someone standing in line to be the food and lifestyle critic of a small hometown newspaper? And for no salary?"

"No salary? Heath was making plenty," Nina said. She stopped suddenly when Grannie came by to taste her pie.

Or did she stop suddenly because I was about to say, "How do you know?"

"I envied you," I told her. "When I read that glowing review of your caramels. Did it boost your sales?"

She shrugged. "Who knows? Did it hurt your sales that he hated your pies?"

"It hurt my feelings," I said confidentially as the judges passed by. "But my sales? I don't think so. I didn't really understand where he was coming from."

"He was from LA," she said.

"I mean I didn't understand his basis for judging food. Maybe if I'd had a chance to meet him like you did. What was he like?"

"How should I know? He bought a caramel and moved on."

I didn't quite understand how she knew that he was from LA and that he was making plenty of money when "he bought a caramel and moved on."

"I can see why he loved your candy," I said. "But what about the bread, the chicken, and my pie? I don't get it."

I realized that Nina's expression had changed. She was looking over my shoulder, her eyes glazed over. I was spending way too much time on the subject of Heath and his reviews. He was gone. It was over. She'd moved on and so would I. Literally.

I wished her good luck and made the rounds admiring a golden-brown onion and cumin quiche in the savory category. The baker, a friend of Grannie's named Olga, said the classic buttery pâte brisée crust was flavored with rosemary, Parmesan, and thyme. It smelled heavenly and I told her I'd love the recipe. I was sure she'd get the savory pie prize until I saw a classic chicken pot pie chock full of chunks of chicken and vegetables, some fist-sized Cornwall pasties, and a cheesy calzoni that looked so authentic I swore it could have come straight from Italy. How were they ever going to come up with a winner? Or two winners, one for savory, one for sweet. I was hoping to get every single recipe, including Blackberry Crumble Pie, Raspberry Cream Tart, and Mixed Berry Cobbler.

Fortunately it was not for me to judge. I

just had to drift around the shop, chatting briefly as I went, careful not to show favoritism, careful not to launch into a tirade about Heath or mention murder in any context. I wanted to turn back the clock to pre-Heath days, and I was sure everyone felt the same way.

When the judges finished their tasting and adjourned to my kitchen to compare notes, I refilled coffee cups and talked with the contestants. All the while our new friend Gay was snapping pictures. What great publicity for me and the shop. Whoever killed Heath had done me and just about everyone else a big favor by giving us Gay. Maybe they'd done a favor for his brother who might inherit some money. Who cared who killed him? Sam did, but not me. Just as long as no one thought I'd done it.

When the judges came out of the kitchen I asked Grannie, as the once and always Crystal Cove Pie Queen, to announce the winners.

"First place in the savory category is the Caramelized Onion and Goat Cheese Pie by Madeline Hooper." The applause was loud and sincere. Madeline, who I'd never met before, flushed, stood, and took a bow. Grannie gave her a French Victorian silver plate. Where had that come from? Gay's flashbulbs flashed. I raised my eyebrows questioningly at the gorgeous plate. Grannie just smiled enigmatically.

"In the sweet pie category, the prize goes to Martha Hutchens for her Snicker's Bar Pie."

I must say I was surprised. I'd thought her pie was clever, but kind of gimmicky. Seeing Martha's surprised look and delighted smile, I clapped loudly and congratulated her when she walked off with Helen's classic tea set. I wondered if she'd find a use for it on her poultry farm.

After the prizes, the judges and I passed out plates and forks so everyone could taste any pie they wanted. I was so overwhelmed with the success of the event and the participation of women I didn't even know, I couldn't eat a bite. Even though I knew I'd be sorry tomorrow. And to think I'd resisted the whole idea.

Since I had all the recipes, I was thinking of making them into a book and marketing it as "The Upper Crust Prize-Winning Pie Recipes." I'd use Gay's pictures to illustrate it if she was willing, and give the proceeds to a charity.

When the crowd finally left and Grannie, Helen, Grace, and Kate had helped me clean up, I drove Grannie and her friends back to Heavenly Acres. I thanked them profusely and they said they'd had a wonderful time. It turned out the silver plate was something Helen inherited from an aunt and was happy to give it away. Especially to Madeline, who she assumed didn't have a plate like that.

"Who does?" I said. "It looks like one of a kind."

"Not exactly," Helen said, "but it is valuable. If you like that kind of thing." Helen was into modern design these days as evidenced by the necklace she wore made of what she called "patina noodles." The silver strands did indeed look like noodles and it made a stunning statement when worn with her black sweater.

Grannie waited until the others had gone inside the stately entrance to the retirement home until she said, "What did you think of Gay?"

"She seems nice, and she's different from Heath. That's a good thing. Had you met her before? You two are colleagues now. Both journalists. Working at the *Gazette*."

"I didn't say anything to her since I'm undercover and she isn't," Grannie said. "I hope I'll be allowed to tell people one of these days." She sighed. "I don't like having secrets from my friends."

"No, of course not," I said. I didn't like having secrets either, but if you break the law and fall into swimming pools or dumpsters, it requires a certain secrecy from even your best friends.

"I have a favor to ask you," she said. "I have a staff meeting at the *Gazette* tomorrow but I can't go. I hope they won't think I'm not interested."

"You have something else going on?" I asked. I assumed, wrongly, I guess, that retired people had nothing to do but an endless series of bridge and croquet games, all optional.

"I'm the caller at the morning bingo game. I was wondering if you'd go to the meeting in my place. I think Bruce, Mr. Scarsdale, will just hand me the letters I'm supposed to answer. I don't see why I have to be there in person. And what if someone saw me? They'd wonder what I was doing there."

"Sure, I'll be glad to go. I'll just hang a closed sign on the store if it's just a quick meeting. But will I need a note from you to say it's okay if I take your mail? I don't think Bruce is very fond of me to tell the truth."

"I don't know why he wouldn't be. Everyone likes you."

"Yes, well . . . maybe he does. Maybe I

273

caught him at a bad moment one day when I dropped in. It was right after the murder. He was probably distressed, seeing it happened on the premises. He seemed curt."

"He's not curt with me, but I notice people are nicer to old people."

"I'll look forward to that," I said.

"Being old?" she asked.

"Having people be nice to me."

She smiled and patted me on the arm. "You tell me who isn't nice to you and I'll give them a piece of my mind," she said.

"I'll make out a list," I said. I smiled to show I was joking. But she didn't look convinced. She looked worried. "I'll be glad when this murder is solved."

"Me too." I watched her walk through the glass doors of the main building lobby. I wondered if Grannie really had to call the numbers at the bingo game. Or did she just not want to go. I did want to go. It gave me an excuse to visit the scene of the crime, get a sense of what was going on there and if anyone suspected me of the break-in.

The next day, I wished Grannie had told Bruce, the *Gazette* editor, that I was filling in for her, because when I walked in, he said, "What are you doing here?"

"My grandmother Louise Denton couldn't make it so she asked me to pick up

274

her mail for her today, I hope it's okay."

He nodded but he didn't look happy to see me. Did he remember I'd come by right after the murder? Did he suspect me of breaking in that night and taking Heath's phone? Or was he just in a bad mood because someone killed his reporter on the premises? He had to be glad Heath had been replaced by Gay.

The first thing I noticed when I arrived at the *Gazette* office was Heath's office door was wide open and Gay was standing in the doorway talking to another man. Gay greeted me warmly and he walked away.

"Come in," she said. She stepped aside and waved me into the office. I tried not to gasp in surprise because how would I know the office had been remodeled if I'd never been there before, but I couldn't believe what I saw. She'd taken over the once-depressing office of her predecessor and re-done it completely. The walls were painted pale robin's-egg blue and Heath's desk had been replaced with an all-hardwood and veneer work station with clean, modern lines. There was not a speck of dust or a sheet of paper on the surface. Her flat screen computer was on a rotating stand. How did she do her work without making a mess? I sure couldn't. I looked around at the abstract paintings on the walls, stunned by the change. No sign of the old couch I'd found the phone in or Heath's old desk. The air even smelled fresh and new with a faint floral scent.

"You've done wonders," I said. But if I'd never been there before, how would I know? Gay didn't notice, she just told me she'd done all the redecorating herself owing to the austerity budget of the newspaper.

"You're here to see how my article is coming along, I bet," she said.

"Actually I've come to the staff meeting in place of my grandmother who's doing some writing for the paper," I said vaguely. "She couldn't make it."

"Then you've never been here before?" she said.

I shook my head emphatically. "Well actually I stopped in to drop off an ad one day, but I've never seen your office." Technically that was true. It was so dark in there that night I hadn't seen much of anything.

"I wanted my office to be an expression of myself," Gay explained. It must have been a challenge seeing she'd taken over the depressing office of a murdered man.

"It looks beautiful," I said. "You've done a great job. I hope you'll stick around for a long time."

"Count on it," she said. "We'd better get on to the meeting."

The conference room wasn't bad. Maybe Gay had revamped it too, because there was a long table with a bouquet of flowers in the middle and folding chairs around it. I took a seat at the end of the table next to Gay and watched as some others came in including Sam. What was he doing there? Dropping off the police beat column that listed the week's criminal activities? He nodded to me and sat down near the door. Probably wondered what I was doing there. Maybe Bruce would just hand me the mail bag and excuse me. That would be best for both of us.

Bruce called the meeting to order and introduced his staff. I was impressed. Heath's murder seemed to have given new life to the small-town newspaper. Though most of us — by *us* I meant Grannie and Sam — were stringers or part-timers, they seemed to have all the bases covered.

Bruce introduced us. "Hanna Denton is here representing one of our contributors. Gay will assume the post of photographer and lifestyle and food critic and of course our Police Chief Sam contributes his crime news." I looked around the table. It was an impressive staff, all things considered. I was sorry I wasn't part of the group.

Bruce went on about how important volunteers were to the success of a small-town newspaper. How lucky they were to have professionals contributing to make the paper what it was. "Our police chief has agreed to expand his role to write a whole article for us this week. It will contain an update on the murder. Well, I'll let Sam fill us in."

"Nothing much to say about the murder," Sam said. "Except our investigation is on-going. We're cooperating with a crime lab in Los Angeles. These things take time. I want to take the opportunity in my article to tell the community that to the best of our knowledge there is no new crime wave. Heath Barr was only a recent arrival in our town and his murder likely had something to do with his past. I won't say anymore at this time. As usual, I advise the community to keep their doors locked, but otherwise enjoy the special environment of trust and cooperation. But I do have a story about the crack-down on the Food Fair by the county officials last Saturday."

I leaned forward. "Has there been any news on that? I'm one of the vendors who was cited. I'm hoping the county has better things to do than bother honest food and craft artisans. And you can quote me."

"I'll do that," Sam said. "First the reason the county singled us out was that they'd had a complaint about conditions. The tipster was anonymous but it might have been someone with an ulterior motive. The complaints were the food that was supposed to be organic was not, or it was not properly made in an official kitchen or improperly stored. All the above were enough to bring out the suits."

"What's to prevent them for returning next week and shutting us down?" I asked. Of course I knew the answer but I wanted to hear what Sam had to say.

"Nothing except they have bigger fish to fry," he said. "Their staff has been cut in half and in a related story, the county officials received yet another anonymous call regarding rodents in the San Pedro supermarket."

Gay gasped. "Rodents?" We all looked around the room. I did my best to act like I had not heard this story before. I don't think anyone suspected, except Sam who knew what he knew and probably still suspected me.

Bruce, the editor, raised his eyebrows. "I'm horrified of course," he said. "But I can't deny it makes for good newspaper reading. Gay, would you be able to get out there to the market and take some pictures for us? If you can get a shot of a rodent, that would be front page material."

She nodded, obviously happy to have such a big story assignment. This was way beyond what she'd been hired to do. If this kept up, maybe the circulation would increase and she'd even get a salary. I mean, how many stories can you write about food and lifestyle in Crystal Cove? But crime? That was a different story. Everyone wanted to read about murders or illegal rats on the loose. Every time we turned around it seemed we had another crime on our hands. I just wished I wasn't involved in any of them.

"Any other reports?" Bruce asked, looking around the table.

Gay told about the fabulous pie contest at my shop. She planned to include photos of the event and recipes with her article, along with a profile of me, how I came to take over the shop, what changes I'd made, and what plans I had for the future. I smiled modestly and thanked the editor for the free publicity.

Then Bruce announced the addition of an advice column. "The writer of 'Ask Maggie' is not here today. She prefers to remain anonymous, but Hanna Denton is here to pick up her mail. Which is considerable since we announced the column last week. I don't know what the citizens of Crystal Cove did all these years without a chance to get anonymous advice from a sage like . . . like Maggie."

"What kind of advice will 'Ask Maggie' give?" Gay asked. "Personal, professional . . . ?"

"Yes," Bruce said. "Anything she can address, she will. Matters of etiquette or family, relationship, behavior. You name it, Ask Maggie will cover it. As for her identity all I can say is that she's a respected member of the community. Known all over town for the wise counsel she dispensed with the products she sold for some thirty years."

Sam gave me a knowing look. I didn't have to tell him who she was. Maybe everyone knew. Or, if they didn't, they soon would. Granny's personality and level-headed advice would shine out of her words.

Bruce handed me a manila envelope. "Here you are. These are Ask Maggie's first letters."

I held the envelope gingerly as if the contents might scald my fingers. I was dying to open the envelope and read the letters. What juicy gossip would be contained in those queries? I could only imagine.

Maybe Grannie would share the contents with me. Maybe she'd ask my help. Or did I lack the wisdom to help anyone when I couldn't help myself? I sighed.

Bruce looked more cheerful at the end of the meeting than he had at the beginning. Was he finally beginning to see that the murder of Heath Barr was a blessing in disguise? That his new staff was a shot in the arm to the otherwise boring newspaper? I hoped so. In fact, he announced that since the murder, circulation was up 15 percent. He had just gone to the portable blackboard to write down the numbers when his new secretary, another volunteer, came to the door and told him there was someone to see him.

"We're in a meeting," he said with a frown.

"I'm sorry, Mr. Scarsdale, but the deputy says he has to talk to the chief right away. He has some bad news."

TWELVE

Sam stood and went to the door. I craned my neck but I couldn't see who'd come in. Who was the deputy who couldn't call Sam on his cell phone? How bad was the news that he had to come in person? If I was his deputy . . . but I wasn't. He'd turned me down. I was having a few words with Gay about her photos of my pie contest when Sam stuck his head in the door and motioned to me.

I excused myself, grabbed Grannie's precious envelope and met Sam and his deputy — a tall, lanky young man — in the hall. My stomach was churning. What kind of bad news was this that applied only to me? Grannie?

"It seems your shop was broken into this morning," Sam said. "Any idea what they were looking for?"

"Besides pies?"

"Let's get over there and you can tell me

what's missing."

Sam drove me to the shop. My heart was racing. At first glance I couldn't see anything out of place. The door had been jimmied open, not even a crack in the glass.

"Anyone could have done it," I said to Sam, relieved to find the shop just as I'd left it. "But in thirty years no one ever has. Why bother? Why not just ask for a pie if you can't afford one? Grannie was known for her charity. No one ever left the shop hungry."

The pies were in the cases, the cold ones refrigerated, the others stacked on the shelves behind the counter.

"Nothing's missing," I said, puzzled but happy to see everything intact.

"Let's go upstairs," he said.

I felt sick to my stomach when I reached the landing and staggered backward. My desk was turned upside down. Bills and old letters scattered over the floor. My dresser drawers were emptied. My lingerie was scattered all over the floor.

I sat on the edge of my bed, my face buried in my hands. I couldn't stand to look at the mess. Or think about who'd been there pawing through my clothes.

Sam stood in the middle of the room. "Well?" he asked.

"I don't know what to say. What on earth were they looking for?"

"The phone?" Sam asked.

"Who knows I had it?"

"You tell me."

"I would if I could. If someone saw me that night, and thought I'd found it, why wait until now to come and get it?"

He shook his head. "Yeah, all they had to do was wait until you left, break into your shop, go upstairs and reach under your bed. Want to file a complaint?"

"Would it do any good?" I asked.

"Probably not. Whoever did this saw your 'Closed' sign on the door. What were you thinking? It was like an invitation to come in."

"So someone was watching me or the store, waiting for an opportunity. But there have been plenty. I've been gone all day some days, the chicken ranch, the pig farm, the dairy farm . . . Why now? Why today?"

Sam must have been tired of hearing my endless questions for which there were no answers.

"What hurts my feelings is that they didn't take any pies," I said.

That got a smile out of him but he also shook his head in dismay. I could just hear him thinking, *That's all she cares about, her pies.* I wished it was true, then I wouldn't feel so violated because someone had been in my bedroom.

"I'm going to get you a padlock for your front door," Sam said.

"Isn't there a saying about locking the barn door after the horse has been stolen?"

"Humor me. Just padlock the damn door."

"Where is the phone by the way?" I asked.

"Sent to the lab. Being analyzed. We should have some voice recognition soon. By the way, your fingerprints are all over it."

I pressed my lips together and nodded.

"And you want to be my deputy," he said with a painful grimace.

I glared at him. "Hey, who found the phone and gave it to you anyway? At great personal risk? You owe me."

He thought about that for a minute. How could he deny it? "How about dinner?" he said at last. "My house. Then we call it even."

I hadn't been to the house he bought next door to Lindsey's. I assumed it was his man cave and no women were allowed in, but maybe I was wrong. Maybe he lured women in with dinner invitations every night. I hesitated for a few moments. It didn't do to seem anxious or desperate.

"Barbecued leg of lamb with couscous and fresh asparagus," he said.

"I didn't know you could cook," I said.

"I had to learn, if I didn't cook I didn't eat."

I knew he was referring to his childhood when his mother walked out on him and left him on his own. My eyes filled with tears. Tears for the kid who was left to fend for himself. Tears for myself. For the mess that someone made of my belongings. Tears just because I was tired of being brave.

"Hey," he said, reaching down to pull me up into his arms. "Don't cry. It's not that bad."

"I'm not," I said between loud sobs. I was crying for lost opportunities, for missed connections, for wasted years. "Go," I said, my voice still unsteady. "Just go and let me clean up."

"Dinner's at seven," he said.

I nodded. I was thinking of what kind of pie to bring. But first I had to clean up the mess in my apartment.

"I don't want Granny to know about this," I said waving my arm at the clothes all over the floor and the emptied kitchen cabinets.

He nodded and then he asked, "Will you be okay?"

"Of course. I'm fine. I'll just straighten up

in here and get back to work."

But of course I wasn't fine. I was a wreck. As soon as Sam left to go back to work, I called Kate. She came right away and helped me clean up. The good thing about her is she didn't freak out, she just spent a minute shaking her head and swearing at whoever did this, then she pitched in and waited for me to vent. Which I did. Eventually.

I insisted we take a break when we'd made inroads on the job. Tossing everything in the laundry and scrubbing the floors. For once I was glad the apartment was small. Finally we went downstairs and I took a bacon, tomato, and cheese quiche I'd made last week out of the freezer and popped it into the oven. It was total comfort food, which I needed badly. While we waited for it to bake, I made a pot of tea. We sat at one of my small glass-topped, ice-cream tables and I answered all her questions. Well, most of them.

"What were they looking for?" she said. I knew that was uppermost on her mind.

"I don't know for sure, but I think it was a cell phone."

She opened her mouth to exclaim and I continued. "See, I had in my possession the cell phone that belonged to Heath, the murder victim. Don't ask how I got it."

"Who me?" she said. "I won't ask how you got the phone, but I don't understand how someone knew you had it and why that someone wanted it enough to break into your place. I don't get it."

"Evidence," I said, pouring tea into two delicate china cups. "I don't know, but I assume there were messages left on Heath's phone that were retrievable and potentially incriminating."

Kate leaned forward, her eyes wide. "So who did they incriminate?"

"I don't know. Sam is trying to find out with some fancy high-tech analysis somewhere. It's hard to imagine who he was talking to. Heath didn't have many friends, at least here in Crystal Cove."

"Forget Heath, that scumbag, for a minute," Kate said. "Who broke into your place today?"

"I don't know that either. Could it be the same person who killed Heath?"

"Let's make a list," she said, reaching for her purse to pull out a notepad and pen.

"First I need some food. I can't think until I eat," I said.

The quiche came out of the oven hot and cheesy and browned on top. It was delicious, if I do say so myself. Kate said so too, for the record. As soon as we'd polished off a few pieces, I cleared the table and we got down to business.

"Possible suspects," she said, pen in hand. "People who hated Heath."

"First the Food Fair people he dissed. That would be Jacques, Martha, Bill and Dave, Lurline and myself, and Lindsey and Tammy. Then there are the Food Fair people he complimented. Nina, the pizza guy, and . . ."

"Why would they kill him? They should be grateful to him," she said.

"It may sound stupid, at least Sam thinks so, but my theory is that they paid Heath to give them good reviews, then when he tried to shake them down for more money, they killed him instead." This time around it sounded lame, even to me, and I could tell by the look on Kate's face, she didn't buy it. That didn't mean it wasn't what happened. "Go on, write it down," I instructed.

She scribbled something on her notepad. "Back to the vendors Heath screwed over," she said. "Can you eliminate anyone besides yourself? Anyone with an iron-clad alibi?"

I put both elbows on the small table and propped up my chin in order to think better. "I don't know and Sam won't tell me who is not on the suspect list, if anyone.

Heath was killed the day of my meeting with the vendors, the ones we're talking about. Which probably means we all had time to slit Heath's throat with our fancy sliceN'dice serrated knives, then show up for the meeting at my shop. I assure you everyone was furious with Heath. Bill and Dave even lost their bank loan because of his lousy review. Not only did Heath slam all of us, but he's the one who phoned in the complaint to the county Health Department before he croaked, which almost shut down the whole fair. At least that's my theory."

"What was wrong with the guy?" she asked.

"Don't ask me. I never met him. Except that day on the phone when you were here. Maybe he was carried away with his own importance. Being a food and lifestyle critic is empowering."

"Now that's he's gone, is the county still on your case about all those infractions?" she asked.

"Let's just say they care more about rats in a grocery store and they're too short-handed and too short on attention span to focus on us too."

"Rats?" she said. "I hope Principal Blandings doesn't hear about this or our goose is cooked."

"Funny you should mention that little escapade of ours. The principal will hear about it because it's going to come out in this week's *Gazette.* It's news, you know. But I can handle him. I'm not a high-school girl anymore. He can't intimidate me or give me detention. I must say getting rid of Heath seems a better idea every day in every way. If I find out who did it, I might just look the other way."

"You wouldn't," Kate said.

"No, I guess not, but I ask myself why are we knocking ourselves out to find his killer this way when we should just forget about it and let the police handle it? They've got labs and computers and a network and connections we can't even imagine." I wasn't sure how many resources a small-town police department actually had, but it was comforting to imagine a vast web of professionals working round the clock on our problems.

"Forget that your house has been vandalized?"

"You're assuming the same person who killed Heath —"

"Aren't you?"

I had to admit I was. "Okay, we can't let the professionals handle our problems. Who wants to solve this mystery more than we do? No one. We've got our list of suspects and now we need a list of questions we want answers to. Isn't that what real detectives do?"

"Sounds good," Kate said. "Question Number One. Who killed Heath? Subset A. Same person as broke into your store? Question Number Two. Why? Question Number Three —"

"Who pushed me into the pool at Jacques' dairy farm?"

"What? You didn't tell me about this. Now I'm getting worried. Unless it was a joke. Did you get hurt? Who do you think it was?"

"No joke. I didn't drown and I think whoever pushed me in was trying to scare me. Sam doesn't believe I was pushed. He thinks I fell in, so he's no help. I think the perps — you know what perps are?" I asked.

She nodded.

"Well, they must have heard about me from Jacques, the cheese guy, and they figured it out."

"Figured what out?" she asked.

"That I knew something that would link them to Heath's murder."

"Do you?" she asked.

"No."

"Then you're safe."

I looked around at the shelves full of pies, the faint aroma of lemon, cinnamon, and ginger lingered in the air and I felt safe and secure in my little world. The mess upstairs was almost forgotten. I reached across the table and squeezed my best friend's hand.

"Thanks for helping me," I said. "I feel better already."

She smiled. "What are friends for? Let's finish this list, then I have to go."

"Let's add some more names."

"I've got the vendors who met with you the day Heath was murdered. Who else?"

"Nina, the salted caramel maker. Her husband, Marty, who mans the booth. Gino, the pizza guy. Barton Barr, Heath's brother."

"Motives?" she asked.

"Nina and her husband could have killed Heath because of extortion, like I told you, although I don't think her husband takes her candy business very seriously, not enough to kill for. Besides, her husband isn't very nice. Do you remember him from high school. He was a total nerd, now he's a jerk. I guess murderers can be jerks, but I don't see why he'd do it. Then there's the pizza guy. And Barton Barr who would inherit whatever family money there was. With Heath gone he'd get everything, if there was anything to get."

"Enough," Kate said, shaking her head. "I'm overwhelmed with data. Let's let all this info settle down. Here's your list. Let me know if you have a breakthrough or if you need me to do something."

I took the paper out of her hand. "Thanks. This helps. I know it does. I'm going to put it under my pillow tonight and maybe the answers will be there in the morning."

She gave me a very skeptical look. "Sounds like a recipe for a nightmare to me. Anyway Sam is just across the street if you feel vulnerable."

"Unless he's at home, which is where he'll be tonight because I'm having dinner at his house."

Kate, who'd been standing near the door, came back and sat down. "I can't believe you didn't tell me you were having dinner with Sam. At his house. Is he cooking for you?"

"I guess so. He's a good cook, at least I think he is."

"I expect a complete report, and I don't just mean the food."

I ignored the suggestive tone in her voice. "He's just doing this to show off, to show me how independent he is. How he does not need anyone. Especially me." I half believed this and half believed he felt sorry for me this morning when he saw the shop.

"I see," she said. I think she thought she saw something that I didn't see.

"I think cooking is a kind of hobby with him. A relief from the stress of his job."

"Chasing murderers, you mean."

"There aren't that many murders," I said. "Sometimes he's out rescuing cats from trees or solving small-town crimes like, I don't know, rounding up stray dogs or looking for lost wallets or writing his small-town crime column for the newspaper. Did I tell you Granny is the new advice columnist. Oops?" I covered my mouth with my hand. "I'm not supposed to tell. You did not hear that from me."

"My lips are sealed," she said, then she got up again and this time she made it out the door.

I baked three pies that afternoon, trying to keep my mind off murder and home invasion. One was a classic apple only I inserted some cheddar cheese under the top crust before baking. Apple pie may not be the world's best pie, but I think it smells the best when baking. Maybe it's the cinnamon, maybe it's the memories. Maybe because it's associated with chilly days and cozy nights around the fire. So why was I making an apple pie in the middle of summer? I guess I just needed a shot of cozy at that moment. Even if I didn't eat a bite of it, just the smell was enough to blot out the scene I'd encountered upstairs.

Next I made another key lime pie with a classic graham cracker crust. I didn't have any fresh key limes so I used bottled key lime juice. My third pie was actually four individual meat pies known in England as pasties. They're basically pie dough used to hold meat, potatoes, and vegetables. The pastie is baked until the dough is golden brown. Pasties aren't fancy, but they're sure good. In the olden days of the Golden West the men used to take pasties into the mines to have for lunch. Which pie should I take to Sam's? He avoids sugar like the plague, but he'll be expecting a pie. Better stick to citrus.

When I walked out the front door that evening on my way to Sam's house, there was a young woman leaning against a car at the curb. She was wearing all olive drab and sensible shoes. She raised her hand in a salute when she saw me.

"Can I help you?" I said. Again, a last-minute pie sale is always a positive possibility.

"I'm Deputy Officer Raleigh," she said.

"From Park City. I'm assigned to watch your shop and put a padlock on the door."

"What? Who assigned you?" As if I didn't know.

"The chief."

"This is ridiculous. Yes, my house was vandalized today, but why would the vandals come back?"

"I don't know, ma'am," she said, which made me feel about one-hundred years old. Especially since she was twenty-one if she was a day. "But I have the combination to the padlock for you."

"I thought you'd be here guarding the store."

"I will, but the chief wants you to have experience with the padlock so this kind of incident never happens again."

"Before you lock the door," I said, "Help yourself to some pie."

She shook her head. "No eating or drinking on duty."

Whose rule was that I wondered as I drove away. Traditionally cops always ate donuts and drank coffee while on the job.

I arrived at Sam's house at seven, pie in hand. After trying out about fifteen different combinations of clothes, from sloppy to fancy and everything in between, I'd finally decided on an off-white short skirt, flat black sandals, and a black sweater with a beaded neckline. I had the list that Kate and I had made out in my purse, just in case we got into the subject of murder and suspects. And when have we not? Still I wouldn't mind skipping the topic for one evening. One evening without worrying about someone breaking into my shop or anyone committing murder. I didn't mind murder so much as long as I wasn't blamed for it.

Sam answered the door. The combination of heavenly smells coming from the kitchen and the sight of Sam at the door of his own house looking sexier than ever in tight jeans, leather sandals, and a blue polo shirt was almost more than I could handle on top of everything else I'd been through, both good and bad. I staggered backward for a moment before I recovered enough to stammer, "Hi."

"Feeling better?" he asked, taking the pie out of my hands.

"Fine," I said. "You didn't need to send a deputy."

"She needed a job, you need a night watchman."

"The home invasion of my home happened during the day," I reminded him as he led the way to the patio behind his house.

"Do you really think the home invader is going to come back?"

"Depends on what he found or is still looking for."

"Why he, why not she?"

"Force of habit. It could be a she. Any ideas?"

I didn't want to start the evening talking about crime or even end the evening that way, so I just shook my head. Then I looked around the patio. Tall palm fronds waved in the evening breeze. Lush bougainvillea climbed the trellis between his house and Lindsey's next door. He poured me a tall drink from a pitcher on a small table.

"Delicious," I said. "What is it?"

"*Poncha.* A Portuguese guy I worked with gave me the recipe. Orange juice, lemon, rum, and honey."

I sat down on a canvas lawn chair, my drink in hand. Even if I thought it was ridiculous to have a deputy watching my shop, it did give me a sense of security. That and the poncha. I refused to worry about driving home either. Sam could take me if he thought I couldn't pass a sobriety test.

I was right about his being a great cook. The lamb roasting on the outdoor grill gave off the scent of rosemary, garlic, and olive oil. When he brought it in to carve, it was brown and crusty on the outside and pink and juicy on the inside. He filled two plates with slices of lamb, a heap of couscous he'd cooked on his kitchen stove, and grilled asparagus.

We carried our plates outside to a rustic picnic table and Sam poured a crisp, dry white Pinot Grigio. I swirled the wine in the glass then I sniffed it. "Mmmmm. Smells like pears."

He nodded. "You have a very good nose." Then he tilted his head to one side and gave me a long look, his gaze traveling up and down my body. Was he checking for concealed weapons? With Sam you never knew. He was always on duty. I was glad I'd worn the right thing. Or had I?

"And your legs aren't bad either," he said with a slight twist of his lips. On anyone else it would have been classified as a smile or even a grin. But Sam? Not so much.

I blushed. Even a woman in her thirties can have a problem accepting a remark like that from an old flame.

"The last person I served this wine to said it was 'innocuous and uninteresting'."

"Obviously someone you should avoid," I said. Wondering if it was a previous girlfriend. But glad I'd passed the test. If there was one.

We talked about wine and food and the town and people in general. The elephant in the room was the Barr murder mystery of course, and we both tiptoed around the subject. Half of me wanted his opinion and the lists Kate and I had made earlier were burning a hole in my purse. The other part wanted a purely social evening. There were so few of those in my life.

Eventually after coffee and a small slice of sweet-tart key lime pie each we sat outside. It was dark except for the tiny lights strung overhead in the trees. That's when we got down to the subject we'd been avoiding.

"Any idea who trashed my house today?" I asked casually, setting down my half glass of cognac which he'd poured from an expensive-looking bell-shaped bottle. I wanted to give the impression that I'd put it all behind me. I wasn't worried or nervous at all. I was just curious, that's all. Surely that was understandable. I just didn't want Sam to think I was a basket case who fell apart every time something unusual hap-pened.

When his cell phone rang I thought he almost looked relieved. He'd rather deal with an emergency than speculate with me about possible suspects. Maybe he was right to avoid delving into mysterious circumstances with me. Maybe our conversations all led to nowhere. He'd made it clear he didn't want my help. Maybe he knew exactly who'd done it and he didn't want to tell me, worried that I would blab or freak out. Who me?

I listened to him ask questions of the caller. Just the usual, who, what, where, and when. But I couldn't tell what it was all about. Until he hung up.

"Gotta go," he said, standing up. "Domestic violence on our favorite street, Mulberry."

"A coincidence or . . ."

"It's the neighbors of Marty and Nina. They say they heard shouting and threats at their house."

"Is that classified as domestic violence?"

"Not yet. I'd rather intervene before it gets to that stage. I'll take you home first."

My eyes widened. Marty and Nina in a fight. "I want to go with you. I promise I'll stay in the car. Unless you need me to talk to her or him. You don't have to use force to break up a domestic fight, do you?"

"Rather not," he said. I followed him inside where he strapped on a gun and put a jacket on over it. "If you come you have to promise not to do anything or say anything. And stay in the car."

I raised my right hand. "Promise. I won't budge and I won't say a word, even though I think it's easier to deal with other people's problems than your own. Isn't that why you're a cop?"

"I don't have any problems," he said, his hand on my shoulder as he locked his front door.

I searched his face under the porch light. No sign of how he meant that remark. As an attempt at irony, a joke, or just the truth as he perceived it.

"If you don't have any problems you're one in a million."

"I could have told you that," he said.

THIRTEEN

Sam opened the official Crystal Cove police car door and I got in. He drove fast and we were on Mulberry Street in a few minutes.

He parked in front of Nina and Marty's house where there was a small crowd standing outside on the sidewalk. Lights shone from every window of their large house. But there was no noise, no voices, no arguing, no music, nothing. Just a hushed murmur from the crowd. Had they killed each other?

"False alarm?" I said hopefully.

A few people came up to Sam as he got out of the car.

"I'm the one who called, Chief," a stocky man in Bermuda shorts and flip-flops said. "Heard lots of shouting. Threats like 'I'm gonna kill you'."

Sam nodded calmly like he'd heard it all before. "Thanks for calling. I'll check it out. People say things but usually don't mean them."

I watched from inside the car while he went to Nina and Marty's front door. I saw him ring the bell, knock, and then walk in. Then I heard voices. A man's voice and a woman's voice. I strained my ears but I couldn't make out what they were saying. I wanted to jump out and ask the neighbors if they'd heard anything else, but I knew better.

A few minutes later I heard Sam say "Good night," to whoever was inside, then he came down the front steps and addressed the group of neighbors.

"False alarm," he told them. "Just a little argument. The Holloways asked me to apologize for alarming the neighbors. But everything's fine now. They've made up and that's the end of it. They appreciate having such vigilant neighbors."

I'll just bet they do, I thought. I bet they hate having the cop come to their door. But how loud was the argument and more importantly, what was it about?

"What happened?" I said once we were headed for his house.

"Nothing," he said.

"Okay, sorry I asked."

"Would you believe me if I told you that Marty had a black eye?"

I turned my head to stare at him with

disbelief. "No."

"Yes," he said.

"Nina did that?" I asked.

"What do you think?" Sam said.

"I can't believe it. Though maybe he deserved it."

"He said he'd walked into a door. He didn't want to press charges or take any action. It was an accident. His own fault. He hadn't called us. He was a little grumpy, I have to say."

"He was that way at the Food Fair when he was minding Nina's booth. How did she look?"

"She looked mad. She looked like she was ready to smack him again."

"So you don't believe the 'walked into a door' story."

He shrugged.

I was deeply flattered that he'd confided in me as much as he had. "What now?" I asked.

"How about a cup of coffee?" he said.

"Sounds good. Why don't we go to my house and you can give your deputy the rest of the night off."

He turned at the next corner and stopped in front of the shop. I gave the poor deputy a cherry pie to take home and Sam told her she'd done a great job. At least he assumed she had. For all we knew she'd taken a nap in her car, which was okay as long as no one tried to break in.

After I'd made coffee upstairs in my tiny apartment, I sat down in the straight-back chair across from Sam and put my elbows on my well-worn kitchen table, which had once been Grannie's.

"What I want to know is how this incident fits into the big picture," I said.

"It doesn't. These incidents as you call them are part of my daily life. They're random. They happen. They will always happen as long as there are people. So don't go trying to make something of it."

"What do you think they were arguing about?"

"I don't know. What do people argue about? Money? Sex?"

"Then she hit him? Why?"

"Nobody said she hit him. Not him. Not her."

"Somebody hit him." I frowned and stirred some cream into my coffee.

"Nobody else at home?" I asked.

"Didn't see anyone."

I was green with envy. Call me nosy, but I wanted to see that house. I wanted to see that black eye too. And I wanted to get a feeling for their relationship, which I couldn't believe was a good one. I'd never seen them together, and I was sure I'd be able to pick up on the vibes between them. I wasn't invited but I could have gone in. There was obviously no danger.

"I don't know about you," I said, "but I haven't crossed Nina off the suspect list."

"The murder suspect list?" he said, tilting his chair back and looking at me as if I'd lost my mind.

"That's the one. This incident tonight just confirms my theory. Nina is obviously capable of violence."

"*If* she socked her husband."

"What are the chances it was a stranger or a run-in with a door? I mean, honestly. Then there's the fact that Heath gave her caramels a good review."

"You're not back to that shakedown theory are you?"

"Why not? I wish I knew if she had one of those sharp knives we all had." I looked at Sam. All he had to say was "Yes, she did and I confiscated it," or "It doesn't matter." He didn't say anything.

"Too bad you didn't have a chance to search the house," I suggested.

"Searching the house, as you put it, requires a search warrant and I don't see any reason for one. Domestic violence is

309

one of the most common crimes there is," Sam said. "And when there's no complaint filed, there's no crime."

"I understand. What I don't understand is how much domestic violence is perpetrated by a woman. Can't be much. We're gentle people. On the whole."

He patted me on the shoulder. "Sure you are," he said. "But it happens."

"Don't humor me, Sam," I said. "I know women commit heinous crimes. Look at Lizzie Borden who took an axe, 'gave her mother forty whacks, when she saw what she had done, she gave her father forty-one'."

"I now know I shouldn't have taken you with me tonight. Now you're convinced Nina and Marty are up to something. Forget it. Forget them."

"Okay," I said.

He gave me a suspicious look. Maybe I should have hesitated before agreeing so readily. I was determined to get into their house on some pretense and check them out. There was something going on and I would find out what it was.

I managed to change the subject back to something innocuous, but my mind was spinning. If Sam hadn't instructed me to drop the whole murder thing, I would have hauled out the list Kate and I made. But if he refused to listen to me, didn't want my help, why should I insist? I'd do my investigating on my own and when I finally had proof I'd hand it to him on a silver platter. I wouldn't ask for praise or recognition or my picture in the paper. All I wanted was to be deputized. Was that too much to ask? That's the way I am, just a concerned citizen, trying to keep Crystal Cove safe for the residents. But it would be nice if he'd thank me.

"You're drifting off," he said.

I sat up straight. How did he know my mind was elsewhere? I pride myself on my ability to look interested even when I'm not. I guess I'm not as good as I thought I was. Or he's better than I thought he was.

"Sorry," I said. "It's past my bedtime. I had a great time. Your dinner was fabulous. And the after-dinner entertainment . . . Just what I'd expect from a lawman."

"Is this what you expected?" he said and he pulled me to my feet and kissed me. I hadn't been kissed like that since high school. And guess who kissed me like that then? I was breathless and shaky. I kissed him back and clung to him, forgetting I was mad at him for shutting me out of his murder case. Sam's kisses had a way of

311

making me forget just about everything. When he finally left, he took my keys and told me he'd bring my car back tomorrow.

"Lock the door and keep your phone under your pillow," he said sternly before he walked out the door. "And if you go anywhere tomorrow, use the padlock."

I nodded and tottered back upstairs. Tomorrow, I told myself, tomorrow I'd figure it out.

But the next day I hadn't figured anything out. Whether I was an idiot to fall for Sam again after all these years, and even more an idiot to think I could solve a murder mystery by myself without the help of lab tests, backup reinforcements, deputies, a search warrant, or even a gun.

So I did what I do best, I made pies. I made another Huckleberry pie, this time from some fresh berries I picked from the patch behind the shop, which Grannie and I had planted many years ago. The berries were at their peak now, a deep eggplant purple and when fully ripe they were better than the most delicious blueberry in the world. I ate half of them before I'd even made the pie crust. Then to switch gears I made four individual steak and mushroom pies, thinking I'd freeze them for later in the season when the days get shorter and it was no longer barbecue season. I'd either sell them or keep them to serve friends. Which reminded me of Sam. He brought my car back, left the keys on my counter, and waved good-bye. That was it. I could still taste the delicious grilled lamb and fresh asparagus he'd made. I could taste his lips and his kisses too.

After I sold some pies, I closed the shop in the late afternoon and padlocked the door. Then I headed out to Jacques' dairy farm to return the robe I'd borrowed the night of his party. Sam didn't know I was going, probably didn't care and couldn't stop me if he did care. Why would he bother? He didn't believe I was pushed in the pool that night, but I did. Is it so strange to want to know why someone wanted to drown you? I'd return the robe and return to the scene of my near death by drowning and maybe I'd realize I was wrong and Sam was right. It was possible I'd merely stumbled. Or I'd have a flash of intuition and I'd recognize the voices I'd heard. In any case it would be good to see Jacques. He made me feel cute and young and carefree. I wasn't sure how I'd explain the robe I was returning. But I'd think of something.

When I got to Foggy Meadow Farm, the

place was buzzing with activity. A tractor was ploughing the fields. The driveway was crowded with commercial pickup trucks. Workers in straw hats lifted bales of hay into the barn where the square dancing had taken place. To think that Jacques was in charge of all this. I was impressed. Under his veneer of casual caretaker, he must be more capable than he seemed. Even the cows on the side of the road looked more alert than the last time I was there. As if they were on a different schedule.

I pulled into the driveway and looked around. A couple of workers waved to me and I waved back. In hopes of returning the robe before I saw Jacques, I tucked it under my arm and went straight to the pool.

It looked just as pristine as the night of the party. No one was in it or lounging around the cabana. I hung the robe in the sauna and went back to the pool. I stood at the edge staring at the water trying to recapture the scene that night, hoping for the mental breakthrough I'd imagined. Nothing. The water sparkled. The sun was warm on my back. I was a good swimmer, I wouldn't have minded being pushed in, so what was the big deal?

"Who are you?"

I jumped back. So much for my sanguine

attitude. I whirled around to see a ruddy-faced guy in jeans and a work shirt, hands on hips looking at me.

"I . . . I'm Hanna Denton, the pie baker. Is Jacques around?"

"So you're a friend of Jacques too? Maybe you can answer a few questions," he said, glowering at me. "I'm Larry Dolan, the owner here."

What was he doing here? What happened to Jacques? Was there a curse on the Food Fair? Was everyone there actually a zombie with a secret life? No, Martha was normal. Lindsey and Tammy were old friends of mine. I would know by now if they were flesh-eating creatures of the night.

"I'll be glad to help if I can," I said politely even though I didn't like this guy's attitude. "I didn't really know Jacques very well. I mean just from the Food Fair."

"The place where he was selling the cheese and pocketing the proceeds?"

Pocketing the proceeds? Was that his crime? "I guess so, if that's what it's about. We're there to sell produce or farm products. Why? Wasn't he supposed to?"

"He was supposed to be taking care of the farm. Then we get a message in New Zealand where we're on a business trip buying livestock that Jacques — if that's his real name — has skeedaddled, hit the road, vamoosed, disappeared."

"Oh no, did he take anything?"

"Just our good reputation and about a few pounds of our best cheese."

"Have you called the police?"

He shook his head. "What can they do? He's gone. I should have known. He was too smooth. His recommendations were too good. He made 'em up."

"Made them up?" I was shocked. "I don't know what harm he did here but actually he did a good job of selling your cheese at the Food Fair on Saturdays. He had a real flair for salesmanship."

"Good at selling himself, that's what he did. Smooth talker. Is that what got you?" he asked.

I didn't like the inference. "He didn't *get* me. I'm in the food business too. I have a pie shop. I thought he was a bonafide farm-sitter, that's what he said."

"He said a lot of things."

"Anything missing besides the cheese?" I asked.

"I'm missing my faith in human nature," he said. "I'll never get that back. Why couldn't the guy stay until the end of summer? Why run off like that?"

Had Jacques killed Heath and left in a

hurry before he could be apprehended? But why? Not just to avenge the bad review he gave to the Foggy Meadow Artisan cheeses which weren't even his at all. Maybe Jacques had a problem with Heath somewhere in his past. Jacques was new here and so was Heath. Who came first? Who followed who to Crystal Cove? If Jacques was a suspect, why hadn't Sam mentioned him? The answer was obvious. He didn't want me to know. He wanted me to think it was someone else so I wouldn't do something crazy like come out here looking for him and tip him off.

"I hope you didn't lose anything else," I said.

"Isn't it enough he ruined our trip? We had to cut it short. We lost time and we lost our trust in people," he said sadly.

I stared at him, trying to figure out if he was for real. Was this angry, introspective farmer as big a phony as Jacques? Was he really Dolan at all? Was he only mad because Jacques took off sooner than expected? I decided to leave before I got pushed in the pool again.

"Sorry about . . . uh, everything," I said. "I still think you had an excellent farm-sitter, whatever his flaws." As far as I knew, he hadn't stolen anything except some cheese and he'd done a good job of caretaking.

Dolan didn't answer. He just shook his head. "Wait a minute. What did you say your name is?"

"Hanna Denton."

"He left a note for you." He reached into his back pocket and handed me a crumpled envelope with my name on it. It was sealed. I couldn't believe Dolan wouldn't have read it. Maybe he had and he'd just re-sealed it.

"Thanks."

I waited until I was halfway home before I pulled off the road and ripped the envelope open.

"Hanna, sorry I had to leave without saying good-bye. It was good to meet you. I'll see you again one day. Who knows. About that night — you're a good sport. Stay well."

Now I was more confused than ever. I couldn't believe Jacques would walk out on the Dolans without a good excuse. Especially abandoning the animals who depended on him. If he had an excuse, he didn't confide in me. Still I was touched he took time to write me a note when he must have been in a big hurry to get out of there. Maybe he wasn't as irresponsible as the Dolans thought. Maybe he left thinking the day laborers would continue to do all the hard work on their place.

Back at my shop I unlocked my front door, grateful for the padlock hanging on the door. Upstairs I finished cleaning my apartment and washing my clothes. Finally I collapsed on the deck behind my kitchen. On my way outside, I noticed the pouch of letters I was supposed to deliver to Grannie. I should go over there, I told myself. She'll want to see what she's got to work with.

I couldn't help being curious. I too wanted to see what she had to work with. I also wondered if I'd be any good at giving advice. I guess everyone thinks they could do it. I looked inside the bag. There were a lot of letters, maybe twenty-five or thirty. Pretty good for a small-town paper. Not so many as to overwhelm Grannie, just enough to make her feel wanted. Surely the editor Bruce was glad to see what a good response they'd gotten.

I sat down in my outdoor recliner chair which along with the small metal table took up most of the small deck. The air was fresh with the damp smell of the ocean. The neighborhood was quiet. Not a sound from the police station across the street. Speaking of the law, I hoped it wasn't against the law to take a quick look at Grannie's letters. Since they were already open, it couldn't be wrong of me to just read a few. After all, one day I might inherit this job along with the one I had. I reached into the pouch and eagerly read the first one.

Dear Maggie,
I'm afraid my husband is fooling around. When I confronted him, he denied everything and he said he'd never do it again. Should I believe him?

Confused

My mind was spinning. For some crazy reason I thought it might be from Nina. Which would explain her husband's absence and her red-rimmed eyes. Or was I getting paranoid, thinking of nothing but Heath's murder?

Dear Maggie,
My brother and I are in business together. I take care of the nitty-gritty, he does the PR. In other words I do the hard work, and he gets all the credit. I'm afraid to walk out on him because he needs me. But I think he's done something illegal like cooking the books because he's acting weird. If I don't report him, am I guilty too?

My Brother's Keeper.

Oh, no, this could easily be from Bill or Dave. Was the "something illegal" killing Heath?

I put the letters back in the bag and leaned back in my chair. But I couldn't stop reading. I was addicted. I reached into the bag again.

Dear Maggie,

I'm a woman in business for myself. I'm smart, successful, and not bad looking. I'm playing the field for now but I don't want to end up alone when I'm old and tired. The problem is I live in a small town and there aren't many single men. Should I go after the only eligible man in town who by the way is smart, handsome, and sexy, or move to a big city where I'll have a wider choice?

Miz Biz

I read the letter again. Was I crazy or was this letter from Lurline? And if it was, by "the only eligible man in town" did she mean Sam? He was definitely smart, handsome and sexy. I put the letter back and took another. Maybe this wasn't a good idea, having an advice column in a small-town paper. If I guessed who wrote the letters, wouldn't everyone else guess too? Or was that the idea? Maybe that was part of the fun, trying to figure out who wrote what about who.

Dear Maggie,
   I'm a single guy living in Smallsville, California. I have some secrets in my past I don't want anyone to know. Nothing terrible, just private stuff, you know? But what happens when I meet a woman who wants to get close? How do I keep things to myself when she wants to bare her soul (and her body) to me? In the past I always just break things off and move on. Or I make her break up with me. She's married by the way, but her husband is out of the picture.
                                    Roaming Romeo

I couldn't help thinking it might have been Heath who wrote this before he was axed. But if it was Heath, who was the woman? There were plenty of married women in this town. How many husbands were "out of the picture"? How would Heath even know there was an advice columnist if it was him? I didn't know and it was my own grandmother. Maybe they'd announced it at a staff meeting and Bruce had asked for submissions to get the ball rolling. Or was it

Sam? I shook my head. Sam writing to an advice columnist? Not in this lifetime. Sam involved with a married woman? Impossible.

I took another and then another letter.

Dear Maggie,

I'm not normally a violent person, but I lost my temper the other night and hit my spouse who deserved it. I know it was wrong to take matters into my own hands, but I couldn't help it. Someone called the cops and now I'm afraid I'll pay the price. I need help. Or I might strike again.

Scared

I stood up and took a several deep breaths. That last letter had to be from Nina, I just knew it was. The other wasn't. Nobody would write two letters to Ask Maggie. The part about the cops was the clincher. But what to do? The first thing I had to do was to stop reading these letters. I had to stop thinking about Heath's murder. It wasn't my problem. Sam said it and I knew it. Everyone I met, everyone I talked to was a suspect. Only they weren't.

I paced back and forth on my little deck trying to decide how I could help Nina before she struck her husband again even though he doubtless deserved it. God only knew what he'd done. Killed Heath? Why? Because he'd written a flattering review of his wife's caramels? That didn't make sense. Nothing made sense.

I had to do something. I was tired of thinking about the murder. Tired of talking about it. It was time to take action. I couldn't sit by while my house was broken into. I couldn't just wait here for something else to happen like a helpless wimp. I had to make it happen on my terms. I would go to see Nina and find out why she smacked her husband. If she did. If not I would gracefully slip away. If need be, I would offer my support. There are places where abused wives or abused husbands can find shelter. No one deserved to be abused. I would sympathize with her or him and convince them to separate.

If Nina was afraid she couldn't make it on her own, I'd tell her there was big business in candy. Look at Mary See and Fannie Mae. I would help her get a leg up the way Grannie helped me get the pie business restarted after her retirement.

But how to broach the subject without letting her know I'd snooped in the Ask Maggie mailbag? That was my challenge. I know.

I'd take a pie. Who can turn down a friend, and I like to think I'm a friend, or at least a farmstand colleague who comes to the door with a pie or a cake in hand?

What if Marty answered the door? Not likely since he was a vet. He had to be at work and if he was there, I'd simply hand over the pie and say good-bye. I'd try not to stare at his black eye and I definitely wouldn't mention it. But I would offer my support as I would to any spouse who needed it.

First I went to Heavenly Acres and gave Grannie her mailbag.

"I'm nervous," she said. "What if I give the wrong advice? And things get worse."

"They can't get worse," I said. "I mean, if someone is so needy they have to turn to an advice columnist they've never met, then they've reached bottom and have nowhere to go but up."

She frowned. Maybe I wasn't making sense. Maybe my mind was on poor Nina. "Anyway, you are the most level-headed person I know. The people of this town are lucky to have someone like you to turn to. Obviously they have no one else or they wouldn't be writing to you."

"Dear Abby was always spot on," she said. "She's my idol. She was funny too."

"You're funny," I assured her. "And some of the letters are funny too. I mean I imagine they might be funny." Like the husband who was fooling around and vowed he'd never do it again, even though he denied doing it in the first place.

Grannie went to her bookcase and held up a leather-bound copy of *The Best of Dear Abby.* "This is where I got the idea for my column. I can never be as good as she was, but I'm going to try."

"If you need any help," I said, "I'd be glad to do whatever I can."

"Thanks," she said, "but this has to be my project. Ever since I gave up the shop and moved up here, I've felt something was missing. Not that I don't love my life here. I do. But I need a challenge." She waved the bag of letters. "This is it."

I left her contemplating her bag of letters. Maybe in a little while she'd get up the courage to delve into the bag. She'd have good advice for all those writers like "Scared," "Roaming Romeo," "Miz Biz," and "My Brother's Keeper." I felt a little guilty that I'd horned in on her new job. The good thing was she'd never know. She had an entirely different approach to the job than I did. Because it wasn't my job. She wouldn't try to figure out who the writers were like I did. And she definitely wouldn't go to their house to help them out. But just as I had to run the pie shop my way, she had to answer the letters her way.

I drove to Mulberry Street and parked down the block from Nina and Marty's house. I walked slowly up the street, hoping I wouldn't run into any neighbors who might recognize me. Or realize that I was a stranger in the neighborhood and therefore out of place. So far, so good.

There was a man mowing his lawn. He didn't give me a second glance. There were kids playing baseball in a back yard. They hit the ball over the fence and I knew I shouldn't touch it but I reached down and tossed it back to them with one hand. I didn't think they knew who threw it.

I gave up trying to be invisible. Instead I marched up the walk to Marty and Nina's house and knocked on the front door, holding my pie in the other hand. I had an excuse for being there.

Nothing. Not a sound. I rang the bell. I waited. Then I walked around the back of the house. The lawn was beautiful and the hibiscus along the fence were in full bloom. They obviously had a gardener. If I were married to a vet I'd have one too. I'd have a shed in back for garden tools and seedlings like they did. I sighed. Some day.

I crossed a brick patio lined with flower boxes and went to the back entrance. I knocked, then waited and finally I tried the door. It wasn't locked. That's the kind of town this was. People didn't lock their doors. Except me. I was supposed to padlock mine. I hadn't done it. If someone broke in again tonight I had only myself to blame. I wouldn't even call Sam. I'd just button my lip and accept my punishment.

I walked into a gourmet kitchen and called "Hello." My voice echoed in the empty house. I always wondered if people who had copper pots hanging over the granite-topped kitchen island and every appliance known to man ever used them. This kitchen was spotless. I was surprised there was not a drop of sticky caramel candy substance. I looked in the pantry. No big bags of sugar either. I tried to picture Nina hovering over this spotless stove stirring the gooey melted butter and sugar with one hand, the other hand holding her candy thermometer. I opened all the drawers. No thermometer. No hot pads. No apron. Maybe she rented a commercial kitchen to make her candy and avoided penalties from the county officials like the rest of us got.

I set my pie down on the stone countertop and walked into the living room. I admit I was curious to see if everything was as first class as the kitchen. It was. From the pine-plank flooring to the antique French fireplace. The furniture was what I call Swedish modern. All white and spare, but very elegant. That's what you can have when you don't have children. French doors led to a garden with carefully trimmed shrubs and vine-covered trellises. I perched on a Louis Something chair and gazed at the charming garden. You'd think French furniture wouldn't fit into this house, but it looked perfect. I was jealous, I admit it. How did an ordinary girl and a nerdy guy end up with the lifestyle I wanted?

Then I told myself to leave and come back another time when Nina was home. I needed answers to some questions. More than that, Nina needed help before she did something worse than socking her husband in the eye.

I stood and turned to go just as I heard footsteps on the front porch. That's what I got for day-dreaming. I ran out of the room as I heard the key turn in the lock. I wanted to shout, "The back door's open," but I didn't. I zipped through the kitchen and out the back door as I heard them talking loudly. They were on my trail.

"Someone's here," Nina said. "I can tell."

"You're crazy," Marty answered.

"I'm serious," she said. "Look, a pie."

Damn, I'd left the pie there in the kitchen. Instead of running out and around the house and back to the street, I raced to the corrugated metal garden shed and closed the door firmly behind me. Now they were outside the house. They were looking for me.

"That was her car on the street," Marty said.

Now how did he know that?

"Go out in front and see if she tries to escape," he ordered.

Escape? I didn't have to escape. Sure I'd entered their house uninvited, but I didn't break in. I walked in. I just hoped they'd go looking for me, then I'd slip out the back way and sneak away. I was breathing so hard I was afraid they'd hear me. I covered my mouth with my hand. Why didn't Marty go inside the house and look for me there, check the upstairs and the closets. Then I could get out of the shed and go home. I should never have hidden here, it just made me look guilty which I wasn't. One of them was guilty.

I stood there for a long time waiting for a sign they were both gone. I sat down on a low rough bench and looked around. A shaft of sunlight came through a small window. On the back shelf there were several large white candy boxes stacked on top of each other. I stood on the bench and reached for a box. It came from an out-of-state Confiserie and the label said, "Sadie's Chocolate Covered Salt Caramels. Ethantown, Vermont" I sat down again with a thud. Nina bought her caramels? That was a shock. She had nothing to do all day, and yet she bought the candy she sold instead of slaving over a hot stove. No wonder it was so good. Even Heath thought so. Was that what she was hiding? If I had to, I would assure her that her secret was safe with me as long as she let me out of the shed. Although I wondered who else knew.

I held the empty box on my lap and looked around. There were garden tools on shelves. A rake and shovels in the corner. Hanging on the wall was an axe and the saw-tooth spatula all the vendors were using. I reached for it. The blade was so sharp I cut my finger again this time. Would I ever learn? Was this the one that killed Heath? If so which one of them did it and why? Suddenly the small shed went dark as if someone had turned out the light. Instead, someone had blocked the small window with a board. I heard banging as if someone was hammering it shut. I jumped up, went to the door and tried to push it open. It didn't budge.

"Help," I yelled. "Let me out." I didn't care if they heard me. I was willing to confess I'd trespassed on their property. They'd seen my car. They'd seen the pie. They knew I'd been there. I had nothing more to hide.

From outside the shed I heard a maniacal laughter. It sounded like one of Martha's chickens cackling. "See anything you like?" Marty said. "Take your time. Look around. You've got all day. Lots of days before anyone comes looking for you."

"That's not true," I muttered. "Someone knows where I am." But how did they know where I was? I pressed my hand over my mouth. Don't tell him someone knew where I was, I told myself. He'd just take me somewhere else. It's better he thinks he's got me cornered. But no one did know I was there. How long before they figured it out? I was getting that closed-in, claustrophobic feeling that I knew so well. I was gasping for breath even though I'd only been in there for minutes. I had to get out of there

"Please let me out," I said sounding

pathetic. "I didn't do anything. I don't know anything."

"Yeah, right. You didn't listen to the phone messages, did you?"

"That's right," I said, suddenly relieved. "I wasn't allowed to."

"Then where's the phone?"

"I don't know."

"I know," Nina said. "Sam has it, doesn't he? And when he hears the messages he'll come looking for me."

"Not you. You didn't do anything." Or did she?

"All I did was sell somebody else's caramels and say I made them. Everyone does it. And they're making a big freaking deal out of it."

"You're wrong, Nina. Nobody is," I assured her.

"Nina, shut up," Marty said.

"No, you shut up. This was your idea. Now look what you've done."

"I didn't have an affair with the asshole, you did," Marty said.

I almost fell over. What was going on here? I didn't want to hear this bickering. How had we switched from illegal caramels to infidelity to murder? If one of them killed him, which one was it?

"Who's the asshole?" I shouted. Now this

was getting ridiculous. Why couldn't they let me out so we could have this conversation without screaming?

"Good question," Marty said. "They're all assholes, every guy she ever slept with."

"That includes you," Nina said.

"Look, I don't know who or what you're talking about. Just let me out and I won't say a word. I can't because I don't know anything."

"Don't know anything? You told your cop boyfriend about the cell phone. He knows I called that phony food critic and what I said."

"No, he doesn't," I insisted, my forehead pressed against the blocked door. *What did you say?* I wanted to ask. "If he knew it was you or Nina he would have arrested you. He'd be here now, but he isn't. He doesn't know anything either. If you let me go I swear I won't tell him. I have nothing to tell him."

"Yeah, I know you won't, because you're not getting out of there. Except on a stretcher."

I swallowed hard. I didn't like the sound of that. I took a deep breath. The time for reasoning with them was over. I picked up the hammer and pounded on the metal door. I made a small dent but I'd never pound my way out that way.

"Let's get out of here," Nina said.

"Thank you," I yelled. Then I realized she'd said, *Let's get out of here,* instead of *Let's get her out of there.* "Wait, I can help you."

"Help me how?" she said. Her voice was loud and strong. Maybe she didn't need my help after all. She'd hit Marty. She could testify against Marty and then get a divorce. What else could I offer her?

"I'll swear it wasn't your fault," I yelled. "I'll swear that you made the caramels in your kitchen so you can keep selling at the market. I'll say I saw the pots and pans and your recipe and the traces of sugar and butter and sea salt. I'll swear you couldn't help it if your husband killed Heath." Here I was taking a chance. I wasn't sure which one of them killed him. Or why.

"Instead of letting you die the easy way, I'm coming in there and use the knife on your throat too," Marty said.

"So you killed Heath," I gasped. I felt like I'd had a shot of adrenaline along with a jolt of pride. I'd figured it out and I'd gotten a confession out of him. Sort of a confession. Wait until Sam heard this. But would he hear? Would it hold up? "But why?" I blurted before I realized I didn't

335

want to know. Yes, it was my chance to unravel this whole mess. If they'd tell me. But after I found out what would happen to me? Would they really use the same weapon on me they'd used on him?

"He was harassing my wife," he said.

"He was not," Nina said. "I don't need you to defend me."

"I won't tell anyone, I promise," I said. "Whoever did it."

"We know you won't because you won't be talking much longer," Marty said his voice right outside the shed.

What did that mean?

I pressed my ear to the door. Then I heard a car. It was nearby. Who was it? Where were they going? If it was Marty and Nina, it didn't matter as long as they left. I'd hack my way out or someone would come and get me. They were outside talking, but I couldn't make out the words. It was dark in there with the window boarded up, but I heard a noise from under the plywood floor. Maybe it was rats. I wouldn't mind, considering the alternative. I got down on my knees and felt around. Nothing. Except I smelled exhaust fumes. Gas. From the car I heard. I stood up so fast I bumped into a shelf and almost fell over. They'd found a way to gas me. Somewhere on the floor

they'd inserted a hose with carbon monox-
ide and it was filling the shed.

I groped around, feeling my way along the
wall until I ran into a long-handled axe with
my fingers. It was so heavy I could barely
hold it let along swing it at the door. At my
first try I dropped it on my foot. I yelped in
pain. I tried again, then I missed the door. I
grunted with the effort of just holding the
heavy axe. This time I actually hit the door.
It made a dent. At this rate I'd die before I
made a hole in the door.

When I stopped to try to catch a breath I
heard voices. A new voice. Someone had
come to rescue me. I tried to shout, but my
voice came out as a whisper.

"Sign here," the new voice said. "What's
that noise?"

"It's nothing. Thanks."

"What's the hose for?"

"We've got rats," Marty said. "We're fumi-
gating."

"Those are some rats."

"No," I wheezed. "It's me. Help."

I picked up the axe again. I was dizzy.
Weak. Sick. Everything went black. I fell
forward. Someone pushed me just like the
night I fell in the pool. The same invisible
person. I couldn't breathe. I was drowning
all over again.

The next thing I heard was loud pounding and a huge crash. I was lying on the floor of the shed but there was light shining on me. It was so bright it hurt my eyes. My head was pounding. I squinted. A big blurry form filled the room.

"There she is," Sam shouted. "Get her some air."

I wanted to tell Sam what I'd heard, but it was all mixed up. He put a mask over my face and I couldn't talk anyway. I felt light-headed and giddy. He picked me up just like he'd done that night at my house and carried me out to the ambulance. By the time we got to the hospital in nearby Hollybrook, my brain was working better. I wanted to rip off that mask and tell Sam not to let Nina and Marty get away. But they wouldn't let me talk. Instead I got rolled into the ER by some med techs and they did a bunch of tests on me.

It seemed like hours later before I was in a bed in a room with some tubes attached to my arm. I picked up the phone on the bedside table and tried to call someone. Anyone. Sam walked in.

"About time somebody came to see me," I fumed. "How long have I been here?" I asked.

"A couple of hours." He sat on the edge

of my bed. He loomed large and he looked tired. "How do you feel?"

"Pretty weak. And my head hurts."

He put his hand on my head. "That's normal."

"Not for me."

"For someone who's been gassed."

"Where are they?" I asked.

"Marty and Nina? They're in custody."

"How did you know Marty killed Heath?"

"I got the report back from the lab. They cleaned up the tape from Heath's phone messages so I heard Marty threaten Heath."

"So you guessed I'd be at their house."

"The delivery man called to say something was funny at their house. A hose from the exhaust on their car was attached to the shed. Then I saw your car on their street. I was . . . concerned."

Trust Sam not to be worried. Not on my account. Concerned, yes. Worried, no.

"Did Nina or Marty confess?"

"They each confessed the other one killed Heath," Sam said. "And they each said it was not their intention to kill you too."

"Oh, they just wanted to scare me?" I asked.

"Little did they know you don't scare easily," he said. "Or else you wouldn't have gone there today, would you?" He frowned at me. He wasn't happy I'd gone to their house, did he know I was guilty of breaking and entering too?

"I admit, I was scared. But how else was I supposed to find out anything?" I said. "You wouldn't do it because you had to have a search warrant. I didn't have to have one. As long as I didn't get caught."

"But you did."

"Am I in trouble?" I asked.

"Big trouble." He leaned forward. He was so close I could see that he hadn't shaved. Too busy saving lives, like mine. "What were you looking for?" he asked.

"I can't remember," I said, rubbing my head. "I've been gassed, you know. But I do know what I didn't find. No evidence of anyone making home-made candy in their kitchen. But wait, there's more." If I could only remember what it was. "Now I know. I went there to help Nina. I was reading Grannie's advice column letters. Don't tell her I told you."

He nodded. "Go on."

"In the bag was an anonymous letter from someone who'd hit her husband. I assumed it was Nina. I thought she needed help, like, you know, anger management classes or something."

"So you came to help her," he said dubiously. "Give her some advice, which she couldn't get from the real advice lady."

"More or less," I said modestly. "Then I found out that One, Nina had been cheating by buying her caramels when the rules of the Food Fair say you have to make or grow the products yourself. And Two, that she was shacking up with Heath to get him to overlook that fact and give her a good review which led to Three, her husband, Marty, finding out and murdering Heath." I closed my eyes for a minute. Then I asked, "Is that enough to convict him?"

"Along with the phone messages and a confession."

"Then it was Marty who ransacked my apartment."

"He figured out who found the phone and he wanted it."

By the time we'd finished this wrap-up I was exhausted. I closed my eyes. I reached for Sam's hand and I squeezed it. I wanted to sleep but there was something I had to say, something I wanted to tell him. "By the way, you may have been right. I might have fallen into the pool that night. Not sure . . ."

"Get some rest," he said. "I'm putting my deputy outside the door here to keep everyone out. No visitors. Oh, and I have something for you." He reached into his pocket, pulled out a gold star and handed it to me.

"What's this?"

"I'm deputizing you."

Tears filled my eyes. "I'm a deputy," I murmured.

He nodded.

I closed my eyes clutching the gold star.

When I woke up Grannie was sitting next to my bed. She was wearing a tailored silk blouse and a pair of trim slacks with low-heeled shoes and she was holding a pie in one hand.

"How are you?" she asked putting her other hand on my forehead to check my temperature.

"Better. How did you get in?

"Next of kin has visiting privileges."

"You look spiffy."

"You like the outfit?"

"Perfect for hospital visiting," I said.

"Sam told me where he found you. I thought I told you not to go into someone's house if they're not at home."

"You did tell me. Of course you did. But how do you get a good look at somebody's kitchen unless they're not at home? I had to find out if Nina really made those delicious caramels."

"Couldn't you have asked Sam to check for you?"

"How would he know if someone had been making caramels in their kitchen? Besides, he's a stickler for the rules."

"And you're not?" She sighed.

"I wasn't before, but now that I'm a deputy . . ." I held the star up so she could see it.

"Congratulations," she said. "I'm not surprised. Sam says he couldn't have solved this murder without you."

"Did he? He didn't tell me that."

"That's because he wants you to stay as humble and unassuming as you are."

"No problem," I said. "Humility is my middle name. Hanna Humility Denton. Make that DEPUTY Hanna Humility Denton. How does that sound?"

"Sounds good," she said. And Grannie is always right. I shared the Georgia Peach Pie she brought with the nurses.

DOUBLE CHOCOLATE
CREAM PIE

Chocolate Filling
3/4 cup sugar
1/3 cup cornstarch
2 squares unsweetened baking chocolate, cut in small pieces
1/2 tsp. salt
2 1/2 cups milk
3 egg yolks, beaten
1/2 tsp. vanilla extract
1 chocolate pie shell, made of crushed chocolate cookie crumbs and butter.(9-inch, pre-baked).

Chocolate Cookie Crumb Pie Crust
1 1/2 cups chocolate cookie crumbs
1 tbsp. sugar
1/4 cup melted butter

Mix ingredients and press into 9-inch pie pan.

Bake at 375 degrees for 8 minutes.

Chocolate Cream Pie Whipped Topping

1 cup heavy cream
2 tbsp. confectioner's sugar
1/2 teaspoon vanilla extract

For the filling: In top of a double boiler, combine sugar, cornstarch, chocolate, and salt. Stir in milk. Cook mixture over boiling water, stirring constantly, for about 10 minutes, or until chocolate mixture has thickened. Continue to cook for about 10 minutes longer, stirring occasionally.

Gradually stir half of the hot chocolate mixture into beaten egg yolks; return egg mixture to the double boiler, stirring well. Cook over boiling water, stirring occasionally, for 5 minutes. Remove from heat; stir in vanilla extract. Pour filling into a baked pie shell.

Chill chocolate cream pie thoroughly in refrigerator, about 3 to 4 hours.

For the topping: In a mixing bowl, beat cream with confectioner's sugar and vanilla extract until stiff. Spread over chocolate cream pie and return to refrigerator until serving time. Store leftover chocolate cream pie in refrigerator.

(Like there's going to be any leftover? I don't think so.)

BUTTERSCOTCH PECAN PIE

Ingredients:
3 tbsp. butter
3 eggs
3/4 cup brown sugar
2 tbsp. flour
1 tsp. vanilla extract
3/4 cup dark corn syrup
3 tbsp. bourbon
2 cups pecan halves
1/2 cup butterscotch chips
1 (9-inch) pie shell of your choice. Hanna uses her all-butter, all-purpose crust.

Preheat oven to 350 degrees. Melt butter in a small saucepan. While butter is melting, beat eggs in a medium-sized bowl. Whisk in the brown sugar, flour, vanilla extract, syrup, and bourbon. Add in butter when just melted. Stir in the pecans and butterscotch chips. Pour mixture into an unbaked pastry pie shell.

Place pie on baking sheet and bake for 50 to 60 minutes, covering pie gently with foil after 30 minutes to prevent crust from burning. Makes one (9-inch) pie.

ABOUT THE AUTHOR

Carol Culver is the author of more than thirty books, including many bestselling Harlequin romance novels. She has a BA in French and studied at the Sorbonne in Paris. This is her second mystery novel in her Pie Shop Mystery series.